SIMMERING
Stu

Books by Pamela Burford

Jane Delaney Mysteries
Undertaking Irene
Uprooting Ernie
Perforating Pierre
Icing Allison
Preserving Peaches
Simmering Stu
Liquidating Larry
Jane Delaney Humorous Mystery Series: Books 1-3 Box Set

Romantic Suspense
Snatched
Going Commando
Storming Meg
A Case of You
Twice Burned (Double Dare book 2)

Contemporary Romance
Rags to Bitches
In the Dark
Snowed
Too Darn Hot
The Boss's Runaway Bride (a novella)

The Wedding Ring matchmaking series:
Love's Funny That Way
I Do, But Here's the Catch
One Eager Bride To Go
Fiancé for Hire
The Wedding Ring Matchmaker Series: Complete Four-Book Romantic Comedy Box Set

SIMMERING *Stu*

A Jane Delaney Mystery
Book 6

Pamela Burford

RADICAL POODLE
P R E S S

Paperback edition published 2020 by Radical Poodle Press
Copyright © 2020 by Pamela Burford

ISBN 978-1-944922-72-6
Ebook ISBN 978-1-944922-71-9

Simmering Stu is a work of fiction. Names, characters, places, and incidents either are products of the author's imagination or are used fictitiously. Any resemblance to actual events or locales or persons, living or dead, is entirely coincidental.

All rights reserved. With the exception of quotes used in reviews, this book may not be reproduced or used in whole or in part by any means existing without written permission from the author.

Interior design by BB eBooks
Cover design copyright © 2020 Patricia Ryan
Author photograph copyright © Jeff Loeser

www.pamelaburford.com

to the memory of my father, Dan, and my father-in-law, Al, two of the best storytellers I ever knew

1
Lifeguard on Duty

YOU KNOW HOW sometimes you say something in passing, or someone says something to you in passing, and only later do you realize the statement could be taken more than one way? Like, *Wow, he didn't know how right he was!* Know what I mean?

Okay, probably not. Anyway, when Martin McAuliffe turned to me and said, "Jane, I have a feeling this is going to be a memorable night," I'm pretty sure he wasn't anticipating the way that night really turned out. Because, I mean, come on. Who could possibly have seen *that* coming?

He uttered these provocative words while steering his 1966 candy-apple-red Mustang into the parking area of a historic bed-and-breakfast inn called The Gabbling Goose, located across the street from the town beach in quaint Crystal Harbor, Long Island. The porch light and first-floor windows of the redbrick inn glowed in welcome, though it was nearly eleven p.m. Moonlight shivered on the inky surface of the bay.

I can hear you wondering why, since both of us possessed perfectly serviceable homes right there in town, we'd decided to shell out the big bucks for a room at The Gabbling Goose.

Well, it was really Martin's doing. He was the one who'd insisted this grand passion that had been smoldering between us for the past year deserved to be, shall we say, brought to fulfillment at a more romantic and, yes, memorable venue than either his one-bedroom apartment above the pub where he tended bar, or the soulless McMansion I'd kinda sorta inherited the previous year.

Brought to fulfillment sounds so much more genteel than *consummated*, don't you agree? (Or any of the earthier synonyms for you-know-what that just popped into your mind. I can, too, read your mind. Deal with it.) In any event, month after month of flirtatious banter and suggestive teasing had brought the slow smolder to a flash point a little earlier that night when Martin and I had shared our first Big Kiss.

I have to admit, after that kiss, he could have fulfilled me in the middle of Main Street and I wouldn't have complained. But I agreed to do it Martin's way because I knew it was prompted by a desire to make the night extra-special for me. Plus it was anyone's guess how long his romantic streak would last—or indeed, how long *we* would last. There were no guarantees where the inscrutable and commitment-phobic padre was concerned.

That's right, I call him *padre*. And lest you get the idea I'd just tangled tonsils with a man of the cloth, let me assure you it's merely a nickname I'd bestowed, owing to the fact that during our first meeting, Martin had been impersonating a priest.

I know. Awful, right?

What's that? You want to know what *I* was doing while he was rocking the priest getup? Well… I might have been attempting to steal a valuable brooch right off a corpse during a wake.

Now, don't be like that. I was an innocent patsy. The client who'd hired me to swipe it for her had insisted it was a worthless piece of junk whose value was strictly sentimental and that she was the rightful owner. Later I learned she'd fibbed on both counts.

My name is Jane Delaney and I perform tasks for paying clients, tasks that tend to bring me into close proximity with the dearly departed. Which might have something to do with why I'm known locally as the Death Diva. Today you might find me checking up on grave upkeep on behalf of a long-distance relative. Perhaps tomorrow I'll be helping a family divide cremated remains or arrange a burial at sea. Pretty tame stuff, right?

And okay, so there's the occasional offbeat assignment, like the brooch thing. Oh yeah, and the time I helped a client cast a death mask of her late husband. Old-fashioned and icky, but nowhere near the ickiest thing I've been paid to do. Plus it was legal and lucrative, my two most important criteria. Last year I facilitated the donation of someone's very old, very dead giant tortoise to the Smithsonian. For that matter, I've arranged oodles of pet funerals. Folks have a tendency to go overboard when it comes to their furry family members, and I can definitely relate. Speaking of which…

"Did you have to bring him along?" Martin cast a disgruntled glance at Sexy Beast, whose front paws were propped on the half-open window, his superpowered canine schnoz hoovering up myriad intriguing scents. My wimpy human nose detected only fresh-mown grass on the chilly breeze, overlaid with the inn's flowering bushes and a hint of brine from the nearby bay.

"The comment period on this issue is officially over, Padre." Once we'd agreed on our destination, I'd made him swing by my place to pick up a few essentials, including my seven-pound apricot poodle. After all, it was too late to get a friend or neighbor to look in on him, and let's face it, Sexy Beast—SB for short—was about as needy and neurotic as they came. If I left him alone all night, even with a pet-sitter, he'd be a gibbering basket case come morning. Not to mention, I'd have felt compelled to rush home at the crack of dawn to reassure him and offer an apologetic Vienna sausage or three. I'd had Martin verify with the innkeeper that the little guy would be welcome in our room.

"Just as long as he doesn't decide to, you know, jump on the bed or anything," Martin grumbled as he positioned the vintage Mustang between a black Mercedes and a gold Lexus, the only other vehicles in the small gravel parking strip next to the inn. Clearly, not all of the B&B's eight guest rooms were occupied, no surprise on a midweek night in early May.

I chewed back a grin. So that's what had the padre vexed—the fear that our long-anticipated (insert your favorite euphemism here) might be interrupted by an adorable yet attention-hogging toy poodle, eager to join in his alpha female's fun new bed game.

Yeah, *new*. Because let's face it, it had been so long since yours truly had played this particular game, I'd almost forgotten the rules. If any new ones had been invented during my downtime, I was confident Martin would get me up to speed before this momentous night was through.

"Not to worry," I assured him as I exited the car and reached into the backseat for Sexy Beast's plush bucket bed, crammed with his toys, snacks, and supplies. The little dog, meanwhile, tested the limits of his leash, avidly exploring. "Once we get settled in, SB will conduct a swift but thorough reconnaissance and be snoring within seconds. It's way past his usual bedtime."

The padre appeared unconvinced. Moonlight glinted off his

short, sandy hair as he retrieved my small duffel from the trunk, along with a knapsack I hadn't noticed earlier. I could only conclude he kept a few overnight necessities packed in anticipation of last-minute sleepovers. I found that particular conclusion more than a little irksome, so I decided not to think about it.

We stood there staring at each other for long moments. The padre's pale-blue gaze felt like a sensual caress as it traced my features, making me wonder how I appeared to him in the moonlight. He shouldered the straps of our bags and reached out to lightly stroke my strawberry-blonde hair, which fell in soft layers just past my shoulders.

He leaned down and lightly brushed his lips over mine, a teasing hint of what was to come. Dear Lord, this man could make even that seemingly innocuous gesture seem triple-X-rated. He placed a warm hand on my back and steered me toward the inn's full-length, covered porch.

Reluctantly I halted in my tracks. "You know what? I'd better give this little troublemaker one last potty break. You go ahead and get us checked in. I'll be around back." I handed the bucket bed to Martin, checked the pockets of my suede jacket to make sure I had a plastic doggie-waste bag, and led Sexy Beast through the parking area and around the side of the big house. He marked a rosebush, a bird feeder, and a wooden fence post before we made it to the huge backyard.

The Gabbling Goose, which occupied two acres of prime Crystal Harbor real estate, began life as a private home in the mid-seventeenth century. Remarkably, the property had remained in the same family during the ensuing centuries. The original structure had been left intact even as expansions and renovations turned it into the elegant establishment it was today.

A couple named Shelley and Woody Bernstein had been the live-in managers of the B&B for about thirty-five years with minimal staff, though at this point they had to be well past retirement age.

As I rounded the house, I saw that a large wooden deck hugged the back of it. Porch lights revealed upholstered seating areas with umbrellas and a fire pit, a glass-topped dining table with a dozen chairs, a large gas grill, and an assortment of potted plants.

Beyond the deck, the manicured lawn lay in moonlit gloom, a landscape of shadows within shadows. The one exception was the free-form swimming pool some distance away, which glowed a shimmering blue-green, courtesy of underwater lights. The pool looked so inviting, I couldn't resist ambling over to check it out. Naturally, Sexy Beast had to investigate every plant, rock… heck, every blade of grass, it seemed. I was happy to let him if the extra activity meant he'd sleep even more soundly.

A stone apron added to the pool's rustic appeal, making me wish it would be warm enough the next day to take a dip. I'd packed a swimsuit, just in case, but the forecast was for a typical early-spring day in the Northeast: partly sunny and just a bit too cool for swimming. I walked along the edge of the pool, squinting through the gloom, and was happy to spy what appeared to be a freestanding hot tub tucked within a stone surround, located a short distance from the deep end. I smiled, picturing the padre and myself lounging in the steamy spa tomorrow morning, sipping restorative mimosas while water jets pummeled our happily sleep-deprived bods.

Sexy Beast seemed to have run out of gas or, um, something and was no longer marking this new territory of his. He was still sniffing like crazy, of course, but I mean, he's a dog. When I came within a few yards of the hot tub, I realized that not only were the underwater jets and lights on, but it was occupied.

"Oh!" I said. "Sorry, I didn't mean to sneak up on you."

The man didn't react, and I bit back a chuckle, realizing he'd fallen asleep in the warm, churning water. The empty martini glass on the tub's rim might have had something to do with that. He sat facing me, comfortably slumped with his head tipped back.

As much as I hated to disturb this guy's snooze, I felt I had no choice. I imagined him sliding down into the tub, and I mean, who knew how much he'd had to drink? Did anyone else even know he was out here?

"Excuse me?" I said. No response. I moved a little closer to the tub. "Sir!" I snapped, with crisp authority. "Hello!" Nada. "Oh, for heaven's sake," I griped.

Sexy Beast hung back, straining against the leash and doing some griping of his own. I didn't have time for this. I had things to do. Important things.

I can hear you snickering. Let me assure you, if you'd ever laid eyes on Martin McAuliffe, you'd know just how important those particular things were.

SB's muttering morphed into sharp barks, which increased in pitch and volume as I snatched him up and marched over to Sleeping Beauty. This close, the moonlight revealed him to be a fairly attractive man of medium build, probably in his mid-forties. His mouth sagged open, but he wasn't snoring.

I reached for his shoulder, intending to shake him awake, but something made me withdraw my hand. Partly it was my dog's behavior. Yes, SB was a nervous little dope at the best of times, but outright hysteria for no discernible reason? He wasn't *that* far gone.

So partly it was Sexy Beast's freak-out, and partly it was something on the cool breeze. Something my wimpy human nose finally registered. Something metallic and slightly sweet.

I got a firmer grip on my shrieking dog and gave Hot Tub Guy a closer inspection. He seemed to be peacefully napping, all right, but something about the tub itself looked wrong—the stone exterior, that is, under and behind his head. I peered around and saw that black paint had pooled on the coping and was dripping down the outside of the tub to puddle at its base.

Oh, look at you, so full of yourself. I know what you're thinking. *Jane, don't you know blood appears black in moonlight?* Well, sure, I'd heard that, too, but it's one of those bizarre factoids you never expect to be able to either verify or disprove.

You will be happy to know I can now verify it, so you don't have to. You're welcome.

Actually, the primitive, reptilian part of my brain verified it a scant couple of seconds before the civilized, mimosa-sipping part caught up. That was all the time it took for reptilian Jane to stumble away from Dead Hot Tub Guy, trip over SB's trailing leash, and execute a face-stinging belly flop in the deep end of the swimming pool.

You know what you don't want to be wearing at a time like that? You don't want to be wearing a heavy suede jacket. I struggled to tread water, whipping my head around, blinded by the wet hair plastered to my face. "Sexy Beast!" He'd sailed out of my arms as I fell, landing somewhere in the pool. "SB, where are you!"

My poor little dog had never learned to swim. Considering how much he detested baths and ran for cover at the first raindrop, I'd always figured it was a lost cause. And yeah, I know poodles have a long and noble history as water retrievers—well, the big standard poodles do, anyway. What can I tell you? There weren't enough Vienna sausages in the world to convince my pampered pooch to get his dainty little paws wet.

"Sexy Beast! Where the hell are you?" Now who was hysterical? Imagine my relief when my panic-stricken cry was answered by a single imperious bark. I finally managed to push the hair out of my face and spied SB at last, halfway down the pool, his little body backlit by the underwater lights.

He was swimming directly toward me, flawlessly dog paddling as if he'd been doing it his whole life. He barked again, in that commanding tone that said: *Stay where you are, Jane. I'm coming for you.*

Good grief. Well, it would have been hard to argue that my tiny dog was the one who needed saving, considering all the flailing and sputtering I was doing. He reached me in record time, latched on to the collar of my jacket, and started tugging me toward the side of the pool.

"What's all the hollering about?" It was the padre, ambling across the lawn toward us.

Oh good, I was afraid I wouldn't completely humiliate myself tonight.

"What are you doing in the pool, Jane?" He reached the edge at the same time I did, and lifted Sexy Beast out. The little furball vigorously shook himself, a spectacular display that progressed from nose to tail—a miracle of physics.

"Sexy Beast fell in," I said, as I made an ungainly attempt to heave myself onto the stone ledge. "What choice did I have? I had to, you know, go in after him."

Martin wore a devilish smile. "What do you say, SB? Is that how it happened?"

"Shut up and help me." I was making zero progress on my own.

He grabbed hold of my arms and started to lift me out. In an amused whisper, he said, "Don't know whether you noticed, but there's a guy asleep in the hot tub over there."

"He's not asleep, Padre. That man is deceased."

"What?" Martin let go of me and sprinted over to the hot tub, while I tumbled back into the cold water. Sexy Beast muttered something in Poodle and jumped in after me.

I gave up on trying to haul myself out in my sodden clothes. Instead I pulled myself along the edge of the pool to the shallow end and its idiot-proof steps. And yes, Sexy Beast played lifeguard yet again, keeping a firm grip on my jacket collar the whole time. I watched enviously as he gave himself another thorough, highly efficient shake.

Shivering, trailing water in my wake, I joined the padre at the hot tub, where he'd already verified my diagnosis of Very Dead and was finishing up a call to 911.

"I'll wait out here for the cops." He was calm and in control, as if finding a corpse in a hot tub were an everyday occurrence. "You go inside and let Shelley and Woody know what happened. Our bags are still in the lobby. You can change into dry clothes. I have a feeling we're going to be here awhile."

But not in the way we'd planned. *Dang it all!*

"You saw the…?" I gestured vaguely toward the, ahem, black paint.

"I saw." Martin sighed. "I know this guy, Jane."

"You do?" I said, wide-eyed. "Who is he?"

"His name is Stu Ruskin. I was his bodyguard."

2
Practical Life Skills

"THOSE TWO SEEM OKAY. Competent. Respectful." Woody Bernstein set a platter of snacks on the coffee table in front of the love seat Martin and I shared in the front parlor of The Gabbling Goose. Cheese, crackers, salami, olives, and fruit.

My stomach whined in gratitude, reminding me how long it had been since I'd put anything in it. Sexy Beast, who'd curled up between the padre and me, was so exhausted by all the activity, not to mention his late-night lifeguard duty, that not even the smell of some of his favorite vittles was enough to interrupt his sound snooze.

"You mean the detectives?" I asked, as I plopped a slice of fragrant cheddar on a water cracker. "Howie and Cookie are more than okay. Not only are they swell people, but they happen to be very good at what they do. I've known Howie forever. Cookie Kaplan joined the force just six months ago, but already I like her a lot."

"Woody," Martin said, "you don't have to wait on us. It's after one a.m. The cops have already interviewed you. You look like you're falling out. Go to bed."

Woody and his wife, Shelley, who managed the B&B, were around eighty years old. Both wore eyeglasses and unobtrusive hearing aids. Woody was on the short side, stocky, with a white ponytail that only served to direct one's gaze to the gleaming bald spot above it. Shelley, a light-skinned Black woman, had a couple of inches on her husband. Her white hair was worn short and natural. The vivid color-block cardigan she'd layered over her long purple dress appeared handmade, as did her large beaded earrings and necklace. Age did not appear to have hampered this lady's sense of style.

Shelley placed a bottle of merlot and three wineglasses on the table. "They're right, dear. If you don't get enough sleep, you'll be useless tomorrow and then it'll all be on me."

This mild guilt-tripping, which I suspect she'd been employing for the past half-century or so, had the desired effect. "Well, if you insist," Woody said, stifling a yawn, "but you have to promise you'll wake me if the detectives have more questions."

"Fine, but they won't. Go on now." Shelley wagged her hand at her husband, who wished us a good night and disappeared up the nearby staircase.

"Since the cops seem to be done with us," she said as she started pouring, "I hereby declare it to be wine o'clock."

"You're an angel," I said, accepting a glass. "I don't know when I've needed it more."

Howie and Cookie had interviewed everyone on the property, starting with Martin and me before moving on to the Bernsteins and the guests who were staying at the Gabbling Goose: a young couple and a family of four. The detectives were conducting these meetings in the large enclosed porch on the other side of the house. Tyler Collingwood, who owned the B&B, had arrived a short while ago and was in with them now.

Within minutes of Martin's 911 call, the property bristled with emergency vehicles and first responders of every description. I didn't see them remove Stu Ruskin's body from the hot tub, but I watched through the front window as the white medical examiner's van pulled away.

The padre took a sip of wine. "Shelley, you must be as wiped out as Woody. I'll make you the same promise you made him. We'll come get you if you're needed."

"Oh, don't worry about me." Shelley settled in an antique-looking armchair with her wineglass. For that matter, all the furnishings and artwork in the elegant B&B appeared to be from a previous century. "I wouldn't know what to do with more than four hours of sleep. I'm a night owl *and* an early bird."

"You'll have to teach me that trick," I said. "I need my eight hours. Six, minimum."

"Good to know." Martin's tone was maddeningly innocent, the fiend. Meanwhile my face heated like a skillet.

Tyler Collingwood joined us in the parlor. The owner of The Gabbling Goose was a little under six feet tall, with a full head of salt-and-pepper hair, a firm jawline, and a confident bearing. Based on the way he filled out his gray silk shirt and close-fitting slacks, I assumed he was either a gym rat or spent every weekend competing in a triathlon. As he scanned the room, I had the impression his intense blue-gray gaze missed nothing.

In short, he was the kind of man it was impossible to ignore. Especially if you happened to be, you know, of the female persuasion. Some men just have that certain something, and he was one of them, despite the age difference. I'd just turned forty a few weeks earlier, and I estimated this man to be in his midfifties.

He extended his hand, and we came to our feet to shake it. "Ty Collingwood." His voice was a rich baritone, because of course it was. "I wasn't ignoring you earlier. The detectives grabbed me as soon as I got here."

We introduced ourselves and Sexy Beast, who roused himself long enough to accept a few brisk pats.

"I would've been here sooner," Ty said, "but I was at a jazz club in Southampton and my phone was silenced. I didn't learn about Stu's suicide until the show ended, and of course, the drive back took an hour and a half."

"Did the cops say it was definitely suicide?" I asked. "I mean, it looks like that, but they wouldn't tell me anything." No surprise there. Howie Werker always played it close to the vest. I usually had better luck cajoling information out of Cookie Kaplan when her partner wasn't around.

"Naturally, they wouldn't commit themselves," Ty said. "The investigation has to run its course and all that, but it's clear they think he killed himself."

"That's the sense I got, too," I said.

"Which means," Martin said, "they must've found the gun."

Ty nodded. "I overheard a couple of cops talking about it. A Glock nine-mil with a suppressor. It was at the bottom of the hot tub."

"Suppressor?" Shelley asked.

"Silencer," Martin said.

Speaking of silence, an awkward one ensued as the four of us contemplated the specific sequence of events that had caused that Glock to end up in that location. I shuddered as I pictured Stu Ruskin placing the barrel of the gun in his mouth.

Ty broke the spell. "I hope this tragic incident didn't completely ruin your stay with us."

"Oh, were not staying here," I said. "Well, we were planning to, but…"

"That's understandable," Ty said. "Let me offer you a couple of free nights to make up for the inconvenience."

"I already gave them a voucher," Shelley said. "Our other guests, too."

"As always, you're on top of everything." He gave her a warm smile. "What would I do without you and Woody?"

"Oh, I don't know," she said, "hire someone younger and sexier?"

"Do they make them sexier than you two?"

"Good point." She rose. "Are you hungry? I can fix you a plate."

"I'm fine, I ate at the club. And anyway, it's late, Shelley. You should be in bed."

"We tried that," Martin said.

"Oh yeah," Ty said. "Ms. 'I only need five hours sleep.'"

"Four." Shelley gave him a knowing look. "Does this club you were at serve my apple crisp? Warm, with vanilla ice cream?"

She'd said the magic words. His eyes widened. "You made apple crisp?"

She turned to us. "There's plenty. Can I interest you? It's my specialty."

"She's not lying." Ty stabbed a finger toward his manager. "Shelley Bernstein makes the best apple crisp on the planet."

"Sounds amazing, but we're still working our way through all this." I indicated the snack platter. In truth, I was hoping for a few minutes alone with the padre, something we hadn't had since he'd made that 911 call.

"We'll take a rain check," Martin said.

Ty and Shelley passed through the adjoining drawing room and into the kitchen while we resumed our seats. I took a healthy swallow of wine.

"He called him 'Stu,'" Martin said. "Did you notice? Like he knew him."

"I noticed. I also noticed that you told me you're Stu Ruskin's bodyguard."

"Was," he said. "I *was* Stu's bodyguard. Part-time for five and a half months, until this past December."

I shook my head, struggling to process this new information. "You're a bartender, Padre."

"Yeah, so?" He shrugged. "There's more to my life than Murray's Pub. The job doesn't claim all my time."

I was well aware there was more to Martin's life than tending bar. During the past year, he and I had shared some intense, even life-threatening experiences, which naturally had brought us closer together. I felt a gut-deep connection with this man that both thrilled and frightened me.

The fact is, I still knew precious little about his background and in particular how he'd come by some of his more, shall we say, practical life skills. Such as picking locks, disabling security systems, cracking safes… you know, basic handyman stuff like that.

He was also skilled at evading my subtle and not-so-subtle attempts to pin him down. Was he a cat burglar? Con man? Bank robber? Something worse? And if so, were we talking past tense? I thought I could live with past tense. Maybe.

It depended on a number of factors. Such as whether he'd ever done time. More important, in my book at least, was the question of whether he'd ever hurt anyone during the course of his, um, activities. That was the make-it-or-break-it question that kept me awake at night. I still didn't know what I would do if I learned the answer was yes.

Oh hell, I knew what I would do. Or more to the point,

what I *wouldn't* do. I wouldn't open my heart to someone like that. And for sure I wouldn't make sexy-time dates with someone like that.

"How long have you done that?" I asked. "You know, worked as a bodyguard."

He was busy poking around in the snack platter for the ideal slice of salami to crown the gob of brie he'd smeared on a slice of baguette. "Oh, about twenty years. No, I guess it's been a little longer than that."

"So here's the big question," I said.

"Why didn't we go to the Hilton?" He shoved the loaded cracker into his mouth and followed it with the last of his wine.

"That certainly would've saved us all this drama," I said, "but the question that occurred to me is this. Why would a person who's contemplating suicide hire a bodyguard? It would seem to be counterproductive and at the very least a waste of money."

"That's my Jane, ever practical. You want some of these grapes before I polish them off?"

"They're all yours. Answer the question."

"I'm as baffled as you are," he said. "I told Howie and Cookie about my time working for Stu, and brought up the obvious inconsistency. I mean, I assume that when someone commits suicide, they've spent some time thinking about it. It's not usually a last-minute decision. But what do I know? I'm no shrink. Plus, it's been five months since I stopped working for him. A lot can happen in five months."

"So, what did they say?" I asked.

"Cookie asked me if Stu ever seemed depressed or suicidal. I said no. Then Howie said people change their minds, and anyway it's too early to say for sure it was suicide."

"But they're definitely leaning in that direction." I poured us each a little more wine. "It's obvious that's what they're thinking."

"Agreed."

"Maybe Stu did change his mind," I said. "Maybe it's why he fired you."

Martin glowered at me. "Cookie said the same thing. Why does everyone assume he fired me? I'm a skilled, experienced bodyguard. I've never lost a client yet."

"Sorry, I just… Why did Stu hire you in the first place? Why did he need protection?"

"The cops asked me that, too. Stu claimed someone tried to off him." Martin paused to let that sink in. "Yeah, I know, but it wouldn't be the first time a client convinced himself that someone was gunning for him."

"Meanwhile it's all in his imagination," I said. "But in Stu's case… What exactly happened back then? I mean, what made him think someone was trying to kill him?"

"He refused to say. Which is less than helpful when you're trying to keep your client alive. And if he knew who the supposed assassin was, he was keeping it to himself."

"Well, let me ask you this, then. During the time you were working for him, did you ever feel his life was in danger?"

The padre shook his head. "I never saw any evidence of it. But I wasn't with him twenty-four seven. Generally he called me in when he had some public event, when he felt particularly exposed."

"Do you know whether Stu replaced you after you quit?" I asked.

"No idea. I certainly wasn't about to recommend the gig to anyone."

"Why not?"

"Because it wasn't just that Stu was withholding important facts," he said, "facts any bodyguard would need to do his job. The guy also turned out to be crooked. The pay was good, but I'm not that desperate for work."

I managed to control my expression. Martin quit a lucrative side gig because the client was crooked? I liked the sound of that. It went against a lot of what I knew, or thought I knew, about the padre. I hoped I wasn't simply grasping at straws.

"Crooked in what way?" I asked.

He offered a wry smile. "You ready for this? He stole a recipe."

"The monster."

"The thing is," he said, "this was no ordinary recipe. You ever heard of a cookie called the Dreamboat?"

"No. Should I have?"

"You probably know it as the MegaMunchGigantiKookie," he said. "It hit the store shelves a couple of months ago. You must've seen the commercials, all the media coverage."

I made a face. "You mean that ginormous, overstuffed, candy-studded monstrosity that weighs more than my head? I've never had the pleasure. I look at that thing and all I see is a week's worth of sugar and fat."

"Since when do you have a problem with sugar and fat?" The padre was well aware of my fondness for junk food.

"There's junk food and then there's Junk, Padre. With a capital *J*. Your basic, run-of-the-mill junk food tastes good and offers a naughty thrill. Maybe even a few vitamins along with the grease and high-fructose corn syrup. Yum."

"And the capital-*J* Junk?" he asked.

"Food only in the loosest sense of the word. I once checked

out the ingredients list for that MegaMunchGigantiKookie. And I'm not even talking about the hard-to-pronounce ones. Did you know there's an entire brownie inside every one of those things? And a caramel center inside of *that*? Oh, plus beer extract and bits of beef jerky for flavor, because what cookie would be complete without beer and jerky? I bet it doesn't even taste that good."

"It tastes awesome," Martin said. "Though I must admit, the original was far superior to the mass-produced knockoff."

"Original?"

"The Dreamboat. It was created in this small bakery in lower Manhattan, The Cranky Crumb, owned by a guy called Henry Noyer. Lives right here in Crystal Harbor, as a matter of fact. He started selling the things about a year ago and they became an instant sensation. Word spread, the Dreamboat became incredibly popular, the bakery had lines around the block. People would queue up an hour before the place opened. Henry had to limit customers to one apiece."

"I take it Stu stole the recipe?" I said.

"Yep. And sold it to Conti-Meeker."

"Wait. Conti-Meeker Pharmaceuticals?" I shook my head, certain I must've heard wrong. "The huge multinational drug company? They're not in the cookie business."

"They are now. The powers that be renamed it the Conti-Meeker *Group* with an eye toward branching out into other products, starting with foods. Once they got ahold of the recipe for the Dreamboat, they fast-tracked production and started cranking them out under the name MegaMunchGigantiKookie."

"How convenient," I said. "So now, after you've choked down a couple of those fat-and-sugar bombs, the same company will sell you your cholesterol medication, your blood pressure drug, and your insulin. Is this a great country or what?"

Sexy Beast blinked, opened his jaws on a giant yawn, and sniffed the air with interest. I offered him a small piece of cheddar, which he scarfed down before turning a few tight circles and resuming his beauty sleep.

"So how did Stu get ahold of Henry's recipe?" I asked.

"That's the thing. Technically, it wasn't Henry's recipe. His wife is the one who came up with it. Well, Georgia Chen is his ex-wife now, but they were still married when The Cranky Crumb started selling the Dreamboat."

"Was she his partner in the business?" I asked.

"Astute question. No. Henry owned the bakery before they got married, and he remained the sole owner during and after their marriage."

"So legally Georgia was considered, what, an employee? I think I read somewhere that if an employee creates a product or invention or whatever, it becomes the property of the employer."

"That's often the case," he said, "because companies make their workers sign contracts to that effect. And Henry was no exception. His business might've been small potatoes, but he was determined to protect it, which meant safeguarding his trade secrets."

"Including the recipe for an insanely popular cookie."

Martin nodded. "So yeah, the contracts his workers signed said that The Cranky Crumb owned any recipes they came up with while working for him. Plus there were the usual nondisclosure and confidentiality agreements. And he kept the recipe in a secure vault, which only he had access to, via a fingerprint scanner."

"Didn't he keep a copy on his computer?" I asked.

"Nope, just paper. Real old-school. I think he was afraid his computer would get hacked. Also, instead of giving his cooks access to the secret recipe, he would mix up the dry ingredients himself and store the mixture in premeasured bags. The baking instructions would say to mix the contents of a bag with the wet ingredients or whatever. With all that security, Henry figured his recipe was safe."

"I'm waiting for the part that goes something like, 'The thing he didn't count on…'"

"The thing he didn't count on," Martin said, "was his wife, Georgia, who he was madly in love with, and who he would never even *dream* of asking to sign a contract—"

"Uh-oh," I said.

"—falling in love with another man and divorcing Henry."

"That still doesn't explain how Stu ended up with the—Oh, wait."

Martin smiled, watching my expression morph from confused to *aha!* "I doubt Stu ever really cared for Georgia," he said. "To him, she was a means to an end."

"So you think Stu wrecked their marriage just to get his hands on this valuable recipe?" I asked.

"I know he did. And so does Georgia."

"So you know her."

"I know her." He didn't look at me as he said this. *Hmm…*

"Tell me about her," I said.

"What's to tell? Georgia's no doormat. The instant she realized what Stu had done, she dumped him."

That wasn't the information I was looking for. Was Georgia beautiful? Alluring?

Did she and Martin have a *fulfilling* relationship? If so, was it over?

"So then," I said, "she wasn't in on Stu's scheme? To sell the secret recipe?"

"If she's to be believed, Stu swiped it from her. His sole reason for busting up her marriage and getting close to her was to gain access to it. He was a grifter playing a long con, and Georgia was his mark."

"Did you consider she might be lying about her involvement?" I said. "That she hated her ex enough to sell the recipe out from under him?"

"She never hated Henry, as far as I can tell," he said. "They were married for more than a decade. Apparently he never fell out of love with her. He was always hoping they'd get back together, right up until he sued Georgia and Stu for corporate espionage."

"Ouch. I guess that would kill the romance. I take it Henry didn't win the lawsuit?"

"Nope. His case was too weak," the padre said. "He'd failed to take the necessary precautions to protect his trade secret."

"Really?" I said. "Despite the fingerprint vault and the cookie mix and all that?"

"His ex-wife knew the recipe by heart, remember. After all, it was her creation. A creation he never took ownership of when he had the chance. Bottom line, it wasn't *his* trade secret."

"It sounds like he trusted her not to share it."

Martin nodded. "With good reason. They had a mutually respectful relationship, even after the marriage was over. Henry knew she was involved with Stu, of course, but neither of them suspected his true motives—until it was too late."

"How do you know all this?" I asked.

"Georgia confided in me."

"I see."

Martin leaned back and draped his arm over my shoulder. It felt good, so I leaned back as well and kind of snuggled against him, to the extent I could do so with a sleepy toy poodle playing chaperone between us.

"Henry must've been apoplectic when he found out what Stu had done," I said. "Did he confront him?"

"Of course. You know what Stu told him?"

"What?"

"He told him that Georgia willingly handed over the recipe as an act of love," Martin said, "that she *wanted* Stu to profit from it."

"And Henry believed it?"

He sighed. "Maybe. Probably, since that's when he decided to sue both of them."

"I'm thinking Stu's conscience might've been eating away at him," I said, "and that's why he decided to kill himself."

"The Stu Ruskin I knew wasn't one for introspection. He was one for self-interest, greed, and covering his tracks."

"So you don't think it was suicide," I said.

"No. I think someone decided to take him out of the picture."

"I wonder what gave Stu the idea to swipe a valuable recipe," I said, "and sell to the highest bidder, so to speak."

"Well, it kind of ties in to what he did for a living."

His fingers began stroking my upper arm. A fine shiver raced through me and it became hard to concentrate. I managed to say, "And what was that?"

"Stu was a cookie rep."

I pulled away from the padre just enough to look him in the eye. "A cookie *what*?"

"Rep—a manufacturers' representative." He pulled me back against him. "The go-between who sells a company's product to a store, which then sells it to people like you and me. In Stu's case, he represented various bakeries, who paid him a commission to get their cookies and brownies and whatnot into restaurants, grocery stores, wherever they sell stuff like that."

"That must be how he met Henry."

"And Georgia," he said. "Stu wasn't content with the hefty commission Henry was paying him to get his Dreamboats into restaurants all over the city. He was looking for a bigger payday."

"And he didn't care if he destroyed someone's marriage in the process," I said. "Not to mention what it must've done to Henry's bakery."

"Between the loss of its signature product and the steep legal fees from the lawsuit, The Cranky Crumb never recovered. It closed its doors a couple of weeks ago."

A deep male voice said, "What can you expect from a Ruskin? Same crime, different era."

3
Same Crime, Different Era

IT WAS TY COLLINGWOOD, reentering the room with Shelley. Clearly he'd overheard the end of our conversation.

Shelley resumed her seat in the antique armchair while her boss remained standing, and poured the last of the wine into her glass. She wagged the bottle. "Shall I open another one?"

The padre and I declined, with thanks.

I was about to ask Ty what he meant by his enigmatic comment when he said, "I'd better get home. Jeanette's no doubt waiting up. She'll be demanding a full report. Oh, Shelley, before I forget, Amy's been asking if you can use some summer help."

"Always. I was about to put the word out. Does she know someone?" She turned to Martin and me. "Amy is Ty and Jeanette's daughter. She put in a lot of summers here herself when she was younger. Well, she practically lived here during weekends and school breaks. And now she's a conservation scientist with the Long Island Environmental Alliance. Isn't that something? Lovely girl."

Ty chuckled. "That 'lovely girl' just turned thirty-two, can you believe it? Anyway, her friend Maggie has a younger brother who's interested in working here this summer. He'll be entering

Cornell's School of Hotel Administration in the fall, so it seems like a good fit."

"If Amy vouches for him," she said, "that's good enough for me. Tell her to give him my contact info."

"Will do." He turned to the padre and me. "Jane, Martin. I'm glad we got to meet, though I must say the circumstances leave a lot to be desired."

We said the expected things, and Ty let himself out the front door.

Martin got right down to it, bringing up something I'd also been wondering about. "Shelley, I know the cops must've asked this, but did you or Woody hear a gunshot?"

She shook her head. "No, no one in the house did, and I don't think anyone went out back after dark. It was too cool."

Not too cool to enjoy a nice soak in a hot tub, I thought. With a 9-millimeter Glock.

"I'm not surprised no one heard anything," Martin said. "Ty said the gun had a suppressor."

"Which brings up another question," I said. "Why the silencer? If you were going to, you know, do yourself in, wouldn't you want your body to be discovered as soon as possible?" Shelley and Martin appeared to give the question some thought. "I mean, Stu might've sat out there in that tub all night if I hadn't decided Sexy Beast needed a potty break. Silencing the gunshot seems like an odd choice for someone intending to kill himself."

I could tell this hadn't occurred to either of them. I wondered if Howie and Cookie had considered the same question.

"Well," Shelley said, "let's hope he left a suicide note. As terrible as that is, how much worse would it be if it turned out someone else did him in?"

The subtext came through loud and clear: How much worse would it be for The Gabbling Goose if an actual murder occurred on the premises?

Martin said, "Was Stu a guest here?"

Her features hardened. "Good grief, no. That man never set foot on these premises in all the years I've been working here. I was shocked when I learned who it was out there."

I said, "It sounds like you might know what Ty meant by that 'same crime, different era' business."

Shelley paused, as if pondering where to start. "The Collingwoods and the Ruskins have a long and contentious history."

"The kind that goes back a generation or two?" I asked.

"Try a dozen or more generations," she said. "Going back to the mid-seventeenth century, when both their ancestors emigrated from England."

Martin and I shared wide-eyed looks. "Seriously?" he said. "That's over three hundred fifty years ago."

Shelley pointed to the large, gilt-framed oil painting hanging over the fireplace. It was a head-and-shoulders portrait of a Colonial gentleman in his late thirties or early forties, wearing a black coat and white cravat. He had long auburn hair and a Van Dyke beard: pointy goatee and mustache with clean-shaven cheeks. The artist had managed to capture what I can only describe as a calculating expression.

"That's Oswald Collingwood," she said. "He came over in 1660 because if he'd remained in England, they'd have hanged him."

Now she had my attention. "For what?" I asked.

"Counterfeiting lottery tickets." Shelley took a dainty sip of wine.

I blinked in surprise. "Lottery tickets?"

"Just the last in a long list of crimes," she said, "but apparently the one that caught the attention of the authorities."

"And for that they'd hang someone?" the padre asked.

"Back then," she said, "folks were hanged, drawn, and quartered for a whole bunch of things that probably wouldn't earn a prison sentence today."

"So Oswald fled to the States to avoid the law?" I said.

"It was the colonies back then," she reminded me. "Within a year, he'd made his way to Long Island and used his ill-gotten gains to buy a large tract of land here in Crystal Harbor. It was a brand-new settlement at that point."

Which is to say, it was a brand-new *European* settlement. I knew that Jeremiah Nevins, who'd founded the town, had purchased the land from the Matinecock tribe in the 1650s.

Martin circled his finger, indicating our surroundings. "This is the tract of land he bought, correct?"

"What's left of it," she said. "Most of the acreage was sold off over the years. Oswald got married, built the original house—we're sitting in the old part—and sired a passel of kids."

"Did he give up his criminal ways after starting a new life here?" I asked.

"Well, he never farmed or took up a trade," she said, "but there's no evidence he was ever arrested either, so it's possible he cleaned up his act. We do know his money ran out at some point, because in 1665 The Gabbling Goose was open for business."

"He turned his home into an inn?" I asked.

"His wife, Sybille, did. I doubt he had much to do with it."

"So Oswald was Ty's ancestor," Martin said. "When did Stu Ruskin's people get here?"

"Percival Ruskin settled in Crystal Harbor shortly after Oswald did, along with a couple of brothers."

"Was he on the run from the law, too?" I asked.

"Not that I know of. Percival operated a tavern in the basement of his house. It was just down the road from here."

"Ty implied that one of Stu's ancestors was a criminal," I said. "Was he referring to Percival?"

"He was referring to a bunch of Stu's ancestors," she said, "not just one. And yes, Percival came under that category. After Oswald's death in 1668, Sybille kept the inn going. It became a popular stop for travelers and gained a reputation for good food and drink, fair prices, and clean sheets. Anyway, she came up with this special alcoholic punch, and it must've been pretty good, because before long, folks from all around were flocking to The Gabbling Goose." Shelley snickered. "Pun intended."

"Oh boy," I said, "I think I see where this is going."

"Once Oswald Collingwood was out of the picture," she said, "Percival Ruskin wasted no time moving in on his widow. He cozied up to Sybille just long enough to steal the secret recipe for Sybbie's Punch. That was her nickname, Sybbie. His tavern started selling it for less money. Which he did by substituting cheaper ingredients, but that didn't deter all those Colonial boozehounds who knew a bargain when they saw one."

"Did he change the name of the punch?" I asked.

"Yep. In his tavern it was called Peg Leg Punch."

"Okay," the padre said, "I'm gonna go out on a limb here—pun *definitely* intended—and guess that our man Percival had a wooden leg."

"He did indeed. Peg Leg Percy, they called him."

"So Sybbie's Punch really was that special?" he asked. "Worth going to all that trouble to steal?"

"What you have to understand," Shelley said, "is that back then, the taverns weren't like the bars of today. If you wanted something besides beer or wine, you were usually looking at rum, hard cider, or applejack—or a couple of those mixed together. They'd all get you where you wanted to go, but Sybbie's Punch would make the trip enjoyable."

I said, "So that's what Ty meant by 'What can you expect from a Ruskin?'"

Martin nodded. "History repeating itself."

"So does The Gabbling Goose still serve Sybbie's Punch?" I asked.

She gave a sad shake of her head. "The recipe's been lost to time. I'd have loved to get ahold of it, even just to offer the punch as a novelty now and then, like around the holidays, but I'm afraid it's gone for good."

"How did Oswald die?" I asked.

"Well," Shelley said, "here's where it gets interesting."

The padre grinned. "*Here's* where it gets interesting?"

"Oswald Collingwood claimed he beheaded King Charles the First," she said.

"Well, that was rude," I said.

Martin turned to me. "You have no idea what she's talking about, do you?"

"Of course I do," I blustered. "I went to college."

"I know," he said. "State University of New York at Stony Brook. Earned your BA part-time sixteen years ago with a three-point-two GPA. Majored in Communications, with an emphasis in Human Relations. Excellent preparation for working with stiffs, by the way."

"A lot you know," I said. "I was already working with stiffs while I got my degree."

"Dead pets, but let's not quibble."

Did I mention? I knew next to nothing about Martin's background, yet he seemed to know every blessed thing about me. Mostly because of those handyman skills I mentioned earlier. Otherwise known as unlawful breaking and entering.

"Okay, so I started out with dead pets," I said. Those early assignments, in case you're wondering, consisted mainly of delivering floral arrangements to the Best Friend Pet Cemetery. I added, "It was my entrée into working with real live, I mean real dead human beings. We're getting off topic." I turned to Shelley. "You were saying?"

She gave me a curious look. "Okay, we're going to come back to that 'working with stiffs' thing. Looks like I'm not the only one with an interesting story. Anyway, back in January 1649, King Charles the First was sentenced to death for high treason. To say this was controversial would be the understatement of the, well, of the seventeenth century."

"The regular executioner refused to do it, right?" the padre said. "The guy that stepped in wore a mask to conceal his identity."

"That's right," she said, "a black mask and a wig. He chopped off the king's head with an ax in one clean blow. The monarchy was officially out and the republic was officially in, until Charles the Second became king eleven years later in 1660."

"You're leaving out a lot of history," Martin said. "Oliver Cromwell—"

"No, no, enough with the history," I said, wondering how the padre knew all this. "Let's get back to Oswald. He claimed to be the guy in the black mask and wig?"

"Oswald Collingwood had an inflated sense of his own

importance," Shelley said, "and he wanted to make sure everyone else thought he was as exceptional as he did. So he cooked up this story about how he was the one who chopped off the king's head. But not until he was safely in the colonies, mind you, because once the new king had been crowned, all those who were involved in the execution of his daddy—and there were dozens of them—were forced to make a run for it. A whole bunch of them were hunted down and killed."

"But Oswald was safe in America?" I asked.

"He thought he was," she said, "with an ocean between him and the king's men. Turns out they were more motivated than he gave them credit for. They shot him dead behind the house as he made a break for the woods."

Behind the house. Where Stu Ruskin had just died. Martin's arm tightened around my shoulders, and only then did I realize I was shivering. And not in the good way this time.

"The irony was," Shelley said, "no one who actually knew Oswald believed his outlandish story. For one thing, the guy was a do-nothing blowhard with a history of skirting the truth. And for another, it was well known that the man who beheaded the king was skilled with an ax. Apparently chopping off heads is tougher than it looks in the movies, and a lot of executions back then... well, let's just say things sometimes got a bit messy."

Martin said, "I take it royal beheadings weren't in Oswald's skill set?"

"The man possessed no skill set," she said, "if you don't count swindling folks out of their hard-earned shillings."

I said, "So Ty Collingwood is still bitter about Percival Ruskin's theft of the secret recipe for Sybbie's Punch? Three and half centuries later? That's some world-class grudge holding."

"There's more to it than that," she said. "Sybille and her

family were convinced that Percival tipped off the king's men and told them where to find Oswald. Percival needed him out of the picture so he could romance his widow and make off with her special recipe."

"Did he?" Martin asked. "Tip off the king's men?"

"I'd bet money on it. What we know for sure is that the events of 1668 triggered a blood feud between the Collingwoods and the Ruskins. It got pretty intense for a while."

"How intense?" I asked.

"Well, it started with Sybille killing Percival to avenge her husband's death."

"Whoa," I said. "Yeah, I'd call that intense. How did she do it?"

"She lured him here under the pretense of letting bygones be bygones. Served him a mug of Sybbie's Punch, only this time it contained a little something extra."

"Don't tell me," Martin said.

"Yep. She poisoned him," she said. "In this very room, as a matter of fact."

The hairs on my nape sprang to attention. "Was she arrested?"

"The constable was her cousin, so what do you think? Rumor was, he actually helped Sybille dispose of the body. She claimed Percival took off for parts unknown, but everyone knew she'd done him in. Didn't matter. The absence of a body meant they couldn't prosecute it as murder."

"So she got off scot-free?" I said.

"Not quite," Shelley said. "The Ruskin brothers decided to take matters into their own hands by setting fire to The Gabbling Goose, with Sybille and her kids asleep inside, not to mention a handful of paying guests. Everyone managed to get out safely, but there was extensive damage to the structure. Much of the house had to be rebuilt."

"Those guys didn't fool around," Martin said.

"Every time one family went on the attack," she said, "the other one retaliated. We're talking theft, assault, kidnapping, attempted murder—"

"Just 'attempted'?" I said.

"No one else died, but it wasn't for lack of trying."

"This feud isn't still going on, though, right?" I asked.

Shelley shook her head. "During the Revolutionary War, a Ruskin ended up saving the life of a Collingwood during battle. Most folks think it was an accident, but if so, it was a happy one, because things finally cooled down between the two families."

"After more than a hundred years of serious hostilities," I said. "It isn't totally over, though, is it? I mean, it's clear that Ty was far from Stu's number-one fan."

"Well," she said, "there's always been an undercurrent of suspicion and resentment. I doubt that will ever change. But the two families have managed to live more or less peacefully in this town for a long time." One eyebrow quirked. "Mostly by keeping out of each other's way."

I recalled Shelley's frigid response when I asked whether Stu had been a guest at the B&B. *Good grief, no. That man never set foot on these premises in all the years I've been working here.*

It would seem the mutual agreement to stay out of each other's way had teeth. And that Ty's disdain for the Ruskins had rubbed off on his longtime employee. I wondered how she'd have responded if Stu had indeed attempted to reserve a room at The Gabbling Goose. I could only assume he sneaked onto the premises to do himself in—sort of a twisted *nyah-nyah* to the Collingwoods.

And if it was murder, as Martin seemed to think? I had a hard time picturing Stu Ruskin slipping into the B&B's backyard simply to enjoy a nice, relaxing soak in a hot tub—only to be shot to death while doing so. By whom? And for what reason? If you think of it that way, suicide seems far more likely.

My musings were interrupted by a muted, metallic sound. A few soft, hollow clangs, then it stopped. Sexy Beast woke with a start. Shelley frowned at the ceiling. "Knock it off, Percy. These folks aren't interested in your shenanigans."

Martin and I exchanged a swift glance. I said, "Uh, Shelley, who are you—"

"You're going to wake up the whole house," she said, still glaring at the ceiling. "Settle down, now."

Clang, clang, clang.

SB jumped off the loveseat and directed three sharp barks at the ceiling.

Shelley threw her hands up, muttering, "I swear, that man is the original attention hog. No shame." Lifting her gaze skyward, she called, "No shame! You're embarrassing yourself, you old fool." To us she said, "Percy just can't stand hearing people run him down."

Against my will, I was forced to acknowledge the obvious. Percy. Percival Ruskin.

Dang. And Shelley had seemed so normal.

I struggled to make my mouth work. The padre had no such problem. "So the place is haunted, huh?" he said. "Percival Ruskin decided to stick around."

"Yeah, he's been a fixture here since he croaked," she grumbled. "The proverbial guest who doesn't know when to leave. For three and a half centuries."

Clang, clang, clang, clang, clang.

SB emitted a long, wolflike howl. I grabbed him and tried to muzzle his little jaws. "Hush, you'll wake everyone up." He jerked his head away and let out one more mournful wail.

"I've got plenty of earplugs, Percy," she told the ceiling. "So bang that thing all you want, but I'm planning to sleep like a baby."

"Um, how does he make that sound?" I asked.

"By banging his pewter cup on the punch bowl. He's still kinda peeved about that whole poisoning thing."

"Ah. I see." To me it just sounded like an old building's old plumbing acting up, but what did I know?

Clang!

Shelley's tone turned sarcastic. "Real mature, Percy. These nice people are very impressed with your antics."

"Pretty cool," Martin said. I knew he was just humoring her. "Do you ever see him or is it just an auditory thing?"

"For someone who likes to make a racket, he's pretty shy about showing himself. Sometimes I catch a glimpse of him in the middle of the night, with his stupid bowl and cup." She tsked in exasperation.

As I watched her drain her wineglass, I found myself wondering whether these ghostly visions tended to be preceded by a glass or two of vino.

"So why does Percy hang out here," he asked, "in the lair of his enemy, so to speak?"

"Well, it's the place he died," she said, "so there's that. But what I figure is, he's waiting for an opportunity to exact vengeance on the Collingwoods."

"For three and a half centuries?" he said. "Seems like it's taking an awful long time."

"Did I leave you with the impression that Percy Ruskin was

bright?" she said. "An organized thinker? The kind of man who got things done? Because if so, I take it back. He was little better than Oswald. What kind of man steals a valuable recipe from a widow who's struggling to feed her kids?"

Clang! Clang! Clang! Clang! Clang!

Okay, that one made me jump, I don't mind telling you. I did my best to muzzle SB, but it was a losing battle.

So Percy Ruskin's ghost is itching to spill Collingwood blood, yet who just met a violent end at the Collingwood ancestral home? Not a Collingwood, but a Ruskin. Talk about unfair. And after all that punch-bowl banging.

"I think I'm about ready to hit the hay," Shelley said, "but first, Jane, I need you to explain what you do for a living. Something to do with stiffs?"

I started with the short explanation, but she was full of questions. The fact is, I didn't mind answering them. It's always refreshing when someone is genuinely interested and doesn't make the *Ew, you do what?* face.

"Stay as long as you like," Shelley said as she made her way up the stairs. "There's still plenty of apple crisp and ice cream, so don't be shy. Just turn the lock when you leave."

Once we were alone, Martin snuggled me against him while Sexy Beast commandeered the still-warm armchair recently vacated by Shelley.

"I'm sorry for the way things turned out tonight, Jane." His words were a warm buzz against my scalp. "I mean, sure, I'm sorry about what happened to Stu, but I also wish like hell..." He sighed deeply.

"I know." I laid my palm on his chest, over his steady heartbeat.

"I guess it's too late to go to your place or mine." His words held a hopeful note.

"After everything that's happened," I said, "it just wouldn't seem right."

He kissed the top of my head. "So let's reschedule. We can spend the weekend in the city. There's a cool new boutique hotel I read about."

I didn't respond, and he angled his head to look me in the eye. I sat up and put a little distance between us.

"Why do I get the feeling I'm not going to like what comes next?" he said.

"Maybe it's just as well things didn't work out the way we planned," I said. "I feel like it's all moving too fast."

"Too fast? Jane, we've known each other more than a year. You and I have something special. Tell me I'm wrong."

"You're not wrong," I said. "It's hard to explain."

"Well, try. Because neither of us is getting any younger. We're middle-aged, in case you haven't noticed."

"I hate it when you say that. I don't feel middle-aged." Middle-aged people had normal, nine-to-five careers, the kind that didn't have *Death* in the job title. Middle-aged people had children, and some had grandchildren. Martin, at forty-three, was about to become a grandfather in a few months, while I was still sitting on my overripe eggs, hoping and praying that someday I'd get a chance to crack one open before its sell-by date.

He tipped my chin, making me face him. "What's this really about, Jane? Is it Dom?"

I shook my head. "You know he's no longer in the picture."

I'd spent most of the past eighteen years regretting my divorce from my ex-husband, Dominic Faso. Since meeting Martin, however, I'd gradually come to recognize that Dom was part of my past. He was a great guy and would always be a friend, but I no longer dreamed of undoing my big mistake.

Our roles had recently reversed. Dom's betrothal to his longtime fiancée, Bonnie Hernandez, had ended for good, and he was eager to put his ring on my finger once more. If you're thinking my relationship with my ex sounds like your basic comedy of errors, you're not far off.

"It's definitely not Dom. There are just too many… unanswered questions." I took a deep breath. "I know very little about you, Padre."

He held my gaze for long moments. "You know what's important. You know what kind of man I am."

"I want to think I do. I guess I just don't understand why you're so secretive."

"I'm not trying to shut you out, Jane. The fact is, there are some things I don't share with anyone." He stroked an errant strand of hair off my face. "I'm not one of the bad guys. Trust me on this."

I was hoping he'd elaborate, provide some actual information. I was past trying to wheedle it out of him.

I closed my eyes and pressed his palm to my cheek. I'd never thought of Martin as one of the bad guys, not really. And yet it was still possible he did bad things, worked with bad people. A seeming contradiction, and one more reason I needed to put some distance between us, give myself time to work it all out.

My eyes were still closed when he touched his lips to mine and kissed me tenderly. "I want you so bad, it hurts," he said, "but I couldn't bear it if you had regrets. I can wait."

4
Live and in Person!

"A *PUNCH BOWL?*" Sophie Halperin gawked at me, a bite of bacon-and-onion quiche quivering on her raised fork.

"According to Shelley," I said, "Percy's ghost bangs his cup on the thing whenever he's annoyed. Which I'm guessing coincides with people taking showers or flushing toilets."

"You mean like air in the pipes?" she said. "That kind of knocking or banging?"

"That's what it sounds like to me, but hey, maybe Shelley's right and it's old Percy, seeking justice."

"I've known the Bernsteins for years," she said. "Never heard about a ghost haunting The Gabbling Goose. Shelley should talk it up. Aren't ghosts supposed to be a big draw for old-timey inns like theirs?"

"Well, the inn's not actually theirs, of course." I lifted half of my croque-monsieur, basically a fancy-schmancy grilled ham-and-cheese sandwich. "It belongs to Ty Collingwood, but the Bernsteins have managed it forever."

"Does Woody believe this ghost business?" She took a sip of sparkling water.

I shrugged, mouth full. It was Friday, about thirty-six hours since I'd made my shocking discovery behind The Gabbling

Goose. Sophie and I had decided to meet for lunch, as we often did, at Patisserie Susanne, a lovely French bakery and café on the ground floor of Crystal Harbor's Town Hall. As the town's mayor, Sophie had an office on the building's top floor, so for her, it was a simple matter of riding the elevator down four flights.

She was in her midfifties, short and round, her chin-length hair mostly gray. Today she wore an outfit typical for her, a colorful abstract tunic with metallic trim over voluminous wide-leg pants.

Oh, and did I mention? Sophie's my best pal.

If there's a heaven, it smells like Patisserie Susanne. There can be no better high than the scent of napoleons, éclairs, macarons, palmiers, and my addiction of choice, chocolate croissants. Not to mention exquisite savory offerings such as pâté sandwiches, assorted quiches and salads, and my decadent croque-monsieur.

The patisserie was bright and cheerful, with abundant sunlight, hanging plants, old-fashioned brass fixtures, and black-and-white floor tiles. Today it was filled to capacity with the usual lunchtime crowd. We'd managed to snag a round bistro table in a corner.

I'd already filled Sophie in on everything I'd learned from Shelley and Martin. I lowered my voice so as not to feed the town's insatiable appetite for gossip. "Don't you think it's kind of a creepy coincidence that both Stu Ruskin and Ty's ancestor Oswald Collingwood were shot to death behind the B&B?" I asked.

"When you put it that way. So you don't think it was suicide." It wasn't a question. Sophie knew me too well.

"Honestly, I don't know. There are a couple of unanswered

questions. Howie and Cookie seem to think his death was self-inflicted."

She swallowed a mouthful of her side salad. "They might be rethinking that initial assumption."

I was instantly alert. This was the kind of insider info I'd been hoping for when I made our lunch date. Sophie Halperin had always been plugged in to the heartbeat of the town, even before becoming the "mayor of this damn burg," as she often referred to herself. Nothing of significance happened that she was unaware of.

"I know the autopsy must've already been done." I tossed back some lemonade.

"Yep. I had drinks with Magda last night."

"Okay, spill." Dr. Magda Temple was the medical examiner, and by all accounts, a thorough and experienced one. She knew her stuff.

Sophie didn't need to remind me to keep the information to myself. Like I said, she knew me. She glanced around at the nearby diners and said quietly, "She found a couple of things during the postmortem that may or may not be inconsistent with suicide."

"May or may not?" I'd been hoping for something more black-and-white.

"The science isn't conclusive. And by the way, this is pretty unsavory stuff, so you might want to wolf down the rest of your sandwich before I get into it." She'd already made short work of her quiche.

"You forget who you're talking to." I punctuated the statement with a nice, big bite of my yummy croque-monsieur.

"Have it your way, Ms. Death Diva." Sophie leaned toward me and said, sotto voce, "Magda said the angle of the gunshot is suspicious."

"You mean like...?" I was about to point toward the interior of my own mouth but thought better of it. No sense taking pains to prevent eavesdropping if we were going to broadcast our conversation through the art of mime. The entire town knew about Stu's death, and how he'd profited from a stolen trade secret. It was all anyone had been talking about for the past day and a half. They also knew I was the one who'd stumbled upon the gruesome scene. I felt my fellow diners' eyes on me.

"Turns out when people kill themselves in that particular way," she said, "the angle of the gunshot tends to be a bit upward and toward the left—if the person was right-handed, that is. Death is due to brain damage."

"Was Stu right-handed?" I lifted the other half of my sandwich.

She nodded. "In his case the gunshot went straight back at a somewhat downward angle, through the neck. Cause of death was blood in the respiratory tract."

Well, she warned me. "And that means someone else was holding the gun?"

"*Maybe.* Like I said, it's inconclusive. And then there's the tongue thing." Sophie watched me set down my sandwich, uneaten. To her credit, she did not gloat.

"Okay," I sighed, "let's have it."

"The bullet went through his tongue."

"And that's unusual?" I asked.

"According to Magda, people who, uh..." Her gaze flicked to the nearest table, where a pair of young businesswomen were quietly studying their phones and ignoring each other. In a whisper, she said, "People who decide to check out that way, they lower their tongue to make room for the gun barrel."

As much as I didn't want to, I asked, "And when it's homicide?"

"The victim tends to automatically put his tongue up, and it gets pierced by the bullet."

"Good Lord." I pushed my plate away.

"But like I said, it's all conjecture. They haven't studied enough cases to draw any reliable conclusions from this sort of evidence."

"So, what did Magda write on the autopsy report and death certificate?" I asked. "It's up to her to determine manner of death. As in suicide, homicide, whatever."

"She wrote 'pending further study' since the police are still investigating. But that's just a temporary thing until they make up their minds. Your turn," she said. "What kind of unanswered questions?"

"What? Oh." I told her about the stumpers raised during my conversation with Martin and Shelley: Why would someone planning to do himself in hire a bodyguard, and why would he use a silencer?

Our conversation was interrupted by the muted sounds of an argument behind the door leading to the café's kitchen: two female voices, shouting in a mixture of French and English. I assumed one of those voices belonged to Susanne Travert, the owner of the patisserie. The young man standing behind the counter, serving customers, wore a *Here we go again* look.

Suddenly the kitchen door banged open and a tall Chinese-American woman stormed out, hollering over her shoulder. "That's it, *je démissionne*! I quit!"

Sophie looked surprised. "That's Georgia Chen. I met her last month at the annual poker tournament."

"Henry Noyer's ex-wife?" I asked. "The woman who invented the MegaMunchGigantiKookie?"

"If you mean the original version, the Dreamboat cookie,

then yes. Didn't know she was working here."

Susanne stalked out after Georgia, screeching, *"Bon débarras!"*

"Good riddance to you, too, Susanne. I'm outta here. *Je ne vais pas revenir.*" Georgia possessed a thick New York accent. Even her French had the drawn-out vowels and brisk, nasal speech pattern of a native New Yorker. Neither woman seemed to care that they were playing to a packed room.

How I wished I had my Parisian hottie, Victor Dewatre, there to translate. I'd met Victor the previous fall when he came to Crystal Harbor following the murder of his brother, Pierre, a local celebrity chef. The two of us hit it off, though we had yet to do anything about it—anything of a, you know, physical nature. Victor had stayed in touch after he returned to Paris. Not only did he urge me to visit, but he'd actually asked me to move in with him there.

As you might have gathered by now, I'm pretty adept at not following through when guys show serious interest. Hey, you don't want to rush into these things.

Okay, you know what? That was not an opening for you to offer your opinion. When I want your advice... Oh, forget it.

Susanne was in her late forties, short and thick-waisted, her dark hair tucked into a turquoise, bandana-style chef's cap. She followed Georgia through the café, hurling invectives in her native tongue.

Georgia turned and stabbed a finger toward her employer. *"Cuire vos propres* damn *biscuits.* You're on your own."

Susanne appeared to be running out of steam. "Zheorzhia, no more of this. *Arrêtez cette bêtise.*"

The women faced off, hands on hips. "Foolishness, is it?" Georgia said. "To want to be treated with respect? *Le respect. Est-ce trop demander?* Is that too much to ask?"

Susanne threw her arms wide in frustration. "*Je te respecte*, Zheorzhia. *Mais le respect va dans les deux sens.* It goes both ways. You must remember who is boss."

Georgia crossed her arms and looked away. "Not anymore."

"*Pour l'amour de Dieu!* You are not really quitting, are you?"

"I should," she grumbled.

Her employer's eyes glistened. *"J'ai besoin de toi ici."*

"I agree." Georgia's chin wobbled. "You do need me here."

Susanne sniffled. "And you need us, too, *non*?"

Georgia bobbed her head as her pretty face screwed up and tears began to fall. The two women threw themselves into each other's arms. A handful of customers clapped, and I got the feeling I was witnessing a regular performance.

Following a lot of tearful jabber and cheek kisses, the two finally separated, Susanne returning to her kitchen, and Georgia—or *Zheorzhia* as I now thought of her—heading for the exit.

Sophie stood and waved her over. "Georgia!"

She stopped in her tracks, looked around, and smiled broadly as she spotted Sophie. "Mayor Sophie! Oh my Gawd!"

They exchanged air kisses, and Sophie introduced me. She invited Georgia to sit with us awhile, which she seemed happy to do.

Georgia Chen appeared to be about my age, perhaps a little older, but still beautiful. Her shoulder-length hair was dyed eggplant-purple, which looked great on her and made me wonder whether I should consider changing up my look. She wore black leggings and a long pink blouse with the sleeves rolled up. I noticed a streak of white flour on her jaw. The scents of cinnamon and chocolate clung to her like the most decadent perfume.

"Your name is familiar," Georgia told me, giving the words a real New Yawk spin. "Someone mentioned you just recently."

Sophie lowered her volume once more. "Jane's the one who found Stu Ruskin's body."

Georgia gaped at me. "Oh Gawd, that's right. That must've been *horrible*."

Sophie put her hand on the other woman's arm. "We're trying to keep our voices down, Georgia. There are enough rumors flying around this town."

"Oh. Right. Sorry." She put a finger to her lips and shushed herself, then turned to me. "They have a nickname for you. The death something?" She shuddered.

I'd been in this person's presence for about two minutes and already had her pegged as your basic drama queen. "Death Diva," I said. "I didn't choose the title. Someone else did me that dubious favor and it stuck."

"Well, I like it." She raised her arms as if pointing to a theater marquee. "The one and only Death Diva! Live and in person!"

If Georgia was broken up over the sudden death of her onetime boyfriend, she had an odd way of showing it.

"Are you and Susanne okay?" Sophie asked. "Looked like you two were really getting into it there."

Georgia wagged her hand. "We just need to blow off steam every once in a while. I'm the best pastry chef she ever had. Sometimes she needs reminding."

"Are we keeping you?" I asked. "Do you have to get back to work?"

"Naw, I'm done for the day. I've been here since five a.m. All the pastries are made fresh every day, and we open at seven on weekdays."

"I knew everything was made fresh daily," I said. "I guess I just never realized the demand that puts on the people who make the magic happen."

"I can't complain," she said. "Susanne gets in at three to start the bread."

"Three a.m.?" Sophie said. "I had no idea."

"And she doesn't go home after eight hours like I do," Georgia said. "It was the same when my ex and me had our own bakery. We'd be there eighteen hours sometimes, seven days a week. At least here I get two days off."

Our own bakery? She might have put in the hours at The Cranky Crumb, but I knew that her ex-husband, Henry Noyer, had been the sole owner.

"How long have you worked here?" I asked.

"What time is it?" She laughed. "Almost a month. I hate working for someone else, but what choice do I have? My ex lost everything, thanks to that rat Stu. Not to speak ill of the dead or whatever, but him dying doesn't change what he was. You gonna finish that?" she asked, eyeing my untouched half sandwich.

I pushed the plate toward her. "Help yourself. It's cold, though."

She shrugged. "Still delish. I gotta hand it to Susanne, everything in this place is orgasmic. Mm-mm…" Her rapturous groan as she took the first bite, combined with the half-closed eyes and shoulder wiggles, served to prove her point.

Sophie said, "So I take it Henry's no longer able to keep up his support payments?"

"What can I tell you? You can't get blood from a stone. He says he'll cough up the arrears when he can, but in the meantime I gotta eat." Which she demonstrated by taking another huge bite of my croque-monsieur.

"It sounds like you and Henry are still on pretty good terms," I said.

She grabbed a paper napkin from the retro dispenser and wiped her mouth. "He just moved back into our house. Well, it's my house now. I got it in the divorce."

"That's very generous of you," I said, "considering, well... Didn't Henry sue you? Over the recipe for the Dreamboat?"

"A misunderstanding," she said. "He thought I had something to do with selling it to Conti-Meeker. Well, what he thought is that I handed it over to Stu so he could sell it, which he shoulda realized I would never in a million years do. But that's what Stu told him and he believed it." She rolled her eyes at the folly of men and their credulous ways.

"So you and Henry are back together again?" I asked.

She sighed. "Naw, he's still sore. Can you blame him? I was so stupid. I mean, I was so *stupid*. How could I have let that rat Stu come between us?"

"As I understand it," Sophie said, "Stu had an ulterior motive. It wasn't you he was after, it was your secret recipe, right?"

Georgia nodded miserably. "He seemed so sincere, so flattering. So believable. And I fell for it hook, line, and sinker. Stupid, stupid, stupid."

"Someone told me Stu was a cookie rep," I said, "and that Henry used to pay him to get your Dreamboat cookie into restaurants and stores."

"Until he betrayed us," she said bitterly. "First by breaking up our marriage and then by swiping the recipe from me and selling it to the highest bidder. The Cranky Crumb was finally taking off, thanks to the Dreamboat. All those years of hard work, all the sacrifices, were about to pay off. Until that rat Stu came in like a wrecking ball and obliterated our dream."

"Do you have any kids?" I asked.

She shook her head. "We decided early on it would just be us," she said.

"What's Henry doing now?"

"Oh, he's just, you know…" she said, "licking his wounds, trying to figure out his next move."

So Henry was broke, so broke he had to move back in with his ex-wife. Apparently he had no job prospects, and it didn't sound like he was making much of an effort in that regard. I could only assume Georgia was supporting them both on her salary from Patisserie Susanne.

I recalled Martin saying that Henry had, at one time, been hoping to get back together with his ex-wife. It sounded like the tables had turned and Georgia was now the one seeking a reconciliation.

"At least you two are living under the same roof again," I said. "That sounds like a step in the right direction."

She shook her head. "Henry stays in his part of the house."

"It's that big a place," I asked, "that you can each have your designated zone?"

"Yeah, it's this big old house that we got for a song back when we were first married. We put a lot of work into it, as in fixing up the place with our own two hands. Gawd knows we couldn't afford to hire the work out."

"Nothing wrong with good old-fashioned sweat equity," I said.

"I mean, Henry's civil when we bump into each other, but mostly he just tries to avoid me. We don't eat together or, you know… anything. He says he's going to move out as soon as he can afford to."

"That might take a while," I said, "if he's not actively looking for work."

"Well, his buddy Steve comes over sometimes, and they make cooking videos in the kitchen. At least, I think that's what they're doing. For job applications, maybe? Henry won't let me anywhere near, and he refuses to talk about it, so…" She shrugged.

Sophie said, "So, Georgia, let me ask you. When you first came up with the Dreamboat cookie, did you have any idea how popular it would be?"

"Oh my Gawd, no!" she squealed, her mood abruptly lightening. "It started out as a joke. Henry and I were goofing around in the kitchen. I was thinking up bizarre ways to use stuff we had on hand in a cookie, and he was egging me on. A bottle of grapefruit-flavored vodka might've been involved."

"Vodka in a cookie?" Sophie said.

Georgia laughed. "No, in *us*! I mean, you'd have to be at least half in the bag to even think of putting jerky and beer and all that other crap into one huge, gloppy, disgusting—" air quotes here "—'cookie,' right?"

"The Dreamboat couldn't have been that bad," I said, "if it was so popular."

"I never said it was bad, I said it was disgusting." More laughter. This woman was good at cracking herself up. And not five minutes after she and her boss had stood there blubbering in each other's arms.

"Once I sobered up," she continued, "I tweaked the recipe, and you know what? It was pretty good, in an over-the-top novelty kind of way. As long as you don't try to eat the whole thing in one sitting, which I know a lot of people do, don't ask me how. So you never had one?"

"No," I said, "but you're making me wish I had. I guess it's too late now. I've been told the Conti-Meeker monstrosity is nowhere near as good."

Georgia blinked back the sheen of tears. Dang, I'd done it now. I shot a panicked look at Sophie, whose expression of amused forbearance told me she had the drama queen's number. Well, and mine, too, I guess.

"But, um," I said, "you can always make them again, right? And sell them, too. Why not? Well, maybe not here at Susanne's. I mean, there's nothing really French about them, and I can't see her letting you…"

Georgia's face began to crumple, and Sophie was giving me that look that said, *Feel free to stop talking.*

"I can never sell them again," Georgia wailed, causing heads to turn. So much for discretion. "That damn Conti-Meeker owns the recipe now—a *pharmaceutical* company, for Gawd's sake. And there's nothing I can do about it. They'll sue me if I even think of selling my Dreamboats again. I'll lose the house. Henry and I will be *homeless.*"

I yanked a handful of paper napkins out of the dispenser and shoved them at her. "Now, now… it'll all work out…" I lied.

"I named the cookie after Henry," she sobbed. "I used to call him my—my—my *dreamboat.*"

I cast another helpless glance at Sophie, whose patience had reached its limit. "All right, Georgia, enough of that," she ordered, reaching over to give the woman's back a few solid thumps. "You got it out of your system. Now, blow your nose."

She obeyed. A hiccup or two and the crying jag was history. I turned to Sophie and mouthed, *How do you do that?* It's not as if she had kids to practice on. Like me, the mayor was childless, though in her case it was by choice. She'd had two early marriages, and apparently they'd been enough for one lifetime.

"So, Georgia," I said, "I'm curious about something. During the time you and Stu were, you know, involved, did you notice whether he owned a handgun?"

"I never saw one," she said. "He must've kept it hidden. Unless he bought it sometime after I dumped him back in December."

"So you don't doubt it was suicide," I said.

Her dark-brown eyes grew wide. "Oh my Gawd, of course not. The cops told me he killed himself."

"Well, I mean, it certainly looks that way." I wasn't about to get into the evidence, such as it was, that hinted at homicide. "Did Stu seem at all depressed to you?"

"Not really, but sometimes it's hard to tell about people, you know?"

"Well, now that you know about the rotten things he did," I said, "do you think he might've been struggling with a guilty conscience?" Martin had discounted that possibility, but Georgia had been Stu's girlfriend for several months and presumably knew him better.

She appeared to give the question serious consideration. "I'm thinking of the lie that rat Stu told Henry—about me giving him the recipe as some sort of gift. Does that sound like someone with a guilty conscience? Or, like, *any* conscience? But there's more."

"Do I even want to know?" I said.

"Turns out that back in November—*before* my divorce was final, mind you—Stu got engaged to his real girlfriend. In case you were wondering how big a rat he really was."

"His *real* girlfriend?" I said. "Meaning the one you never knew about."

"Not until it was too late to save my marriage. Of course, she didn't know about me either."

Sophie said, "So getting back to the recipe, how *did* Stu get his hands on it?"

"You ready for this?" she said, in a voice that carried, until I gestured for her to keep it down. She leaned forward, prompting us to do the same. "I don't have the recipe written down anywhere—not on paper, not in my computer, not in the cloud or anything. Nothing ever seemed secure enough, and no one had to tell me how valuable that thing was." She laughed. "Well, Henry did tell me, constantly, 'cause he knows how scatterbrained I can be."

So Georgia Chen had a modicum of self-knowledge. How refreshing.

"Was it copyrighted?" I asked.

She shook her head. "In most cases, copyright doesn't apply to recipes. I just know that rat Stu must've run himself ragged looking for it, and all that time—" she tapped her noggin "—it was right up here."

"I'm assuming he somehow tricked you into revealing it," I said.

She took a deep breath and exhaled it forcefully. "So my divorce becomes final in early December, right? And Stu says let's celebrate, though I gotta tell you, that's the last thing I felt like doing." Her chin quivered.

Sophie said, "What kind of celebration did that rat Stu have in mind?"

Hearing Georgia's own pet name for her detested onetime paramour coaxed a watery smile from her. "A nice dinner in the city, before heading back to my place for a special dessert."

"Let me guess," I said. "The special dessert was a couple of fresh-baked Dreamboat cookies."

"He hung around the kitchen the whole time I made them," she said. "At one point I noticed him recording video on his phone. Just for fun, he said. I told him to stop and delete it because, you know, the whole trade-secret thing."

"And did he?" Sophie asked.

"He said he did. Then he propped the phone on the backsplash and walked away from it. I didn't realize till later that he kept it running. He got the whole thing. All the measurements, the process, everything."

"So then all he had to do later," I said, "was watch the video and write it all down."

"I was so *stupid*," Georgia said.

"You were trusting," Sophie said. "There's a difference. You had no way of knowing how ruthless the guy was."

"Stu Ruskin spent months trying to locate that recipe," I said. "He deceived you, manipulated your emotions, did whatever he had to, to get what he wanted. You're not the first person to be taken in by a smooth-talking con man."

"When did you find out what he'd done?" Sophie asked.

"Well, about two weeks later, Henry calls me. I'm at Stu's house, we're about to head out to some fancy business function. Henry tells me he just got this scary letter from Conti-Meeker's lawyers. They own the recipe for Dreamboat cookies now, and if he doesn't stop selling them, they're gonna sue him to kingdom come."

"Did Henry think you had something to do with it?" I asked.

"I *did* have something to do with it," Georgia said, "only it took me a while to figure it out. I was… well, I was a wreck after Henry's call, completely distraught. Trying to work out how a pharmaceutical company could have ended up with our secret recipe. If it wasn't for Martin, I might've gone off the deep end for good."

The word *Martin* was a string, jerking me to attention. I looked at Sophie. Sophie looked at me.

As I groped for a response, Georgia barreled ahead. "He was Stu's bodyguard. Well, just part-time, whenever we were going somewhere that made Stu nervous. A crowded concert, maybe, or a charity dinner. Or like this business thing that evening." She wore a suggestive, just-between-us-girls smile. "I gotta admit I looked forward to having Martin around, if you know what I mean."

I stopped her right there and explained that I was acquainted with the gentleman in question and that I wouldn't want her to reveal anything that might embarrass either of them.

Just kidding. What I really said was, "No, I don't think I know what you mean, Georgia. Why don't you tell me?"

Sophie kicked me under the table. I kicked her back.

"Oh my *Gawd*. This guy Martin?" Georgia raised her palms in a *Wait for it* gesture. "We're talking drop-dead delish, top to bottom. Gawdlike shoulders, pale-blue eyes you just wanna dive right into, and a killer booty. I mean, how are you supposed to concentrate on anything when you've got a guy that hunkalicious—" she giggled like an adolescent "—guarding your body?"

I opened my mouth to pursue this line of questioning, but Sophie cut me off. "So, what happened that evening?" she asked. "After Henry's call."

"Stu didn't seem all that surprised by the news," she said. "I started screaming at him, demanding answers, getting myself more and more worked up. He ordered me out of his house, but

I stood my ground until Martin grabbed me and got me out of there."

"To protect Stu?" Sophie asked.

"That's what I thought at first, but no. He put me in his car—it's this sexy vintage Mustang, *red*!—and drove to the town beach, of all places. I mean, it was December and it was dark and it was *freezing*, but we walked on the sand, and the cold air kind of cleared my head, you know? He asked a lot of questions and helped me put the pieces together. Later he did a little digging and confirmed our suspicions."

Sophie said, "I take it that was the end of your association with Stu Ruskin."

"Martin's, too." With a kind of dreamy half smile, Georgia said, "I always expected a bodyguard to be a big, dumb side of beef in a suit. But Martin is smart and sensitive and... well, he kind of saved my sanity that night, like I said."

I'd heard quite enough about sweet, sensitive Martin and his killer booty. "Why did Stu hire a bodyguard?" I asked. "Was he in any particular danger?"

"He claimed he was." Her dubious expression said it all. "He said someone tried to kill him. What I think? I think it just made him feel important having a bodyguard hanging around. I mean, only big shots have bodyguards, right?"

5
The Everlasting Torment of the Damned

THE DAY OF Stu Ruskin's funeral was one of dazzling sunshine and above-average temperatures for mid-May, in stark contrast to the dismal proceedings at Whispering Willows Cemetery. I was able to dispense with a coat over my customary funeral attire of gray skirt suit, white blouse, black pumps, and faux pearls.

Stu's younger brother and executor, Gilbert, had chosen to commemorate his only sibling's passing with an abbreviated graveside service. No viewing, no church or funeral-home service, no post-funeral reception, no flowers, no clergy, no hymns, not even a eulogy. Gilbert himself officiated, with an assist from his sour-faced wife, Darla.

Obviously, the parsimonious Gilbert Ruskin never considered wasting money on a professional Death Diva to coordinate that which required little coordination. I was attending as a civilian. The more I learned about Stu, the more intrigued I became—the most intriguing question, of course, being how he'd ended up in the Gabbling Goose's backyard hot tub with a ventilated cranium. I thought perhaps his funeral would give me a little insight into Stu Ruskin the man.

Dozens of looky-loos were on hand, people who'd never met the deceased and were motivated strictly by morbid curiosity. These vultures jostled for position near the open grave, straining for a glimpse of the cheap casket Gilbert had selected for his brother: fiberboard covered in blue cloth.

And lest you think that was a criticism, let me assure you there's nothing wrong with cheap caskets. I myself happen to be a fan of them and am gratified on the rare occasion when a client chooses the proverbial plain pine box over thousands of dollars' worth of mahogany or bronze. Over the years I've turned down several under-the-table payoffs from funeral directors trying to get me to coerce my grieving clients into spending far more dough than they needed to. Those establishments get blacklisted.

My attitude regarding funeral spending clearly puts me in the minority in this affluent town, which is home to more than its fair share of snooty, judgmental people. I stood on the outer edges of the crowd, barely able to hear Gilbert's rushed rendition of the Twenty-Third Psalm over all the snickers and sarcastic whispers.

We were in the newest and least desirable section of the cemetery, far from the entrance and nowhere near the coveted (and pricey) historical precinct where Crystal Harbor's founding family and assorted local luminaries had been laid to rest, including several of Stu Ruskin's ancestors. No gentle hills or shade trees broke up the monotony of this low-rent subdivision, where even the grave markers were required to be flush with the ground.

Stu had not died destitute. As I understood it, his business as a cookie rep had been thriving even before he chose to augment his legitimate earnings with the sale of a purloined recipe.

There'd been more than enough money for a traditional funeral, with plenty left over for Gilbert, his sole heir. Apparently Stu had two grown children from an early marriage, but had been estranged from them for years. They must really have despised their father to boycott his funeral.

I could only assume Stu's brother held the same low opinion of him—with good reason, as I'd learned—and saw no reason to waste money on the bells and whistles that accompanied most funerals in this town.

"Did you know him?"

It was my ex-husband, Dom Faso, coming to stand beside me. He looked painfully handsome in a dark-blue suit that caressed his six-two frame as if it had been sewn right onto him. Which it kinda had been, considering that almost all of Dom's clothing is custom-made. Yeah, he's rich, as in filthy, stinking rich, thanks to his successful chain of Janey's Place vegetarian cafés.

Right about now you're guessing he chose the name of his business before our divorce eighteen years ago. How clever of you. As for your other question: I am not, nor have I ever been, a vegetarian. Dom, however, has shunned animal flesh since before we met in Mr. Bender's eighth-grade Spanish class. For the longest time he held out hope I'd come to my senses and turn veggie. But, I mean, bacon.

Janey's Place started out as a lone food truck way back when. There were now more than thirty locations in the Northeast, and I happened to know Dom was casting his gaze toward the West Coast. Both the flagship store and corporate headquarters were located right there in Crystal Harbor.

I took his arm and steered him some distance from the crowd as Gilbert stumbled in his reading, so intent on reaching the end of the psalm that he skipped an entire verse and had to backtrack. *You need to preparest that table, Gilbert. That cup's not gonna runneth over by itself.*

Well, of course I know the Twenty-Third Psalm by heart. Look who you're talking to.

I answered Dom's question. "I never met Stu, but I've been chatting with people who did, and it's made me want to know more. What about you? Did you know him?"

Dom nodded. Both his thick, wavy hair and his eyes were a deep, dark brown that never failed to remind me of espresso. "Every time our paths crossed," he said, "Stu treated me to the hard sell. He wanted Janey's Place to carry some of the lines he repped."

"What, you mean cookies and pastries?" I asked. "In a health-food café?"

He shrugged. "He was a salesman, and I have thirty-four stores. I guess he figured if he could get one item in to start, we might eventually become a lucrative account. I respected his efforts, but it just wasn't for us."

I looked toward Stu's gravesite, where Gilbert had blessedly finished butchering the psalm. His wife, Darla, had commenced reciting a stern Old Testament passage, in a loud, shrill voice. When she got to the part about stealing and lying, she became even louder and shriller. *Honey*, I wanted to tell her, *you can holler all you want, but your brother-in-law is past the point of redemption.* Likewise, I was fairly certain her hectoring was wasted on the assembled vultures.

I said, "What do you think of this scaled-back funeral?"

"If it serves the family's emotional and spiritual needs, it's not up to me to judge," said Dom, the nicest guy in the world. "This is for them, Janey. They're the ones who are grieving."

I couldn't help myself. "Are they, though? I get the feeling Gilbert and his wife think Stu got what was coming to him."

"You can never know what's in someone else's heart." He glanced around as if to ensure our conversation was private.

"But…?" I prompted. "Come on, Dom. Spill."

He lowered his voice. "What I heard is that Gilbert was looking into other options. Before he read Stu's will."

"Other options? What do you…? Oh." Death Diva Jane understood what *options* meant when it came to the disposal of human remains. Death Diva Jane had seen it all. "So he was looking into cremation? Obviously Gilbert wanted to keep costs down, and cremation is a fine, economical alternative."

"I don't have to tell you what's even more economical, Janey."

"Ah. Well, medical science needs bodies, Dom. There's nothing wrong with that. I've facilitated quite a few anatomical bequests." At no charge to the family, I might add. "But Stu had other ideas? You mentioned his will."

"He specified that he was to be buried in this cemetery, following a funeral. I'm assuming he had a more elaborate service in mind."

"And he couldn't have anticipated all these curiosity seekers." I peered into the crowd. "Is that Nina?"

Dom followed the direction of my gaze. "It is indeed. Are you surprised?"

"Can't say I am, no."

Pretty, petite Nina Wallace was one of those snooty, gossipy types I mentioned, but she was oh, so much more. A ruthless, entitled backstabber, she'd employed every dirty trick in the book to beat Sophie in the recent mayoral election. Thankfully, the Town Council caught on, overturned Nina's sham victory, and reinstated Sophie for another three-year term. As I watched, Nina bent her head to the woman standing next to her, the pair of them making little effort to stifle their giggles.

I continued to scan the crowd and spied a few more people I knew. A gray-haired man detached himself from the cluster of so-called mourners and headed toward the exit.

Dom was watching me watch him. "He looks familiar," he said. "I think I've seen him around town. Do you know him?"

I nodded. "That's Ty Collingwood. He owns The Gabbling Goose. I'm surprised to see him here. He and Stu Ruskin weren't what you'd call best buds."

"Speaking of the B&B, I heard you were the one who found Stu's body." He placed a big, comforting hand on my back and leaned in close. "How are you dealing with that, Janey? Are you okay?"

"I'm fine. I mean, it was a shock when it happened, of course, but it's not like I've never seen a dead body before."

"Yeah, but a violent death like that is different." After a moment, he added, "So, what were you doing at The Gabbling Goose? Was Collingwood looking to hire you for some Death Diva thing?"

I could always tell when my ex was making an effort to sound casual. Plus he was nibbling his bottom lip, a lifelong tell that meant he wasn't being completely upfront. He was worried that I'd been at the B&B for some purpose that had nothing to do with my Death Diva business and everything to do with Martin McAuliffe.

I had zero intention of confirming his suspicions. For one thing, it was simply none of his business. But mostly, I had no desire to cause Dom pain. A few weeks earlier he'd declared his love for me, along with a bone-deep need to marry me again and give me the babies we should have had long ago. He'd been working hard to woo me ever since, though with no encouragement on my part.

And yeah, I know that after all those frustrating post-divorce years of watching Dom commit himself to a string of other women, and become a father three times over, I didn't owe him a darn thing. But I also didn't need to rub his nose in my newly resurrected love life. If indeed it was resurrected. The jury was still out.

I scanned the crowd as I attempted to change the subject. "Ty has no use for my services, as far as I can tell, except perhaps—get this!—to help exorcise the inn's resident ghost."

Which was Dom's cue to say, *Ghost? What's all this about a ghost?* Instead he said, "Then what *were* you doing at The Gabbling—"

"Is that Howie?" I said. The tall, dark-skinned man striding on the fringes of the crowd had his back to me, but I'd been friends with Detective Howie Werker long enough to recognize him just from his walk. "It *is* Howie. Which means Cookie's probably around here somewhere."

"What reason would the detectives have to work the funeral of a suicide victim?" he asked. "Howie was probably friends with Stu. That's why he's here."

"You knew Stu," I said. "Can you picture him and Howie tossing back a couple of cold ones at Murray's Pub?"

Dom tipped his head in a way that said he was forced to agree.

The crowd showed signs of restlessness as Darla flipped pages in her bookmarked Bible, finding one dire passage after another with which to condemn her deceased brother-in-law to the everlasting torment of the damned.

"There she is." I pointed to the other side of the throng, where Detective Cookie Kaplan ambled in our direction while scrutinizing the crowd, her sharp gaze moving from face to face. "Does that look like someone just paying her final respects?" I asked.

He frowned. "I thought they decided it was suicide."

"That was the initial assumption, but there are some lingering questions."

He stared at me. "How do you always manage to get in the middle of stuff like this?"

"Who says I'm in the middle of anything? *Sh!* She's coming this way."

"Funny running into you here, Jane," Cookie said as she joined us. Her curly brown hair was pulled back in a messy bun. She wore burgundy-framed eyeglasses and funky earrings made from an old animal-cracker tin. "You told us you didn't know Stu."

"If you're going to arrest everyone who showed up out of curiosity, I don't think you brought enough handcuffs." I didn't want her thinking I was one of the tittering vultures, so I added, "And for the record, Stu and I had mutual acquaintances. So I almost kinda knew him."

I didn't notice Howie sneak up behind me until he said, "Who are these mutual acquaintances?" He and Dom nodded hello.

Oh brother. "Have I ever told you I hate it when you go all cop on me, Howie?"

He gave me a scary-looking scowl. "Are you going to answer the question or do I have to take you downtown and beat it out of you with a rubber hose?"

"Not fair," Cookie said. "It's my turn to beat it out of her with a rubber hose."

"Sounds kinky," Dom said. "Can I watch?"

I said, "I've been to your cop shop, Howie. There's nothing 'downtown' about it. But just to humor you, I'll answer your question. The mutual acquaintances are Ty Collingwood and Georgia Chen. Ty was here earlier, but Georgia's a no-show."

"Her ex is here, though." Cookie tossed her hand toward the crowd. "Henry Noyer."

I brightened. "Really? What does he look like?"

Howie glowered at his partner. "We've talked about this, Cookie. We do not give information to Jane Delaney. Jane Delaney is going to get herself killed one of these days sticking her nose where it doesn't belong." He turned to Dom. "You have anything to add to that?"

"Nope," Dom said. "I think you covered it."

I smacked Howie's shoulder. "Listen to you, you big kidder. As if I don't share useful information with you when I have it. What we have here is a symbiotic relationship." I made a back-and-forth gesture. "Give and take. You scratch my back, I scratch—"

"I forbid you to involve yourself in this case." Howie crossed his arms. "Is that clear?"

"Oh yeah," Dom drawled, "that'll work."

"I mean it, Jane," Howie said. "Leave the snooping to—"

"So you're thinking it's murder, right?" I said. "You're talking about this case as if it's a, well, a case. As in homicide, not suicide."

Cookie chuckled. Howie turned to Dom. "Do you have *any* influence with her?"

My ex gave me the kind of slow, sensual smile that used to turn my innards to pudding. And okay, so it kinda still worked, despite my best efforts to resist. "Janey's always been her own woman," he said. "That's one of the things I love about her."

My heart stuttered. It was one thing for my ex to use the *L* word when it was just the two of us, but a more or less public statement like this was... well, I didn't know what it was.

Yes, I did. It was confusing. I mean, I was officially over Dom. This was an established, unambiguous fact that required no further reflection. It certainly didn't require the warmth I felt creeping into my cheeks, or the difficulty I was having constructing a coherent thought.

What were we talking about again?

The crowd was beginning to thin out as Darla Ruskin continued browbeating everyone within hearing. I almost envied the guy in the econocasket, who was beyond his sister-in-law's biblical scolding. To my knowledge, Stu had never stolen an ox or a sheep, but if it turned out he had, her audience now knew the appropriate punishment.

I turned to Cookie, who was always more appreciative than her partner of that give-and-take thing I mentioned. "You do think it was murder, don't you?"

She preempted Howie's objection with an *I've got this* gesture. "We're still investigating, Jane. Standard procedure in situations like this."

"Did the gun belong to Stu?" I asked.

Howie surprised me by answering for her. "Yes. It was legally registered. So if you've convinced yourself it was homicide, you can see it's not so cut-and-dried."

"Did he buy the gun while Martin was still his bodyguard," I asked, "or after?"

This was news to Dom, I could tell. His imagination started filling in the blanks, and not in a good way. He said, "McAuliffe was mixed up with that thief Stu Ruskin? Why am I not surprised?"

Cookie seemed to know where I was going with my question. "Stu bought the gun five months ago, shortly after Martin quit."

"And did he hire another bodyguard to replace the padre?" I asked.

She shook her head. "Nope."

"Five months seems like a long time to work up the nerve to kill yourself," I said. "So either he wasn't in any particular hurry to get the job done, or he bought the gun for self-protection, once he found himself without a bodyguard."

Cookie and her partner exchanged a look. It was clear they'd already had this discussion.

"There's something else that's probably already occurred to you," I said, "but let me throw it out there anyway. Do you guys consider it at all strange for someone to use a silencer when committing suicide? Especially when the person has got to know his body will be sitting outside all night if no one hears the gunshot. Exposed to, you know, the elements." Some of which possessed fangs and hearty appetites.

"It depends," Howie said. "That's one of those seeming inconsistencies we seasoned detectives are accustomed to dealing with."

That "seasoned detective" thing was a running gag between us, usually deployed whenever I got too nosy. I wasn't about to bring up the other inconsistencies, the ones Sophie had learned from Dr. Temple, the medical examiner. They were told to me in confidence, and Howie wouldn't be too pleased knowing that the results of Stu's autopsy were being dissected, so to speak, over quiche and a fancy grilled cheese.

I asked, "Did you find fingerprints on the gun?"

Howie raised both palms. "That's enough, Jane. My patience is—"

"Did he leave a suicide note?" I asked. "He didn't, did he, or you wouldn't be working it as a potential homicide. Which we all know you are, so spare me."

"Since you've answered your own question," Howie said, "I won't bother responding, except to remind you that suicide notes can be faked. You going to trivia Wednesday?"

Murray's Pub held a trivia contest every Wednesday night. Sophie and I were semi-regulars, and so were the detectives. Dom, however, had no particular fondness for trivia. Plus, Martin would be behind the bar. Speaking of things Dom had no particular fondness for.

"I'll be there," I said, "unless something comes up. You guys want to partner with me and the mayor?"

"Sounds good," he said. "I'll get there early and grab a table."

Cookie tapped her partner's arm and nodded toward the gravesite, where only a handful of people lingered—actual friends and relatives of the dearly departed? I supposed it wasn't outside the realm of possibility. Gilbert had managed to pry his wife's dog-eared Bible out of her hands and was clearly preparing to hightail it out of there.

"We need to have a word with the brother," Cookie said. "See you Wednesday, Jane. I'll come up with a good team name."

I chose our team name last time: A Mayor, a Death Diva, and Two Cops Walk Into a Bar.

Dom watched them walk away, then said, "I have to go, too, Janey. I have a meeting." He leaned down and kissed me on the lips before I could do anything about it. Because, you know, I would've stopped him, but I guess he was too quick. Or something.

Oh, don't start. You'd be conflicted, too. Don't deny it.

"Listen. Before you leave." I squinted toward the people ambling away from the open grave. "I have no idea whether Henry Noyer is still here. Have you met him? Do you know what he looks like?"

"Why do you want to talk to him?" Dom's dark eyebrows pulled together.

"Who said I want to talk to him? Maybe I just want to see what he looks like. I mean, I've heard so much about him."

The look he gave me reminded me he can read my mind. "I don't know what the guy looks like, and if I did, I wouldn't tell you. Howie's right. Leave this mess alone." He checked his watch—some hideously expensive Swiss thing—then pointed a stern finger at me. "You hear me, Janey?"

I laughed. He shook his head in exasperation and walked away. I watched him stride toward the cemetery's gate, all masculine grace and self-assurance. That self-assurance extended to his relationship with me, though not obnoxiously so. While he seemed confident we'd end up together, he didn't take it for granted.

Dom had asked me out on several romantic dates, all of which I'd politely turned down. He continued to invite me to family events, most recently Easter dinner and his mom's birthday party. I couldn't exactly say no to those since I'd always attended in the past. And the fact was, I liked his kids and his parents. I even liked his other two ex-wives, Svetlana and Meryl. Yeah, I'm gonna say it. Dom has good taste in wives.

He'd invited himself over a few times to watch movies we

both loved, or to binge-watch a favorite TV show, always bringing wine or beer and delicious homemade snacks. Well, that's not exactly a date, is it? The snacks, by the way, were of both the vegetarian and meaty persuasions. That alone should tell you how serious he was.

And lately he'd been showing up at places where he knew, or just guessed, I'd be. Didn't it strike you as odd that he'd taken time out of his busy workday to attend the funeral of a cookie rep he'd probably met a handful of times? One he himself had described as "that thief"? Dom knew me. He knew I wouldn't be able to resist checking out Stu's funeral, unrepentant snoop that I am.

He was waging an impassioned battle to win me back, and I'd be lying if I claimed I was immune to it. If nothing else, it was intensely flattering, especially after all those lonely years I'd pined for him. It didn't mean I was going to acquiesce now, when I was finally over him.

Which I was. I was definitely over him.

I looked toward the gravesite and saw the detectives talking with Gilbert and Darla. The last few funeralgoers were wandering away. The show was over, having provided ample material for Crystal Harbor's gluttonous gossipmongers.

As I headed for the nearest walkway, my path began to converge with that of a man dressed too casually for a funeral, in my humble opinion. And okay, so my opinion isn't all that humble. Guilty as charged. I mean, would it have killed this guy to throw on a sport coat over his T-shirt, or at least swap it out for a shirt with buttons and no logo? He was there to pay his respects to a deceased individual, after all, not to mow the grass. And a ball cap? Really? *Harrumph harrumph.*

In the next instant I gave thanks to Saint Flipflops, patron saint of inappropriate funeral attire. The man was about fifteen feet away when the yellow design on his navy-blue tee finally registered: the words *The Cranky Crumb*, complete with a whimsical cartoon image of a cookie wearing a suitably irascible expression and shedding crumbs. His navy ball cap sported a smaller version of the same logo.

The man himself appeared to be in a pleasant enough mood. He was of medium height, with a slim build and heavy-lidded dark-blue eyes, now directed at the walkway we were both headed toward. He had not noticed me noticing him.

"Henry!" I called.

He halted and looked around, his amiable expression turning suspicious as I jogged up to him. "Do I know you?" His voice was pleasingly raspy.

I extended my hand and held it there, more or less forcing him to shake it. "I'm Jane Delaney. I was hoping to run into you here."

"Sorry, I'm not talking to the press." He walked swiftly away, making it difficult to keep up with him. But keep up, I did.

"I'm not the press," I said. "You might've heard of me? Folks around here call me the Death Diva." What the heck. My weird moniker had been known to open doors before. Or at least intrigue people long enough to make them hear me out.

Henry frowned as his pace slowed. "Yeah, I heard of you. Can't remember where."

"Maybe Georgia mentioned me. Your wife and I kind of had lunch together yesterday."

He stopped walking and faced me. "Ex-wife. And she didn't mention you because the two of us don't sit around chatting about how our day went. We don't speak unless it's absolutely necessary. What do you want?"

"I just..." What *did* I want from Henry Noyer? I opted for honesty. "I know what Stu Ruskin did to you, to you and Georgia. The more I learn about him, the more questions I have. Frankly, I find it hard to believe he committed suicide."

"What's your stake in this?"

"My stake?"

"Were you and Ruskin friends?" he asked. "Lovers?"

"No, no, nothing like that," I said. "I didn't know him."

He treated me to a disdainful once-over. "So you're just another rubbernecker fishing for gory details you can impress your friends with over wine spritzers at Murray's Pub. You should be ashamed."

As Henry started to leave, I blurted, "I'm the one who found him. In the hot tub."

Slowly he turned to face me. "I remember now. That's where I heard your name. Your nickname. Someone told me it was you that found him."

"Yeah, well, the whole town's talking about it." My tone did not convey pleasure, and I sensed I'd passed some test, judging by the softening of his expression.

Henry stared off into the distance for a while. Finally he said, "Come on," and led me across the walkway to the cemetery's ritzier neighborhood, marked by rolling hills, elegant plantings, and feathery weeping willow trees, already in leaf. Not to mention a profusion of upright granite. We sat on a stone bench under one of the trees.

He said, "So you don't think Ruskin ate his gun."

"The jury's still out," I said, "but there are too many unanswered questions to just assume it was suicide."

"What kind of questions?"

I hesitated, wondering how much to reveal. Not the autopsy stuff, certainly, but I knew I wasn't the only one wondering about the silencer and the fact that Stu Ruskin had employed a bodyguard—for a few months, anyway. I shared those details with Henry, who seemed to give them some thought. He struck me as a sober, contemplative person, unlike his ex-wife, Georgia, with her hot-and-cold-running emotions. Well, don't they say opposites attract?

That thought brought to mind the padre and our kinda sorta relationship. I hoped he and I weren't *too* opposite. At least when it came to questions of ethics, morals, and criminal tendencies.

"I didn't know his gun had a silencer," he said. "I did know about the bodyguard. Ruskin always was a pretentious jerk."

"So you don't believe his life was in danger?" I asked.

"I know he said it was. He claimed someone tried to kill him. That's what Georgia told me. If you ask me, it was BS."

"So you and Georgia were still talking after she left you?" I asked.

He looked at me as if trying to decide how much of a blabbermouth I was.

"Anything we discuss stays between us," I said. "It's part of the Death Diva code of honor."

One side of his mouth quirked up. "Are we doing Death Diva business here?"

I smiled, too. "I can invoice you if you like. It's ingrained in me, the confidentiality thing. My lips are sealed." Unless I learned something of an illegal nature, in which case they'd get unsealed faster than I can say, *I'm not a priest or a lawyer, so next time keep your big yap shut.*

He sighed. "Georgia never slipped around or lied to me.

That's not her style. Once she became involved with Ruskin, she came right out and told me. As gently as she could, but still. It was the worst day of my life."

I recalled Martin telling me how badly Henry wanted her back. At first. "Had she ever done that before?" I asked. "Um…"

"Been unfaithful?" He shook his head. "Never. Me neither. We were married for twelve years. And they were good years."

I thought about Stu Ruskin, about everything I'd learned about him. "How does a man like that manage to…?" I shook my head.

He watched me trying to make sense of it. "Steal a woman like Georgia?"

Or any previously faithful wife, I thought. Obviously Henry still considered his ex to be pretty special. The admiration was mutual. Just yesterday, Georgia had called Henry her "dreamboat." Clearly an eye-of-the-beholder thing.

"You never met the guy," he said. "He could be… well, I guess the most accurate term is 'charismatic.' Especially when it came to women, but it didn't hurt his business either."

A charismatic salesman. Yeah, I could see how charisma might be a valuable personality trait for someone in that line of work.

I said, "So he had some kind of special hold over Georgia. Until she found out what he'd done." After a moment I added, "You thought she was in on it. Selling your trade secret to Conti-Meeker."

"That's what Ruskin told me at the time." He stared into the distance.

"But now you know she had nothing to do with it," I said.

"How could she have been so careless?" It was the most animated I'd seen him, his face flushed, his features hard.

"But she didn't know he was—"

"She should have!" he said. "They were together for months. How could she not have figured it out by then?"

What could I say to that? I sensed Henry struggling to rein in his emotions. He took a deep breath, yanked off his ball cap, and ran his fingers through his brown hair, which appeared in need of a trim.

He sounded subdued, almost defeated, when he said, "I was devastated when Georgia left. It almost killed me. I would've taken her back. For the longest time, I kept waiting for her to come to her senses, to see that bastard for what he truly was. She wouldn't listen to me. Georgia… she tends to see only the good in everyone." He grimaced. "Until it's too late."

Out of the corner of my eye I noticed activity at Stu's gravesite. Gilbert and Darla had left, and cemetery employees had begun to close the grave.

"Your turn. Why did you come here today?" I indicated Henry's Cranky Crumb T-shirt and cap. "To make some kind of statement? I hate to tell you, but the creep in the casket is past caring."

He glanced down at his shirt. "I have a bunch of these. They're all that's left of a bakery I owned for sixteen years. Started it when I was just twenty-six. A kid. I put everything I had into that business."

"What about Georgia?" I said.

"What about her?"

"Did she put everything she had into it?" I asked. "While you two were together?"

He was quiet for a moment. "Yeah. Yeah, she did."

"So why *did* you come here today?" I asked.

"I could say it was to make sure he was dead, but without

being able to peek inside the box..." He shrugged. "Did anyone bother to drive a stake through his heart?"

"Take my word for it," I said. "Stu Ruskin is no more."

"That's right." He looked at me. "You saw him. After."

"Just one more thing that can be counted on to jolt me awake in the middle of the night," I said.

"I saw you talking to those cops," he said. "The tall Black dude and that woman with the glasses and curly hair."

"Howie Werker and Cookie Kaplan," I said. "How do you know they're police detectives?"

He gave me a look that said, *You're kidding, right?* "They weren't exactly trying to blend in."

"Maybe they were being deliberately conspicuous," I said. "Hoping someone would approach them with information."

"So, what do your cop friends think about Ruskin's so-called suicide?" he asked.

"The official line? Too early to tell. They're still investigating."

"And unofficially?" he said. "You must've gotten a sense of which way they're leaning."

The detectives' very presence at the funeral told me which way they were leaning, but I was uncomfortable having this conversation with a near stranger—one who had every reason to despise the deceased. "Not really," I said. "We'll just have to wait."

Henry's expression told me I wasn't fooling him, but all he said was, "When they find out who did it, I hope I get a chance to shake his hand."

6
A Sweet Little Old Lady from Central Casting

VINCENT VAN GOGH kept fussing with the bandage covering his left ear. It was held in place by a long strip of white fabric, which passed under his chin and disappeared beneath his blue cap, trimmed in black fur. A shapeless green jacket completed the look. You might recognize this fetching ensemble from his famous *Self-Portrait with Bandaged Ear*, completed in 1889.

Vincent sat at one end of a ponderous leather sofa in the large, wood-paneled office of Sten Jakobsen, attorney-at-law. A human-size cactus sat at the other end.

And yeah, there was indeed an actual human inside the bulky green neoprene cactus costume, which was studded all over with lethal-looking but harmless rubbery spines. A large pink blossom adorned the top of the cactus, which extended almost a foot above Lola Rutishauer's scowling, green-painted face, framed by an oval opening in the neoprene. The unwieldy costume thwarted her attempts to cross her cactusy arms in annoyance.

Vincent van Gogh—real name Austin Rutishauer—spoke

up. "I'm getting rid of this itchy thing." He whipped off his cap and started to untie the bandage. At fifty-two, he was three years younger than his sister, Lola, but at the moment he came across as a whiny toddler.

Sten Jakobsen responded from behind his massive mahogany desk, speaking in his usual slow, precise way. "As has been explained to you, Mr. Rutishauer, failure to adhere to every detail of the requirements laid out by Opal Stenger will nullify any claim you might have to her estate."

"Aunt Opal was a damn crackpot," Austin snapped as he retied the bandage and jammed the hat back onto his head. "No, I take it back. That woman was certifiably insane. What kind of sadistic nut makes her heirs wear dopey costumes to the reading of her will?"

His sister decided the rhetorical question merited an answer. "A sadistic nut with eighty million in the bank, mansions in Crystal Harbor and Palm Beach, and a six-thousand-square-foot penthouse apartment on Fifth Avenue with a view of Central Park. Go ahead, Austin, ditch the costume. More for me." The glint of anticipation in her eyes told me she was mentally redecorating those six thousand square feet.

I observed all this from the comfort of a cushy leather chair tucked into a corner near a potted tree. If my client Opal Stenger had required *me* to don a silly costume that day, I would've obeyed without complaint. Trust me, it would have been way down on the list of embarrassing things I've had to do during my bizarre career. Happily, she'd made no such demand, which meant I was free to wear the same forgettable outfit I'd worn to Stu Ruskin's funeral the day before: the gray skirt suit, pearls, and plain black pumps I thought of as my Death Diva uniform.

Opal was not, in fact, certifiably insane, though it would be hard to argue with "crackpot." She had her own reasons for scheduling this particular meeting, and specific ideas about how she wanted it conducted. Which brings us to the costumes.

I'd delivered them to her relatives several days earlier. You can imagine how that went over. However, once they'd accepted that there was no arguing with their aunt at this point, they'd grudgingly accepted her terms: wear the embarrassing costume or be cut out of her will.

Opal never had children. Her closest relations were Lola, Austin, and their cousin, Clive Rutishauer. Speaking of which…

"Where the heck is Clive?" Austin said.

Lola had to shift her entire neoprene-clad body to squint at the big brass clock on the credenza. "He's seven minutes late. Let's start."

"We will proceed when all parties are present," Sten said, "not before." The lawyer was in his early seventies, his amber gaze sharp behind wire-rimmed glasses, his blond hair nearly as white as his trim beard. Sten's erect six-four stature, noble bearing, and quiet intelligence gave him an imposing presence that he'd used to good effect during his long career in the law.

I said, "If Clive doesn't show up soon, I'll give him a call. Would you like some water or soda? Coffee?"

"What I'd *like*," Austin said, "is to find out how much cash I'm getting and which one of those mansions is mine so I can sell it and retire."

I couldn't fault the man for his impatience. He'd been a salesman in a children's shoe store for the past thirty-four years.

The door swung open and Bigfoot lumbered into the room.

Lola's jaw dropped. "You have got to be kidding me."

"Actually, that kinda makes sense," Austin said.

He was right. There was a reason Opal Stenger chose this

particular look for her nephew Clive. A big guy in both height and girth, he filled out the shaggy, apelike costume, which included a full-head mask with little eyeholes. Predictably, it also featured huge feet that slapped the Oriental carpet as he crossed the room to Sten, who stood to greet him.

I stood, too, and made introductions. Sten shook Bigfoot's massive paw. "Thank you for coming today, Mr. Rutishauer," he said.

"Call me Clive." Bigfoot gave a sad shake of his big head. "Poor Aunt Opal. I can't believe she's gone. She was a hell of a lady, I'll tell you that."

Lola snorted. Austin rolled his eyes.

"She made it to eighty-three," Clive continued, "but if you ask me, she went far too soon. It's not fair. That wonderful woman should've lived to a hundred."

Lola emitted a bark of laughter. "Another seventeen years putting up with that harpy?"

"More to the point," Austin said, "another seventeen years working our butts off until we're too old and used-up to enjoy our inheritance."

"Aunt Opal could've thrown us a few million anytime she wanted," Lola griped. "She wouldn't have missed it. But no, the stingy old bat made us wait till she croaked."

"That's not fair. You two never got to know her like I did." Clive wagged a big, furry finger at his cousins. "When's the last time you visited her?"

"Why would I willingly spend time with that horrible woman?" Lola said.

Austin backed up his sister. "She was abusive."

"'Abusive,'" Clive scoffed. "Poor little Austin, the boy without a backbone. I like that Aunt Opal never took crap from anyone."

"Yeah, you can do that," Lola said, "when you've inherited zillions from a husband who was old enough to be your grandpa."

"And what about her fantastic sense of humor, huh? Pulling a stunt like this from beyond the grave?" Clive indicated his woolly self, laughing. "Trademark Aunt Opal, am I right?"

"Clive," I said, "can I get you something before we start? Coffee, tea—"

"I'll take a beer."

"Um, I'm afraid we're all out," I said. "How about a soda?"

"Nah, that's okay, then. Nothing for me."

I invited him to have a seat. He got into the part, striding with a gorillalike swagger, swinging his long arms, and emitting the occasional simian grunt before settling his shaggy bulk in the center of the sofa. Between his sheer size and his widespread knees, Lola and Austin ended up squashed against the armrests. Sasquatch appeared to be a fan of manspreading. Who knew?

"We're just waiting for one other person," I said. "As soon as he gets here, we can—"

The door opened and I spent long, dumbfounded moments struggling to process what I was seeing. An eighteenth-century nobleman stood leaning against the doorframe with ankles crossed, insouciantly posed as if in a period painting. It was a case of visual overload as my stunned gaze skidded over the elaborately embroidered ice-blue frock coat and ivory waistcoat; the frothy lace cascading from sleeves and throat; the gold-trimmed knee britches and blue silk stockings; the ivory satin shoes with jeweled buckles and high, stacked heels; the gigantic powdered wig; and finally, the full-on makeup and rouge—historically accurate, believe it or not—complete with a small, black beauty patch on the left cheek.

Opal's niece and nephews lost no time before debating the newcomer's identity. Lola claimed he was their aunt's studly accountant, a man equally at home in both spreadsheets and bedsheets. Austin insisted he was the studly plumber Opal kept on call twenty-four seven because dangerous leaks can happen any time of the day or night. In her bedroom. Clive claimed they were both wrong and that this guy was her studly personal chef. Which led to the inevitable gag about Aunt Opal's prodigious appetites, and if you didn't see that one coming, you haven't been paying attention.

Lola said, "He's too tall for the chef, and too young for the plumber."

"Well, you can forget about the accountant," Austin said. "He quit the biz to become a monk."

"I hope this doesn't mean we have to split everything four ways." Lola glared at the weirdo in the doorway. "Who the heck *are* you, anyway?"

"Eez eet not obvious?" the man drawled, in a snooty French accent. He bowed, with a flourish. "Zee Marquis de Sade, at your service."

I finally managed to find my voice, which came out as more of a growl. "Excuse us." I grabbed a fistful of the marquis's lace jabot and hauled him through the doorway, past Sten's gawking paralegal and receptionist, and down the hall to a vacant conference room. I slammed the door shut.

"What the *hell*, Padre?"

"Did I misunderstand zee theme of zee day?" Martin asked, still all Frenchy, still striking a foppish pose.

"You know very well the costumes are for Opal Stenger's heirs." I gave him a good, hard shove. Alas, he was immovable. The fancy shoes added several inches to his six-foot frame. I found his elevated height, in conjunction with the outlandish makeup and wig, more than a little unnerving.

"You also know that Sten hired you for security," I said, "in case one of Opal's unloved ones decides to get physical. How are you supposed to do your job dressed like that? And why the Marquis de Sade, of all people?"

"Beats me."

Well, I walked right into that one.

Why did we need security? you ask. I knew Opal's three heirs expected their aunt's estate, which was worth close to a hundred million bucks, to be divided equally between them. I also knew they were in for a surprise. Sten was concerned about their reactions. Once he learned about Martin's side gig as a bodyguard, he decided he was just the fellow to keep order during this unorthodox meeting.

I was tempted to demand Martin go home and change, for all the good it would do me. However, we were already running late, and I was eager to get this whole thing over with.

"Well, at least take off that idiotic wig," I said, "and wipe off the makeup."

"Nonsense. Eet eez all part of zee *ensemble*." If anything, the marquis's French accent was growing more pronounced. "And if you continue being zo mean, I weel not tell you what zee gendarmes are saying about our dairly departed 'ot-tub enthusiast."

All right, now he had my attention. The padre had at least one loquacious buddy on the force. I pictured Martin sliding free beers across the bar at Murray's Pub last night and being rewarded with the latest cop-shop gossip.

I jumped as someone knocked on the door and cracked it open. Sten's paralegal stuck her head in. "Um, Mr. Jakobsen wants to know when—"

"In a minute, Jeanie," I said, as politely as I could manage. The instant the door closed, I turned back to Martin. "Okay, spill."

He dropped the accent. "They're definitely leaning toward a finding of suicide."

I made no attempt to conceal my surprise. "I saw Howie and Cookie at the funeral yesterday. Looked to me like they were at least keeping an open mind."

"I don't know the specifics," he said, "but it seems there just isn't enough compelling evidence to indicate homicide. For what it's worth, I think they're getting pressure from Bonnie. She probably wants to close the file on this one."

Bonnie Hernandez, Dom's ex-fiancée, happened to be the town's chief of police.

"Did they find a suicide note?" I asked.

"Nope."

"I know you thought he was murdered."

"Still do," he said.

"But—"

"There's more. Have you been wondering whether they recovered fingerprints from the gun?"

"Yes!" I said. "Please tell me they did."

"They didn't."

"Dang!" I said. "Because it was in water?"

He shook his bewigged head. "Because it was in *warm* water dosed with sanitizing chemicals. But guns just don't hold fingerprints well. The textured surfaces, for starters."

"Really?" I said. "Someone should tell the folks who write all those TV crime shows."

"Come, *ma chérie*." Martin opened the door and ushered me

through it. "Zee othairs weel begin to wondair what we are up to in here." He punctuated this with a lascivious Gallic chortle.

"Are you *trying* to channel Pepé Le Pew?" I asked. "Because if so, you nailed it."

Back in Sten's office, I made no attempt to explain the marquis's presence. Whatever stories they'd concocted were preferable to the truth.

You see, guys, Sten and I are pretty sure that one or more of you are likely to be Very Disappointed by what is about to transpire here today, so we brought in the Marquis de Sade in case you decide to express that disappointment in a socially unacceptable and potentially lethal fashion.

The padre took up a position near the sofa, one hand on his hip, the other dangling a lace hanky. What did it say about me that he still looked kinda sexy, even now?

Okay, you can just keep it to yourself. Not every question needs an answer.

Sten, being Sten, didn't so much as bat the proverbial eyelash in the face of the bodyguard's preposterous getup. "Before we proceed with the formalities," he intoned, at his signature glacial pace, "your aunt requested that each of you, in turn, share your favorite memory of her."

Lola and Austin groaned in unison. "Do we have to?" Lola whined. "I mean, is this another one of that crazy old bat's moronic requirements before we finally get to find out how rich we are?"

"This part is compulsory, yes," Sten said.

"It doesn't have to be long," I offered. "A few words will do."

Clive waved his shaggy arm and said, "Ooh! Ooh! Can I go first?"

"By all means," Sten said. "I applaud your enthusiasm, Clive."

"Well, when I was a kid, I just loved hanging with my aunt Opal."

Lola slumped in her seat, to the extent she could do so while encased in all that green neoprene. "Oh, here we go."

"I was nine." The eyes peering out of the Bigfoot mask squinted in concentration. "No, I guess I'd already turned ten. It was the summer after fifth grade."

Austin did that rolling motion with his arm, telling his cousin to get to the point.

"Okay, okay, so you know how many cats my mom had, right?" he asked his cousins. "I loved Mom, but face it, she was the original cat lady. I never got a clear count, but there were at least seven or eight at any given time."

"We remember the darn cats," Lola said. "What about them?"

"So Aunt Opal comes over for dinner one day and she brings this big bakery cake for dessert. Decorated all fancy, with flowers and what-all. And right in the middle, in elegant script, it says, 'Your house smells like a litter box.' I laughed so hard, my mom sent me to bed without supper. But it was worth it."

"Thank you for sharing your special memory." Sten turned to Austin. "Mr. Rutishauer?"

"My favorite memory of Aunt Opal is when this one over here—" Austin tossed his hand in my direction "—called to tell me the old broad had dropped dead."

"Argh!" Lola smacked her cactusy forehead. "Wish I'd thought of that one. Okay, let me see... Well, there was that time Aunt Opal let me drive her to Jones Beach."

"So?" Clive said.

"So I was eleven," Lola said. "I had to stand up to reach the brake pedal in that baby-blue Caddy she had back then. Aunt Opal was totally calm, coaching me the whole way. We almost got creamed getting onto the Meadowbrook Parkway, but I got us there."

Austin thought about it. "Actually, I've gotta admit, that sounds kind of cool."

Sten said, "Well then, if we are all finished…" He turned to me and nodded.

I rose and crossed to a door that connected to the adjacent office. I opened it and said, "I think we're ready for you."

"Not *another* heir," Austin griped. "They're coming out of the woodwork."

In the next instant he was gawking, along with the others, at the woman who'd marched into the room.

"Whaddaya know," Lola said, as she took in the newcomer's sleek white hairdo, vivid orange lipstick, purple silk pantsuit, and heavy diamond jewelry. "This one's done up like Aunt Opal."

"That *is* Aunt Opal, you idiot!" Clive launched himself off the sofa and ran over to wrap her in a furry embrace.

"You're—You're not dead?" Austin sputtered.

Opal turned her steely gaze on her hapless nephew, making him flinch. "I take back all those cracks I made about your mental capacity, Austin. You're *twice* as dumb as I thought."

Lola sprang off the sofa, nearly taking a header on the coffee table, thanks to her cumbersome costume. Martin stuck close to her as she stalked over to Sten's desk and slammed her fists onto it. The official Marquis de Sade security detail stood ready to do battle with a cactus, should the need arise.

"You lied to us!" she accused the lawyer. "You told us she was dead."

"Correction," I said, "*I* told you your aunt Opal was dead. *I* told you today's meeting was for the reading of her will. Mr. Jakobsen never said any such thing."

It was true. Being the conscientious lawyer he is, Sten wasn't about to directly lie to his client's relatives. That didn't mean he was above playing along with her little charade. At this point in his long career, he wasn't averse to pushing the boundaries.

Austin was on his feet now. "So this was all, what? Some kind of sick joke? Just a way to make us all look foolish?" He yanked off his cap and bandage, and tossed them onto the carpet. Turned out he actually looked a lot like the great artist he was meant to impersonate, right down to the red hair and perpetually mournful expression.

His sister was beginning to figure it out. "No, this was a way to trick us into telling her what we really thought of her. She was probably behind that door the whole time, listening to our conversation. Right, Aunt Opal?"

Opal said, "At least you're not as dumb as your brother. Which isn't saying much."

Austin began to panic, clearly envisioning millions of pictures of George Washington slipping through his fingers. "All those things you heard me say, Aunt Opal, I didn't really mean them. They were… well, they were kind of a joke." He tried to laugh, but it came out as a sad little wheeze. "I think I said something like… oh, I don't know, that you were 'certifiably insane'? Who would take that seriously?"

"According to you, I'm also 'abusive,'" Opal said, with a flat little smile, "and a 'sadistic nut.' Oh, wait, that one's true. I'm cutting you out of my will. Sadistic enough for you?"

The padre spoke up. "Nothing eez evair sadeestic enough for *moi*." When this was met with blank stares, he added, "Not to boast, but zee word *sadeestic* comes from my name."

"Who the hell invited the Marquis de Sade?" Opal demanded. "Are you related to me? Never mind, I like your style. I'm putting you in my will."

Martin executed another flourishy bow. "You are too kind, madame."

"What am I going to do now?" Austin wailed. "I was counting on that money. As soon as I heard you were dead, I bought a Maserati and a timeshare in the Hamptons."

"You just keep proving my point," Opal cackled.

Lola wheeled on me. "This is all *your* fault! You lied to us. You set us up."

She flew at me, a big cartoon cactus with vengeance in its heart. Martin moved like lightning, seemingly unencumbered by his elaborate suit of clothes, enormous wig, and high-heeled shoes. He grabbed Lola around her middle and flung her onto the sofa.

Never breaking character, he wagged a beringed finger at her and said, "You weel behave yourself, madame, or suffair zee consequences."

"It was supposed to be mine!" Lola struggled against her bulky costume in an attempt to sit up. "The penthouse apartment. A third of all that money. What did I ever do to deserve this?"

Opal said, "You mean besides running me down to anyone who'd listen? Getting in touch with me only when you wanted something? It's been going on for decades. You think I don't have feelings, just because I don't fit the mold of a sweet little old lady from central casting?"

Lola gave up trying to sit and instead rolled off the sofa onto the carpet, then grabbed the coffee table and pulled herself to her feet. She stabbed a green finger toward her brother. "It was

Austin, Aunt Opal. He was always running you down. I stuck up for you. Punish him, not me."

Austin gaped at her, the picture of outraged betrayal. "You called her a stingy old bat, not five minutes ago. And a whaddayacallit. A harpy."

"Don't forget 'horrible woman,'" Opal said. "That one's my favorite. If either of you ever had the guts to say those things to my face, I'd at least have a little respect. As it is, you're both out of my will and I'm leaving everything to your cousin Clive."

Bigfoot blinked in surprise. Clearly he was the only one in the room who hadn't seen that one coming. "Aw, Aunt Opal, I don't know what to say." He hugged her again. "Except I hope that inheritance doesn't happen for a long, long time."

"Well, my doctor says I have the heart of a twenty-year-old marathon runner," she said, "so you might get your wish. In the meantime, I'm going to take Lola's suggestion and do what I should've done ages ago."

Lola looked alarmed. "*My* suggestion?"

"I'm giving Clive a big chunk of his inheritance right away," Opal said. "You were right. Why make him wait?" She put her arm through his shaggy one. "Let's blow this joint, big fella. You can afford to buy me a beer."

7
You'll Never Take Me Alive, Suckers!

"WELL, WHO'S THIS hefty guy?" I stood in the foyer of The Gabbling Goose, keeping a solid grip on Sexy Beast's basket tote as the biggest house cat I'd ever seen nudged my ankles, nearly knocking me over. SB peered over the edge of the tote, his little nose working overtime as he attempted to compartmentalize this strange new creature.

My nose was working overtime, too, but not because of the cat. Ambrosial scents wafted from the direction of the kitchen. Someone was baking.

"I guess you didn't meet Toby when you were here last week," Shelley said. "She was probably down in the basement, hunting."

"Hunting?" I said. "You mean, like, for mice?"

"Best mouser we've ever had." She lifted SB out of the tote and gave him scritches, while he kept a wary eye on the supersize brown tabby at our feet. "The Gabbling Goose has always had a cat around to keep the critters under control, starting way back in Oswald and Sybille's time. Sybille was quite accomplished with a needle and she actually embroidered some of the cats' portraits. They're hanging in the dining room."

Toby's body was over two feet long. A thick, bushy tail added at least another twelve inches to her overall length. A long, shaggy coat, extravagant chest ruff, oversize paws, striking green eyes, and furry, tufted ears added to her distinctive appearance. She didn't so much meow as trill, a sort of musical purr.

"This has to be a Maine Coon," I said. "Aren't they the largest domestic cat breed?"

"Right you are," Shelley said, as she set SB on the rug. He scrambled right back to me, begging to be picked up. I hesitated, not wanting to appear overly protective of my nervous little poodle, but let's face it. The inn's resident mouser was easily twice his weight, and appeared even larger with all that fur. She might see him as simply another species of vermin in need of eradication, albeit one with a meticulously trimmed apricot coat and neatly clipped nails.

Shelley's knowing gaze told me I was doing a poor job of concealing my trepidation. "Don't worry about Toby. She's more dog than cat if you ask me. Your basic gentle giant and very friendly—well, as long as you're not a mouse."

Sure enough, Toby appeared curious and even playful, nudging and sniffing SB, gradually putting him at ease. I witnessed no tail twitching on Toby's part, no hissing, no unsheathed claws.

"How about that, SB?" I said. "You made a new friend."

It was late afternoon, about half past five. Once that bizarre meeting at Sten's office had finally adjourned, I'd grabbed a quick lunch at Janey's Place: my usual papaya-ginger smoothie, a so-called healthy drink so yummy I could forget it was supposed to be good for me.

Yeah, that's right, I'm a picky little kid who has to be tricked (even by herself) into consuming food with redeeming nutritional value. Your point?

Following lunch, I took Sexy Beast for a long walk on what had turned into a bright, sunny afternoon, after a miserable gray start to the day. Then I tried to concentrate on some Death Diva paperwork while SB watched a rerun of *Sesame Street*, his favorite TV show. However, my mind kept sliding back to Stu Ruskin and my unanswered questions. It was one of those questions that had brought me back here to The Gabbling Goose.

Okay, you're right, I should've just left the whole thing alone. It was none of my business and all that. But looking at it objectively (which, as you know, I always do), it was clear that the cops (specifically my ex-husband's ex-fiancée, the chief of police, not that that had anything to do with it because I'm, you know, so objective) had jumped to the conclusion that Stu Ruskin had done himself in, despite compelling evidence to the contrary. And, I mean, it's not like I was conducting my own investigation or anything. I'd just gone to The Gabbling Goose to satisfy my curiosity on one little point. Perfectly understandable and not at all presumptuous or meddlesome, right?

Okay, you're not the boss of me, and I'll be presumptuous and meddlesome if I feel like it.

A burst of muted feminine laughter from another room told me Shelley and I weren't alone. Too bad. I was hoping for a nice private chat with her. "You're probably busy," I said. "I'm taking you away from paying guests. I just had a quick question, but I can come back some other time."

"No guests here at the moment," she said. "We had the nicest group of ladies staying with us for a few days—a 'wench convench,' they called it, isn't that cute?—but they left this morning, and no one else is expected until after dinner. Woody's upstairs getting the rooms ready. He actually enjoys cleaning, and I'd rather take care of reservations, payments, all that managerial stuff."

"Sounds like a match made in B&B heaven," I said.

"Well, plus Woody has become so forgetful and confused," she added, sotto voce, "it's really better if I take care of the business end of things."

Sexy Beast must have decided Toby was all right. He lowered his chest in the classic doggie play bow, an invitation that was not lost on his new friend. They began to chase each other around the room. SB yipped happily, while Toby emitted the occasional birdlike chirp.

"Come." Shelley led the way through the adjoining drawing room, a cozy sitting area with a fireplace and comfortable antique furnishings. The walls were filled with old paintings and framed embroidery, the latter no doubt the work of Sybille Collingwood.

My gaze lingered on a rectangular wooden coffee table whose glass top protected a large embroidered panel depicting the exterior of The Gabbling Goose as it appeared back in Colonial days. I would have liked to linger and examine it more closely, but Shelley didn't pause, so I followed her into the huge country kitchen, which managed to retain its Colonial flavor despite the ultramodern appliances.

"Oh my Gawd, it's the Death Diva!" Georgia Chen wore a hot pink bib apron adorned with dozens of pin buttons, displaying everything from promotional advertising to jokey one-liners to sappy inspirational messages—*The harder I work, the luckier I get!*—to vintage political slogans. Richard Nixon and George McGovern shared equal billing on Georgia's apron.

The pastry chef was in the process of sliding filled muffin tins into the oven. A couple of dozen finished muffins cooled on racks on the granite counters. Blueberry by the looks of them, and some that looked and smelled like apple-walnut.

She shut the oven door and rushed over to wrap her arms around me. It was only our second meeting and already I was getting the Big Hug. "So glad to see you, Jane," she gushed. "What are you doing here?"

"I was about to ask you the same question," I said.

"You're looking at the new, official pastry chef for The Gabbling Goose." Georgia executed a snappy salute.

"Don't tell me you actually quit your job at Patisserie Susanne."

"Nah. Mondays and Tuesdays are my days off. Amy got me this gig, she's such a doll. Have you two met?"

Georgia directed this question over my shoulder. I followed her gaze and saw an attractive thirtyish woman entering from the enclosed porch.

"I don't think so." The woman crossed the room to shake my hand. "I'm Amy Collingwood."

I introduced myself. So this was Ty's daughter.

She frowned in concentration. "Your name sounds familiar."

Shelley was pulling dessert plates out of a cabinet. "Jane was here last Wednesday night. She's the one who found Stu's body."

Amy's eyes widened. "That's right, I remember now. Dad mentioned meeting you."

Amy Collingwood had medium-brown hair pulled back in a practical ponytail, and eyes the same shape and blue-gray color of her dad's. She wore a teal blouse and gray dress slacks, and I assumed she'd gone straight to her family's B&B after work. I recalled Shelley proudly mentioning that Amy was a conservation scientist with the Long Island Environmental Alliance.

Georgia addressed Shelley. "So the ones in the oven are lemon-poppy. Once all the muffins have cooled, I'll wrap most of them for the freezer and you can serve them all week. Next time I'll make chocolate babka and cinnamon buns. I won't even *think* about apple crisp, 'cause Amy told me that's your specialty. Can't wait to try it." She rinsed her hands at the sink and dried them on an embroidered tea towel.

"Wait a minute. Is that…?" I took the damp tea towel from her and shook it out. An exquisite floral pattern had been meticulously stitched onto linen that appeared quite old. "Is this an antique?"

"Shelley insisted I use it!" Georgia cried, as if I'd accused her of some unspeakable act.

"Oh, that," Shelley said. "That's some of Sybille's work. We have dozens of her pieces. Napkins, tablecloths, pillowcases—"

"And you *use* them?" I gaped at her. "Embroidery from the seventeenth century?"

"Would you prefer we lock them away in some trunk where no one can see them?" she said. "Sybille put a lot of work and love into those things. She wanted them to be used and enjoyed."

"Well, but won't they get destroyed?" I asked.

"Does that thing look like it's been destroyed?" she asked, not unreasonably. "It's not like we scrub the floors with them. We use them gently and clean them even more gently. Don't worry, these pretty things will outlast us all."

Amy was laughing. "You're not going to budge her on this subject, Jane. Don't even try."

"Now for the important question." Shelley plunked the

dessert plates onto the oak table in the center of the room. "How do we know these muffins are any good? We'd better make sure."

"You can never be too careful." Amy transferred several muffins from the cooling racks to a small platter. "I'll put on a pot of coffee."

"You know what goes even better with muffins?" I withdrew a bottle of good Cabernet from my tote bag and wagged it.

The ladies greeted this idea with enthusiasm, and within a couple of minutes we were sitting around the table, enjoying a late-afternoon snack of warm muffins and first-rate vino.

"Oh my Gawd," Georgia cried, "look at that cute little dog!"

Sexy Beast and Toby had made an appearance, heading straight for the food and water bowls near the back door. SB slaked his thirst before sniffing delicately at the kibble in Toby's food bowl, finally deciding to take a pass. Poodles are notoriously picky eaters. As far as my discerning pet was concerned, if it's not people food or his preferred brand of gourmet dog food, it's not worth taking a chance on.

I made the introductions, and Georgia lavished abundant love on my little guy. "We should introduce Sexy Beast to my boxer, Jackson. They could have a play date."

"Bring Jackson next time you come," Shelley said. "We're dog-friendly here, and as you can see, Toby doesn't discriminate."

SB ate up the attention before joining Toby on her plush kitty bed, the two of them snuggling like cross-species lovers. SB started licking the cat's head, a spa treatment she appeared to appreciate, judging by her half-closed eyes and trilling purr. I'd never known Sexy Beast to cough up a hairball, but something told me he might find out what it's like.

I reached for a warm apple-walnut muffin. "I'm curious how you two know each other," I said, looking from Georgia to Amy.

"Oh, we met at the patisserie," Georgia said. "Just about a week ago, right, Amy?"

"Six days ago, to be precise," Amy said. "Wednesday morning. I popped in before work to pick up a birthday cake for a coworker. Georgia wrote the happy-birthday message in icing and added a few extra garnishes."

"So we got to chatting, and whaddaya know, it turned out we had someone in common." Georgia frowned in concentration. "Didn't I tell you about Amy? I'm sure I mentioned her."

"I don't think so." I lifted my wineglass and took a sip.

"Yeah, yeah," she said, "I told you that her and Stu got engaged while he was seeing me."

I blinked at Amy. "That was *you*?"

"I'm afraid so." Her expression was grim.

Shelley reached over and squeezed her hand, her sympathetic expression downright grandmotherly. Amy placed her free hand over Shelley's and gave her a warm smile. I recalled Shelley mentioning that Amy, as a kid, had spent a lot of time at The Gabbling Goose when school wasn't in session, and had worked there as a teen during summer vacations. The two were clearly very close.

"Amy," I said, "I have to ask. Were you still engaged to Stu last week? When you met Georgia at the bakery?"

She nodded. An angry flush stained her cheeks. "The two of us compared notes. Turns out I'd been seeing Stu for a couple of months when he got involved with Georgia this past June. I still had no clue about her when we got engaged in November."

"Meanwhile I dumped him in December," Georgia said,

"after he stole the cookie recipe and sold it to Conti-Meeker. I didn't know about Amy at the time, of course. I only knew he was a home-wrecking rat thief."

"And I didn't know anything about the whole cookie scandal while it was happening," Amy said. "It was dumb luck, meeting Georgia at the bakery last week. I learned that the man I was engaged to marry, the man I'd been planning to grow old with, had—" her voice cracked "—had betrayed me. I was so stunned, I nearly dropped the cake."

"What did you do?" I asked.

"As soon as I got in my car, I called Stu," Amy said. "He tried to weasel out of it, of course. He denied even knowing Georgia. I guess he thought I was too dimwitted, or too besotted with him, to see through his BS. But I was having none of it, and finally he was forced to admit it. He tried to make it sound like Georgia was this conniving seductress who worked her dark magic on him."

At this, Georgia let out a shrill laugh, which startled Sexy Beast and Toby in mid-lovefest. "Yeah, that's me, a real femme fatale."

I wondered what, if anything, it meant that this little drama occurred last Wednesday, mere hours before Stu Ruskin—or someone—put a bullet in his brain.

"I take it you called off the engagement," I said.

"Right then and there," Amy said, "over the phone."

"Did he try to change your mind?" I asked.

"Did he ever. He was distraught, almost desperate. Insisted we meet face-to-face to talk it over. No way. I was done."

Georgia said, "I hope that rat gave you a big freakin' ring and I hope you sold it for a lot of bread."

"I had no intention of keeping that ring *or* selling it," Amy said. "I knew Stu was visiting an account in the city, so I called my work to tell them I'd be late and drove straight to his house. He'd given me a key, which I left on his coffee table, along with the ring."

"Gawd!" Georgia groaned. "You never give back the ring. Not after the rat shows his true colors. Don't you know anything?"

Amy's expression turned bleak. "What I know is it was never me he wanted. I figured that out before we got off the phone. Stu was using me. I was a means to an end."

"Well, it's all over now." Shelley squeezed Amy's hand again—more an admonition this time, I sensed, than a gesture of sympathy. "We don't need to get into all that."

Sure we do. I topped off their wineglasses. "What did Stu expect to get by marrying you?"

Amy spread her arms. "All of this. The Gabbling Goose and surrounding acreage. The Collingwood ancestral estate."

I started to ask why that was so important to him when the answer walloped me upside the head. "It all goes back to the blood feud, doesn't it? Between the Collingwoods and the Ruskins."

Shelley answered for her. "Stu Ruskin's ancestors never managed to hold on to any property. A bunch of losers, all of them. Their original homestead in Crystal Harbor changed hands countless times over the years. You know that Sunoco gas station just down the road? That's where Percival Ruskin's house was, with the basement tavern."

The tavern where Peg Leg Percy sold his version of Sybbie's Punch back in the seventeenth century, after stealing the recipe.

"Stu knew I'd be inheriting all this someday," Amy said. "He figured that marrying me was the only way to get his hands on the Collingwood estate. He probably saw it as a way for the Ruskins to finally stick it to the Collingwoods after all these years."

"But you won't inherit this place for a good long time," I said. "I mean, your parents are, what, in their mid-fifties? Your father looks to be in great shape."

"Dad works out a lot," Amy said, "but it's all about cardiac rehab—he has a heart condition. The Collingwood men tend to die young. And my mom is six years older than him and has her own health issues. Stu knew all this."

"He wouldn't have owned the property, though," I said, "even if you two were married."

Amy grimaced. "He knew me well enough to know I'd make my husband joint owner. I get sick thinking about how close I came to handing over my family's legacy to that… that…"

"The word you're groping for is 'rat.'" Georgia tore off a piece of her apple-walnut muffin, inspected the texture, gave a satisfied nod, and popped it into her mouth.

"So the feud really isn't over, is it?" I asked Shelley. "You told me things had cooled down between the two families, that they basically keep out of each other's way. Sounds like Stu never got the memo."

"He got the memo, all right," she said, "he just had no interest in keeping the peace. He had no interest in anything that didn't directly benefit Stu Ruskin, and he didn't care who he hurt in the process."

Amy picked at her blueberry muffin, her expression glum. "He was so smooth, so believable. So easy to fall in love with."

"Don't I know it," Georgia said. "The guy was a sociopath, you ask me."

"If I'd only known at the time."

One of Shelley's gray eyebrows arched. "Your dad tried to warn you."

"Don't remind me." Amy looked chagrined. "I wish I'd listened to him."

"He tried to talk you out of seeing Stu?" I asked.

"Of course. I didn't take him seriously. I mean, would you have? Knowing it all went back to that ridiculous feud?"

"What did your father say when you two got engaged?" I asked.

"Oh, I didn't tell him. And I never let him see the ring. The only person I told is sitting right here." Amy laid a fond hand on Shelley's shoulder. "And I swore her to secrecy. Not even Woody knew."

Shelley said, "You thought your dad would come around eventually. I knew better. I was just praying you'd come to your senses before the wedding. You refused to hear anything critical about your fiancé."

"I can be pretty stubborn, I admit it," Amy said.

"Well, you come by it honestly," Shelley said. "The Collingwoods and Ruskins are nothing if not stubborn."

I said, "To keep a family feud going for three and a half centuries? Yeah, I'd say that's the definition of stubborn."

Amy turned to Georgia. "You called Stu a sociopath, but I have to disagree. From what I understand, sociopaths have no conscience."

"My point precisely." Georgia tossed back the last of her wine and grabbed the bottle. "Gawd, you of all people should know that rat didn't have anything resembling a conscience."

"Then why did he commit suicide?" Amy asked. "For sure it wasn't because I broke up with him. I figure he could no longer live with what he did to you and Henry, and everyone else he ever cheated and stole from."

"Oh, honey, you are so sweet but so naïve." Georgia's New York accent grew stronger with every sip of wine.

"The other day you seemed to think it was suicide," I told Georgia. "Have you changed your mind?"

She shrugged. "I suppose anything's possible, but yeah, I could totally believe he offed himself, for his own sick reasons. Like maybe he was some kind of serial killer or something, and maybe the FBI was closing in and he was like, *'You'll never take me alive, suckers!'*"

Amy wore a lopsided smile. "Isn't it too bad Georgia has no imagination?"

She laughed delightedly. "Never been accused of that."

I smiled at the jest, but inwardly I was still trying to figure Georgia out. On the one hand, she clearly had despised her onetime boyfriend, that cheating rat Stu, and for good reason. He broke up her marriage, and not because of any deep love he felt for her, but to steal a valuable recipe. As a result, Henry's bakery, The Cranky Crumb, went down the tubes, forcing both him and his ex-wife to scramble to support themselves.

On the other hand, while Georgia had a mercurial temperament, she didn't seem like the type to hold a grudge. But what did I know? This was only our second meeting.

Henry was more of a wild card. He'd made no secret of his hatred for Stu Ruskin when we'd chatted in the cemetery after the funeral. He'd seemed to be pumping me for information, trying to find out how much I knew.

Then again, maybe he was just making conversation and I was reading too much into it. Not that I ever, you know, do that, but there's a first time for everything.

I said, "Georgia, there's something I've been wondering about."

"Shoot."

Unfortunate choice of words, but okay. "Stu tricked you into revealing the recipe the same day your divorce was finalized, right? You said it was early December?"

"December third."

"And Henry found out about it a couple of weeks later when Conti-Meeker's lawyers sent him that threatening letter?" When Georgia nodded, I said, "What I want to know is, why did Stu keep seeing you once he had the recipe? Why not dump you immediately?"

"That's easy," she said. "He was afraid that if he ended it too soon, I'd figure out what he was up to and alert Henry and maybe manage to blow up the Conti-Meeker deal. He had to keep me dumb as a stump until the deal was done."

"Henry must've been pretty upset when he got that letter," I said.

"Oh, he was beside himself. I never saw him so angry."

Which brings us to…

"You told me Henry stays in a different part of the house," I said. "I assume that means you're not always aware of his comings and goings."

I thought I was being pretty darn subtle until Georgia said, quite amiably, "You want to know if he was home when Stu died. You're still thinking maybe it wasn't really suicide."

Smooth, Jane. "No, really," I said, "I wasn't implying—"

"Henry was at his mom's place in Queens all day," she said, "fixing a million and one things around the house 'cause she's too cheap to hire a handyman. I heard him come in a little before midnight. I was bundled up in bed, binge-watching all my favorite rom-com flicks, back to back."

"Even though you had to be at the bakery at five the next

morning?" I asked.

"Yeah, pretty stupid," she laughed, "but those feel-good movies are like a drug. Once I start, I have a hard time stopping."

"That beats what I was doing," Amy said. "I was home alone all evening, reading conservation journals and feeling sorry for myself. I'd just broken up with Stu that morning. I hadn't a clue that he… well, I didn't learn that he killed himself until hours later. Dad let himself into my apartment and woke me up to break the news to me. That's when I told him about the engagement and our breakup. Needless to say, I didn't get any more sleep that night."

I said, "I'm assuming the detectives interviewed you?"

"I called Detective Werker myself the next morning," she said, "and stopped by the police station after work to talk to him and his partner. They seemed particularly interested in the breakup—as if that had anything to do with Stu's suicide."

"How can you be so sure it didn't?" I asked.

"Well, he was upset, like I said, but not in a sad or depressed way. It was more like someone whose fabulous business venture suddenly collapsed."

"Ah, irony," Georgia said.

"Which I realized later, when I thought about it," Amy said, "wasn't far from the truth. I was the linchpin in this grand scheme of his to 'win' that stupid old feud."

I hadn't seen either Amy or Georgia at the funeral. Little wonder, considering their history with the deceased. Ty, however, had made an appearance.

I turned to Shelley. "So you had no idea Stu had come onto the property and was having himself a soak out there in the hot tub?"

She shook her head. "Woody and I had our hands full inside. We had six people staying with us, and they kept us hopping. Cocktails, snacks, board games, charades. I didn't mind. I like being busy, and they were interesting folks. Good conversation."

It would seem this personable woman had found her ideal vocation all those years ago. She would have made a great cruise-ship director.

"Speaking of cocktails," I said, "I can't help but wonder about the glass Stu had with him out there."

"Glass?" Georgia said. "You mean like a drinking glass?"

"A martini glass, to be precise. It was sitting on the rim of the hot tub." I shrugged. "I mean, I know he wasn't a guest here, so I was just wondering where he got hold of the drink. There are no other places within walking distance that serve cocktails."

"Those detectives asked me about that glass," Shelley said. "It was one of ours, all right, etched with the Gabbling Goose logo. The only explanation I could think of, and this is what I told them, was that Stu must've slipped in through the back door when no one was looking and poured himself a stiff one. It wouldn't have been all that difficult."

"Really?" I said. "You wouldn't have heard him moving around in here, opening cupboards and mixing a drink?"

"We were all in the front parlor for most of the evening," Shelley said, "and with music playing and lively conversation, he could've slipped in and out of the kitchen pretty easily."

"Did the cops take the glass with them?" I asked.

"I assume so. It wasn't there after they left."

Amy remained silent during this exchange, although she was intimately familiar with The Gabbling Goose and must have had some opinion on the feasibility of her ex-fiancé successfully managing a stealth cocktail grab. She stared glumly down at the muffin she was systematically shredding, and I could only imagine she had mixed emotions regarding the sudden death of a man she'd loved enough to become engaged to, a man who had not only cheated on her, but had turned her into an unwitting pawn in their families' centuries-old blood feud.

Stu Ruskin, serial user of women. It might not be the worst of his crimes, but it was pretty reprehensible in my book.

"The cops talked to me, too." Georgia wore a silky smile. "That Detective Werker is delish."

"And married," I said. Howie and the lovely Lillian had been happily hitched for many years.

"I know, I know." She flapped her hand at me. "I saw the ring. No harm in looking—or fantasizing about tall, dark cops and their handcuffs. You met him, Amy. Does Detective Delish do it for you?"

"No one does it for me anymore," she said. "I've sworn off men."

Shelley failed to restrain a skeptical snort.

Georgia laughed. "They're not *all* rats."

"So, what do you think now, Shelley?" I asked. "Did Stu commit suicide?"

"Yes," she said with finality. "That's what the liquid courage was for. Wouldn't surprise me if he was drunk before he got here. Don't ask me why he did it. Someone that mean and calculating, who's to say what drove him?"

I said, "Isn't it possible someone else used the hot tub that evening—before Stu showed up or even at the same time—and that this other person left the martini glass there? One of your guests, maybe? You couldn't be expected to know where every single person was at any given—"

"No, absolutely not," Shelley said. "I would've known."

"How?" I said. "I mean, you told me you had no idea Stu was out there, so how could you have known there was no one else?"

"I didn't make anyone a martini that night," she said.

"Maybe they helped themselves to the booze. Isn't it possible?"

Amy spoke up. "Do you mind if we talk about something else? I'm sorry, I just…"

"No, *I'm* sorry," I said, and meant it. "It was insensitive of me to keep talking about this." Amy hadn't appeared bothered by our earlier conversation regarding Stu and his death, but I guessed she'd reached her limit.

Shelley patted Amy's back and murmured something soothing in her ear. Georgia got up to check on the lemon-poppy muffins in the oven. At some point Toby had slipped away, probably to terrorize any rodents foolhardy enough to cross the threshold of this historic B&B. Sexy Beast roused himself from his nap, stretched luxuriantly, gave himself a good shake, and commenced the restless pacing that told me it was time for a potty break.

I grabbed a plastic bag out of my tote, clipped SB's leash onto his harness, and told the others we'd be back in a jiffy.

The sky was still light on this late afternoon in mid-May. I love this time of year, when the days grow not just warmer, but longer. The brine-scented breeze was balmy as I stepped onto the deck. Now that I could actually see the inn's two acres in their entirety, I spied flower and vegetable gardens, a charming grape arbor, picnic tables, and a wealth of trees.

One impressive specimen stood out from the others. It was a huge oak tree, located in the dead center of the property. The massive main trunk was easily twenty-five feet in circumference, its many stout limbs curving in all directions, a few nearly touching the ground. I smiled. A wonderful tree for climbing.

My attention soon shifted to the hot tub—or what was left of it. Three workmen were busy dismantling the tub, reducing the stone exterior to a pile of rubble and disconnecting the pipes, filter, and heater. It was a noisy operation, requiring a bunch of scary-looking tools. I spied a reciprocating saw, which I assumed would be used to reduce the liner to manageable chunks.

I recognized Ty Collingwood from the back. It was a nicely sculpted back, clad in a slim-fitting hunter-green sweater over jeans that were just snug enough to advertise what Georgia would have called a killer booty. He stood halfway between the deck and the hot tub, arms crossed, watching the men work.

Ty's body language told me he might not be eager for company, and I debated taking SB around to the front of the house instead. At that moment the little guy gave an imperious bark, demanding to know what the holdup was.

Ty glanced over his shoulder. It took him a second to recognize me, then he smiled and waved us over.

I returned the smile. "Give us a minute. Sexy Beast has important business to attend to." I led him to a Japanese maple at the edge of the yard, which he watered with enthusiasm while executing an impressive doggie handstand intended to lift his leg as high as possible—the canine version of false advertising. Instinct told my puny shrimp of a poodle that the higher on the tree he peed, the bigger he would appear to any dogs that came sniffing around later.

Men!

Ty nodded in greeting as I joined him. I kept a tight hold on SB's leash, not wanting him to interfere with the workmen or get hurt as they tossed debris onto the growing pile.

"The good news," Ty said, "is that the pool and spa don't share water lines, so I won't have to drain the pool and somehow get it sanitized."

I could have recommended a crime-scene cleaning service to, shall we say, rehabilitate the hot tub. My friend Denny Pinheiro was a real pro when it came to such unsavory work. However, I couldn't argue with Ty's decision to obliterate the site of Stu Ruskin's violent demise.

"Are you going to replace it?" I asked.

Ty pointed to the deck. "I'm having one installed up there. A recessed eight-seater with all the bells and whistles. There's already a nice, thick cement foundation under the deck, so the weight shouldn't be an issue. They'll start this week."

"Nice," I said. "It might be more convenient for wintertime use, too, to have the spa a few steps from the back door."

"That's what I was thinking. In any event, I couldn't leave this thing out here." He gestured toward the work being done a few yards away. "We've already had a few ghouls sneak onto the property to goof around and take pictures—even before the crime-scene tape came down. You'd be surprised at the sickos out there."

"Actually, I wouldn't."

He glanced at me, and I saw the instant he got it. "Oh, right. Look who I'm talking to."

"Trust me, Ty," I said, "I could tell you stories that would make your trespassing ghouls look like Boy Scouts helping an old lady cross the road."

"That wasn't my only reason for getting rid of the tub. None of us need to be reminded of what happened every time we come out here."

"Well, I, for one," I said, "think you're doing the right thing."

He tipped his head in acknowledgment.

SB tugged at the leash, trying to get closer to the action. I picked him up and exchanged kisses for dog-breath licks, and he settled down in my arms with a disgruntled sigh.

"It's quite an accomplishment," I said, "keeping this property in the family for three and a half centuries. And nothing less than astonishing that The Gabbling Goose has been open for business all that time. You should be very proud."

"I'm just continuing the work of my ancestors," he said, "most of whom faced tougher challenges than I ever have. And not just from the Ruskins. This place has survived a devastating fire, the billeting of both British and rebel troops during the Revolution, financial collapse during the Great Depression, and the Great Hurricane of 1938, which blew the roof right off the building and dropped a sailboat into one of the upstairs bedrooms."

I tried to picture it. My imagination was not up to the task.

"Do you have a day job?" I asked. "I mean, aside from running The Gabbling Goose."

He offered a self-deprecating smile. "Shelley and Woody run the place. I just take the credit. As to your question, I was fortunate enough to inherit a bit of money. My day job, if you can call it that, is investing it."

As if summoned by the sound of her name, Shelley appeared on the deck with a tray laden with sandwiches and chips, which she placed on the glass-topped dining table. Amy followed with a pitcher of lemonade and glasses.

Shelley hollered across the lawn, "Aren't you boys done for the day? You've been at it for hours. You're going to faint from hunger."

Three sweaty, dusty faces looked to Ty for permission.

"Don't look at me," he told them. "I wouldn't cross her if I were you. That woman's mean as a snake."

"Go inside and wash up first," she ordered as they gratefully crossed the lawn and ascended the steps to the deck.

Once we were alone, I said, "So you like jazz, huh?" At his questioning look, I reminded him, "The other night you mentioned you were at a jazz club in Southampton."

With his phone silenced. Which was why he didn't get the news about Stu's death until the show ended.

"Oh, right," he said. "Are you a fan?"

"I love jazz," I lied. "Was it a good show?"

"Outstanding. The Manny Molina Trio."

"Wow," I said. "Lucky you."

"In hindsight, I wish I'd stuck closer to home, maybe gone for a beer at Murray's Pub instead. Shelley and Woody shouldn't have had to deal with this mess on their own." He jerked his head toward the debris field that used to be an elegant hot tub.

"For what it's worth," I said, "after the initial shock, they were calmly professional."

"I'm sure they were, but I worry about them. Those two aren't getting any younger."

"Well, as for Murray's," I said, "I'm guessing your wife prefers cool jazz in Southampton to a cold pint at the local pub."

"Jeanette's no fan of jazz. Plus, she's something of a homebody. Her idea of a good time is curling up with a book and a cup of tea. Fortunately for me, she doesn't mind if I go without her."

"Oh, so you went alone?" I asked. "I always like to go with friends who, you know, love jazz as much as I do."

Sexy Beast raised his little head to stare right into my eyes, and I could swear he was thinking, *Are you proud of yourself, Jane? Lying to this nice man?*

I tore my gaze away as Ty said, "Yeah, it was just me that night. Most of my friends refuse to stay out late on weeknights, the old fuddy-duddies, and I have no problem enjoying live music alone. Sometimes I even prefer it."

The workmen exited the house, seated themselves at the table, and dug in to the sandwiches and lemonade. With a gentle hand on my back, Ty steered me far enough from the deck to keep our conversation private.

I said, "That was a quite a nasty surprise you got last Wednesday after the show."

"Shelley left a voicemail and a text, telling me to call right away. She sounded rattled, and nothing ever gets to that woman, so I knew it had to be something serious. Still, when she told me about Stu, I could hardly believe it." He paused. "On the other hand, a little part of me wasn't surprised."

"What do you mean?" I asked.

"You never met Stu Ruskin, did you, Jane?"

"No, and from what I've heard about him, I wasn't missing much."

"The man would do anything to get what he wanted," Ty said. "Well, except work hard and treat people decently. I wish I could say it was just him, but that seems to have been the pattern with all the Ruskins, down through history."

From what Shelley told me, the first Collingwood to set foot in the New World was no saint either. Oswald was a counterfeiter of lottery tickets, in addition to other crimes, not to mention lazy and self-aggrandizing. *Yeah, I chopped off King Charles's noggin. That was me. Guess you could say I had an ax to grind ha ha.*

I refrained from mentioning it. Instead I said, "So when you say you weren't surprised by the news, does that mean you think Stu was murdered? Like maybe he crossed the wrong person and his bad behavior finally caught up to him?"

"It's possible," Ty said. "If it *was* suicide, for whatever reason, then his choice of venue was calculated to make life as difficult as possible for me."

"Or for Amy," I said.

He looked at me. "You know about that?"

I nodded. "I also know you didn't approve of their relationship."

He gave a mirthless laugh. "Talk about an understatement. I didn't know they were actually engaged. I only found out after Stu was dead. That was my second shock of the night. At least she had the sense to dump him."

I said, "Then you also know Stu was involved with another woman at the same time he was seeing Amy."

"Georgia Chen," he said. "Damn fine pastry chef. She's in there now, whipping up some muffins or something. Did you meet her?"

"We actually met a few days ago," I said. "I like her."

He glanced over his shoulder, ensuring we still had privacy. "A little excitable, maybe. Very different from my daughter. I'm surprised they hit it off. They don't have much in common, after all."

Well, except for a certain dastardly, dead ex-boyfriend.

I said, "What Stu did to Georgia and her ex-husband, Henry Noyer, is unconscionable."

Ty shrugged. "He was a Ruskin."

Same crime, different era.

"I know about Percival Ruskin stealing Sybille

Collingwood's punch recipe," I said. "Shelley told me."

"I've spent my whole life looking for that recipe. Not just in there." He jerked his head toward the house. "I've contacted every relative I could find, scoured public and private libraries, the Crystal Harbor Historical Society, countless university archives, every Colonial cookbook I could dig up." He heaved a frustrated sigh.

"That's a lot of effort to go to," I said, "for an old recipe."

"It's more than an old recipe, Jane, it's a pivotal piece of the Collingwood legacy. Look what Percival Ruskin did to get ahold of it. He led the king's men to Oswald Collingwood. They shot him right where that giant oak tree now stands." He pointed to the humongous tree I'd admired earlier. "Sybille planted an acorn on the very spot where her husband was gunned down, and put a curse on anyone who cut it down."

A deep shiver ripped through me as I stared at the distant tree. A few minutes earlier, I'd pictured children scrambling all over it, laughing, jumping off the lowest branches—as they'd no doubt done for generations. Now, all I saw was a threatening tangle of twisted limbs and menacing shadows.

"Once he'd gotten Oswald out of the way," Ty said, "Percival wooed Sybille just long enough to steal the recipe for her popular punch—in case you thought Ruskin men using Collingwood women for their own greedy ends was something new."

"Sybille got back at him, though," I said. "Didn't she poison him?"

"She sure did, and can you blame her? It's fair to say that recipe ignited the centuries-old feud between the Collingwoods and the Ruskins. I'd hoped to lay my eyes on it before I die." He sighed again. "At this point, I have to face the probability that it's lost to history."

Amy had mentioned her father's heart condition. A sense of his own mortality no doubt played a part in his quest for that missing piece of the Collingwood legacy.

"Isn't it possible," I asked, "that the recipe was handed down in the Ruskin family? I mean, Percival went to all that trouble to steal it. Maybe his descendants safeguarded it and it's still around, hidden somewhere."

Ty was already shaking his head. "The Ruskins squandered everything they ever got their hands on. Real estate, money, you name it. No one in that family ever managed to hold on to anything."

Except a grudge, I thought.

8
Paging the Death Demon

THAT NIGHT THE ghost of Percival Ruskin came to me in a dream. He was in my kitchen, mixing something in his pewter punch bowl.

"Hey, Jane. You thirsty?" One might assume British-born Percy would have an accent to match his country of birth. This was not, in fact, the case. He sounded like Robert De Niro in *Taxi Driver*.

"I sure am, Percy." I wasn't lying. My dream self had wandered into the kitchen for the express purpose of guzzling the two-liter bottle of orange soda I'd stashed in the fridge. I'd never felt so parched. It may or may not have had something to do with the three slices of Buffalo chicken pizza I'd wolfed down shortly before bedtime.

The significance of this encounter was not lost on my unconscious mind. Here was my chance to recover the recipe that had cost two men their lives and sparked a centuries-long blood feud. "So tell me," I said. "What goes into this punch?"

"Oh, a little of this and a little of that." Now Percy didn't just sound like De Niro, he looked like him, as well.

Even asleep, I thought to ask, "Is the recipe written down anywhere?"

"You know who would know?" Percy said. "Stu. You should ask him."

"I can't, he's dead."

"You talkin' to me?"

"That's different," I said, "you're right here in my kitchen. Stu is six feet under, and he's not making house calls. Hey, that's my tequila!"

Percy was pouring every last drop of my precious añejo tequila into his punch bowl. That bottle had cost a bundle and should have lasted a year or more, doled out in stingy, infrequent shots.

Next he upended a bottle of grapefruit-flavored vodka over the bowl. Didn't someone recently mention grapefruit-flavored vodka?

"Are you sure this is the correct recipe?" I said. "It doesn't look very Colonial."

He dipped his pewter cup into the mixture and tasted it, then uncapped a bottle of beer and poured it in. "If there's anything I know how to make, it's Dreamboat cookies. Where do you keep the jerky?"

I opened my eyes in the darkness of my bedroom, feeling the dream slipping away, dissipating like fog. I concentrated on replaying it, committing it to memory, though I couldn't say why, aside from a vague sense that it contained some nugget of truth.

Then I sat up, slid my feet into my fuzzy slippers, and went in search of the orange soda.

AT AROUND THREE in the afternoon I was sauntering down Main Street, headed for my red, secondhand Mazda, which was parked around the corner. It had been a productive day so far, and I was feeling pretty good about myself.

I'd spent the morning with an address book that had belonged to a client's brother, a classical studies professor who'd succumbed to a stroke while engaged in illicit acts with the wife of the department head. The official story was that he'd been struck down while volunteering in a soup kitchen. Yeah, good luck selling that story.

In any event, I'd been hired to make phone calls to friends and distant relatives, gently notifying them of the death and providing visitation and funeral info. It wasn't my first time performing this sad task, and it's never easy. I've found that most people take the news reasonably well, especially when the death is expected or the deceased was well on in years.

Once in a while, though, someone totally loses it. Usually I can calm them down on my own. In one instance, however, which occurred nine years ago, a middle-aged man named Bart became so distraught over the news that he threatened to jump out the window of his fifteenth-floor apartment. I happened to have a land line back then in addition to my cell, and without breaking our phone connection, I managed to call 911 and quietly alert the cops to the situation. They responded swiftly and saved Bart's life.

The weird thing was, Bart wasn't even close to the deceased. They'd been college roommates thirty years earlier, and their only interactions since then had been occasional "likes" on Facebook. I figured poor Bart must have been at such a low point in his life that it took very little to push him over the edge. Okay, poor choice of words, but you get my point.

Fortunately, that morning's death-notification session went smoothly. After lunch, I hied myself to Crystal Harbor Ceramics, a pottery gallery and studio there on Main Street owned by an artistic young couple, Poppy and Beau Battle. A regular client of mine, Veronica Sheffield, had decided the cremated remains of her recently deceased uncle Edwin merited a handmade urn that reflected his enduring devotion to Australia—a country, I should add, he'd never visited except in the occasional movie and magazine article.

I met Veronica at the gallery to discuss the project with the Battles. And no, she didn't actually need me for this transaction, just as she hadn't needed me for ninety-nine percent of the bizarre assignments she'd hired me for over the years. But Veronica had more money than she knew what to do with, and she relished displays of conspicuous consumption, particularly when a deceased individual was involved. Don't ask me why. I'm a Death Diva, not a shrink. Every time she hired me, she made sure everyone in town knew about it.

Fine with me. Not only did I receive my fee, I scored plenty of free advertising to boot. A win-win.

And in case you're wondering, Veronica arranged for Beau Battle to craft an urn in the shape of—you guessed it—a cartoon kangaroo. Yeah, I know, but you can't buy taste.

So there I was, making my way down Main Street, greeting other pedestrians and wondering what kind of takeout to pick up for dinner (burgers or Thai? Or hey, how about pizza? Haven't had that since last night) when a rapid knocking brought me up short in front of a store called Mike & Mary Pat's Kitchen Emporium.

My friend Maia Armstrong was on the other side of the big display window, beckoning me into the store. I entered and gave her a hug. "I thought you bought all your cooking gear wholesale," I said. Maia was a successful local caterer.

"I'm not here as a customer." She nodded toward the back of the store, where there was a demonstration kitchen fronted by a curved granite counter with seating for fifteen. "I'm teaching a class on paella in a little while."

Only then did I notice her taupe chef's jacket. Her magnificent cloud of shoulder-length Afro coils had been tucked under an artfully twisted head wrap in shades of orange and purple.

"I didn't realize you were holding classes here," I said.

"It's only my third time at Mike & Mary Pat's." Maia glanced at a couple of young guys near us who were comparing high-end woks before steering me into an aisle filled with big-ticket coffeemakers and espresso machines, devoid of customers at the moment.

"To be honest," she said, "I get a lot of affluent suburbanites who own these fully stocked, state-of-the-art kitchens and never make a darn thing in them except coffee and cocktails. They come to this store and plunk down big bucks on complete sets of Le Creuset cookware and Shun knives, and then they never touch them. It's all for show."

"What a waste," I murmured, thinking of the fully stocked, state-of-the-art kitchen I'd inherited from Irene McAuliffe, along with the rest of her big, fancy house. Of course, strictly speaking, the house didn't belong to me yet. It belonged to Sexy Beast during his lifetime. Which, if you'd known Irene, you would not find the least bit surprising. I wasn't much of a home chef myself, but at least I didn't pretend otherwise.

"So most of them are here to drink wine," Maia said, "eat the samples, and socialize. Which, when you think about it, isn't the worst way to spend a couple of hours. And a few of them, believe it or not, actually want to learn how to cook."

"Go figure." I became aware of a middle-aged woman hovering at the periphery of my vision, clearly a store employee waiting for the opportunity to get a word in. I turned and was surprised to realize I recognized her.

Maia said, "I'd better get back there and set up. But listen, Jane, it's been too long since we had a girls' night out. I'm thinking dinner and a show in the city. Maybe get Sophie in on it?"

"Sounds perfect," I said. "I'll call you tomorrow."

Once we were alone, the saleswoman smiled and said, "I see you know our Chef Maia. Are you here for her paella class?"

"Oh. No, I'm, um… I just came in to browse," I said, thinking fast, loath to squander this chance encounter. Before she could ask what I was looking to buy, I said, "You're Stu Ruskin's sister-in-law."

Darla Ruskin blinked. "Have we met?"

"No. My name's Jane Delaney. I was at the funeral." I made myself add, "You and your husband conducted a lovely graveside service."

"Thank you for saying so. Stu wouldn't have wanted a lot of fuss."

I didn't know about that. The Stu Ruskin I'd been learning about had probably anticipated a much more elaborate sendoff than he'd received. From what I understood, his brother and sister-in-law had done, and spent, the minimum necessary to satisfy the requirements of his will.

Darla Ruskin was just under average height, her graying dark-blond hair cut in a short, serviceable style. She wore a drab brown jacket dress identical in style to the black one I saw her in at Stu's funeral. "So you knew my brother-in-law?"

"Not exactly. Well, not when he was alive, anyway." Watching Darla's eyes bug out, I hastily added, "I'm the one who found him. After he, um…"

Her features hardened. "Committed suicide."

Well, maybe he did and maybe he didn't. That wasn't a conversation I intended to have with her. Instead I said, "Do you mind if I ask you a question?" I was still thinking about that strange dream and Percival De Niro's punch bowl.

"I'm afraid I'm busy, Ms. Delaney. It's just me and the owner here today, so if you're not looking for anything in particular—"

"It'll just take a minute," I said. "And please, call me Jane."

She opened her mouth to tell me to get lost just as an attractive, fiftyish man who was obviously her boss popped his head into the aisle. He didn't look like a Mary Pat, so by deductive reasoning I identified him as Mike. Would I have made a great detective or what?

Mike said, "Darla, I could use you—"

"Tell me about *this* one, Darla!" I slapped a possessive hand on the nearest coffeemaker, a contraption made by Jura that was so imposing and complicated, it would have looked right at home on the International Space Station. *Houston, we have a latte.*

Mike's eyes widened fractionally. He bestowed an approving smile, made a *carry-on* gesture, and disappeared.

Before his employee could stomp off after him, I said, "One little question, Darla. It'll take no time at all. I'll even consider buying…" I peeked at the price tag on the Space Station coffeemaker. Now it was my turn to go bug-eyed. "What kind of fanatic would spend six grand on a coffeemaker?"

"Our customers appreciate quality, and they're willing to pay for it." Darla double-checked that no one was within earshot and turned her disapproving glare on me. "I heard about you, you know."

"What?" I was still reeling from sticker shock. "What do you mean?"

"I was told that someone called the Death Demon discovered my brother-in-law's body."

"It's actually 'Diva,' not—"

"And that you make a living doing disgusting things to corpses," she said.

"Okay, there's a lot of misinformation going around—"

"I would like you to leave the store, Ms. Delaney." She crossed her arms over her chest. "Now."

I stood my ground. "Did Stu ever mention a recipe?"

I saw her mentally debating whether to answer the question or toss me out on my keister. The look I gave her said, *Just try it.*

Finally she huffed in exasperation. "Are you talking about the recipe that was stolen?"

"Yes!" My heart kicked. "What can you tell me? Did Stu have it?"

"Well, of course he did," she said. "That's what started all the fuss, isn't it?"

"Fuss? I'm not sure I—"

"We were visiting Stu," Darla said, "my husband and I, when that awful man showed up. Not that we enjoyed going over there. Gil and his brother never got along, and Lord knows I had no fondness for him either, but family is family, that's what I always tell Gil, and it was our duty to look in on his brother once a month, him with no wife and no contact with his own children because, let's face it, they couldn't stand him, but we did the right thing, even following his kooky burial instructions to the letter, and—"

"Okay, okay, I get the picture," I said. "Let's back it up a bit. What's this about an awful man coming by? What happened?"

"I was getting to that," she sniffed. "This man just barged into the house and attacked Stu. I can't recall his name."

"Attacked him how?" I asked. "Did he have a weapon?"

"None that I saw," she said, "aside from his fists. And he was yelling all kinds of terrible things. It didn't last long. They exchanged a few punches before Gil managed to separate them."

I thought about Ty Collingwood and how he'd felt about his daughter's relationship with Stu Ruskin. Sounds like he might've decided to take matters into his own hands. Or more accurately, fists.

"When did this happen?" I asked.

"Around the end of June," Darla said.

Which was shortly before Martin started working for Stu. Could this fistfight be the so-called attempt on Stu's life that had prompted him to hire a bodyguard? A bit of an overstatement in terms of lethality perhaps, but the timing certainly fit.

"What kind of terrible things was the man saying?" I asked.

"Oh, things like 'Leave her alone' and 'I'll make you sorry' and 'You better watch your back.' Along with some very bad language. Never in my life have I seen anyone so angry," she said. "If Gil and I hadn't been there, well, I don't like to think what might've happened."

I said, "But what does this have to do with the recipe?"

"Isn't it obvious?" Darla said. "Stu only took up with that woman to get his hands on it. He never would've bothered with her otherwise."

"Took up with…? Oh. You're talking about *Georgia*. So it

was Henry who barged into Stu's house."

"Right, that was his name. Henry Something," she said. "The baker who invented that ridiculous cookie."

"Henry Noyer," I said, "and it was actually his wife who invented it. Well, Georgia Chen is his ex-wife now."

"All the misery Stu caused." She gave a sad shake of the head. "And for what? So he could die a little richer."

Stu had told Martin that someone attacked him, but refused to identify the perpetrator. Which made no sense. Wouldn't he want his bodyguard to know who to be on the lookout for?

The answer came to me in the next breath. The last thing Stu would have wanted was to draw attention to the con he was pulling on Georgia. A fistfight with her estranged husband? Something that juicy would have had tongues wagging and might have led to someone putting two and two together and figuring out what he was really up to. I'd be willing to bet Georgia herself still didn't know about the fight.

I recalled what Henry had said about Stu's claim that someone tried to kill him. *If you ask me, it was BS.* It would seem he was speaking from firsthand knowledge. Henry's intention, at that point anyway, hadn't been to kill Stu but simply to beat the tar out of him for stealing his wife.

"I guess I wasn't specific enough," I said. "It's not the cookie recipe I'm interested in. It's an old Colonial recipe for a kind of punch—called Sybbie's Punch, or maybe Peg Leg Punch. I thought you might know whether Stu had it in his possession. Or perhaps your husband does, or even one of their cousins, if they have any."

Darla's eyes narrowed in suspicion. "Why do you care about some old recipe?"

I thought fast. "It pertains to an assignment I'm working on.

I'm not at liberty to divulge details, other than to say the recipe belonged to the Collingwood family—specifically Sybille Collingwood—but one of Stu's ancestors, a man named Percival Ruskin, swiped it way back in the seventeenth century."

"An assignment?" She grimaced. "You mean that Death Demon stuff?"

"It's Death *Diva*, and not everything I work on involves satanic rites, animal sacrifice, or grave robbing. Sometimes I like to take all those extra body parts that are just lying around and sew them all together, see what I can come up with. Sort of a fun, rainy-day craft activity for the kiddies."

And before you tell me I just blew it, let me assure you it was already a lost cause. I could see it in her mean little eyes. This woman had zero intention of sharing any information with me, even if she knew anything about that old recipe, which she probably didn't.

One look at her stony expression and I knew it was time to skedaddle. As she trailed me to the door, I said, "You know, Darla, if you ever get bored selling pots and pans, I could always use an intern. You'd spend most of your time mopping up entrails, but hey, the job comes with dental. Just tell me you'll think about it."

9
Waltz Right In

"SO YOU DIDN'T get anything out of them?" Martin uncorked a bottle of fine sipping tequila—the luxury añejo brand I favor and which he kept concealed behind the bar just for me—and dispensed a generous shot into a small snifter, which he slid across the bar.

"I learned nothing I didn't already know." I lifted the glass, inhaled deeply, and took a dainty sip of the tequila, which caressed my gullet like velvet fire.

We were in Murray's Pub, where Martin could be found behind the bar most nights. As always, antique wall sconces bathed the room in a warm glow, and the bluegrass music was kept to a reasonable volume. The original wooden floors, wainscoting, and bar top, scarred but lovingly maintained, exuded the subtle, intoxicating perfume that can only result from more than a century of spilled beer and good times.

It was a little after nine on Thursday night. A few of the barstools were occupied, and about a third of the tables and booths. The padre and I leaned across the bar and kept our voices down to discourage eavesdroppers.

We were discussing my visit to the pub the previous evening for the weekly trivia contest. Sophie and I had, as planned, teamed up with Howie and Cookie. It was Cookie who chose our team name: If You Ask About Stu, We'll Slap Handcuffs on You. That jolly rhyme was my first clue that the detectives were prepared to resist all my subtle and not-so-subtle attempts to extract information about the case.

It's not as though I'd been stingy in the sharing department. I'd told them everything about my encounter with Darla that morning. Well, maybe not *everything*. I might've left out the part about satanic rituals and mopping up entrails. It turned out Howie and Cookie already knew about Henry's fistfight with Stu. Darla's husband, Gilbert, had told them about it when he was questioned after his brother's death, and Henry himself had confirmed it.

"Don't you consider that fight significant?" I'd asked the detectives, while we were supposed to be putting our heads together to come up with an answer to the question: *What breed of dog won Best of Show during the most recent Westminster Kennel Club Dog Show?* Sexy Beast loves watching dog shows. Or rather, he loves lounging on a pile of pillows on the ivory leather sofa in the family room and barking at the contestants. Alas, SB never thought to tell me who won top-dog honors. Our team's best guess was Irish setter. The correct answer turned out to be Papillion.

"I mean, I know you guys think it was suicide," I continued, "but aren't you obligated to follow up on leads like this?"

Howie set down his beer glass. "Stu Ruskin and Henry Noyer throwing a few punches over a woman ten months before Ruskin's death is not what we seasoned detectives call a lead."

Even Sophie tipped her head as if to say he had a point. The traitor.

"Okay," I said, "but what about Stu stealing Henry's cookie

recipe? That's *another* motive. Come on, guys, I'm doing your job for you."

Cookie said, "That whole cookie thing, Stu selling the recipe to Conti-Meeker, Henry receiving the cease-and-desist letter, that all happened back in December. Five months ago. If Henry was going to murder Stu over that, why would he have waited so long?"

"I'll tell you why." I gestured with a French fry. "Henry was trying to keep his bakery afloat that whole time. The Cranky Crumb. He managed to stay in business until a couple of weeks before Stu died when he was finally forced to close up shop. That's when it really sunk in, how Stu Ruskin had destroyed both his marriage and the business he'd spent so many years building."

Sophie said, "She actually has a point." *Gee, thanks.*

"I'm right, aren't I?" I nodded vigorously. "Darn right I'm right. Now, about that martini glass that was sitting on the rim of the hot tub. I'm assuming you sent it to the lab. Any results yet?"

Unsurprisingly, the detectives had refrained from answering that question. In fact, they'd ignored all further attempts on my part to discuss the case. To add insult to injury, our team had come in last.

Martin listened to me whine for a while about how unfair Howie and Cookie had been. "Hold that thought," he said, before moving away to pour a pitcher of beer for Poppy and Beau Battle, who'd come in with a couple of young friends.

When he returned, he said, "What do you know about that martini glass?"

"Only that it was no longer there after the cops left."

"But how did Stu get ahold of a cocktail?" he asked. "If no

one even knew he was out there in the hot tub."

"Shelley thinks he snuck into the kitchen and poured himself a drink on the sly."

"You look like you're not buying that," he said.

I shrugged. "I guess it's not outside the realm of possibility, but something about it just doesn't ring true. Since the cops are so sure it was suicide, who knows whether they even sent that glass for testing?"

Martin wore the hint of a smile. "They did."

I slapped my palms onto the bar and leaned forward. "Tell me! What do you know?"

His pale-blue gaze scanned our immediate surroundings, as if to assure himself our conversation wouldn't become grist for the Crystal Harbor rumor mill. He rested his forearms on the bar, and now we were practically nose to nose. The fresh, masculine scent of his skin teased my nostrils, making me a little giddy. Or maybe it was the tequila. Whatever the cause, I found it difficult to concentrate on what he was saying.

Until I heard the words "lab results," followed closely by "martini glass." It seemed his contact in the police department, whoever that was, had come through.

"So, what did they find?" I asked.

"Well, what you and I didn't notice, because it was so dark out there behind The Gabbling Goose, was a little reddish liquid in the bottom of the glass."

"I did see a curly piece of orange peel," I said.

"It was lemon peel. They're still analyzing the components of the drink, but they did determine there were no drugs in it."

"So it's not like someone knocked Stu out with, say, a date-rape drug and then did him in," I said.

"You told me you didn't buy it, Stu slipping inside the inn to pour himself a drink, and I have to agree." Martin's fingers shifted on the bar top to stroke the tender inside of my wrist. "It would've been tricky enough if he was just splashing some vodka into a glass, but a drink that color? With a lemon twist? There's a bit of mixology going on there."

"You're the bartender," I said. "You tell me. What kind of cocktail do you think it was, and how long might it have taken to throw together?"

"In a kitchen we can assume Stu was not that familiar with. For sure he wasn't a regular visitor at The Gabbling Goose."

Martin straightened as a customer teetered up to the bar on four-inch-high platform sandals. I recognized Cheyenne O'Rourke, a local teen who worked part-time at Janey's Place, Dom's health-food joint. The only reason she'd been hired in the first place, and had avoided being fired, is that her dad, Patrick O'Rourke, was the manager.

If you open the dictionary to the word *shiftless*, you'll see a picture of Cheyenne, complete with the alarming tattoos scrawled on the sides of her neck: the names *Brian* and *Sean* (two former beaux), both crossed out with prominent tattooed *X*'s. Cheaper than laser removal, I suppose.

Oh, but what did I spy, smack-dab on the front of her neck? You guessed it, a brand-new tattoo: the name *Neal*, executed in big, sloppy letters and surrounded by a jittery heart. How, um, romantic.

Cheyenne had stringy, highlight-striped hair, light brown eyes unclouded by anything resembling deep cogitation, and a doughy figure which she'd stuffed into a yellow, python-patterned crop top and fuchsia leggings adorned with little green iguanas. The stratospheric sandals were faux crocodile. Somehow I just knew the reptilian theme was entirely coincidental.

Martin sighed. "Cheyenne, we've been through this. You're underage. I can serve you a Coke."

"A lot you know." She wagged an ID in front of his nose. "I'm twenty-one."

"Did you suddenly age two years overnight?"

"You can't refuse to serve me. I got proof." She tossed the card onto the bar. "Gimme a frozen margarita."

Martin lifted her ID and examined it, front and back. "This is pretty impressive."

"No kidding," she snapped. "Frozen margarita. Use the mango mix. Extra salt."

To me he said, "This has to be the worst fake license I've ever seen. And trust me, I've seen a lot."

"That thing's real!" Cheyenne cried. "I even checked off that they can take my organs. After I'm, like, dead, though."

"I hope you didn't pay too much for this piece of junk," he said.

"A hundred and—" She clamped her mouth shut and produced her phone. "If you refuse to serve me, I'm calling the cops."

"Excellent idea," he said. "It'll save me the trouble of confiscating this card and reporting you."

"You can't do that!" she barked. "That license belongs to me. I got it at the, um... the place where they hand out licenses."

"It's too flimsy, for starters." Martin flexed the card back and forth. "And the features are way out of date. This photo's in color, not black and white, and there's no ghost image."

Her face crinkled in perplexity. "Why would there be a picture of a ghost? You're making this stuff up."

"What year were you born?" he asked.

"Twenty..." Cheyenne wore a crafty expression. "Wait. Is that a trick question?"

I could no longer contain myself. "Of course it's a trick

question! Good grief, we all know you weren't born in…" I took the card from Martin and peered at the birth date. "Ninety seventy-five?"

Her expression turned mulish. "Who says I wasn't?"

"Oops, what do we have here?" Running my fingers over the card, I discovered that the edge of Cheyenne's fuzzy glamour shot was slightly raised. I picked at it and easily peeled up her photo, revealing a picture of a middle-aged dude with a mullet and shaggy beard.

"You ruined it!" Cheyenne snatched the card out of my hand. "What am I gonna do now?"

"Here's an idea," Martin said. "A little out there, but it just might work. Wait till you're twenty-one to order alcohol in a bar?"

"You're the meanest person I ever met." She sniffled, blinking hard to produce tears.

"Yeah, that's not going to work," he drawled. "I strongly advise you to cut up that bargain-basement ID. The next bartender might very well turn you in, and you're looking at a five-hundred-dollar fine and possible jail time. Is it worth it?"

Cheyenne appeared to give the question serious consideration.

"Okay," I said, "the answer is no. It's not worth it."

"It's not fair." She gestured toward my half-empty snifter. "*You* have a drink."

"I'm forty."

Her expression of combined horror and disgust made me want to grab my phone and turn her in myself. It was with profound relief that I watched her stomp out of the pub.

I slumped onto the bar. "That was exhausting. What were we talking about?"

"Stu's red drink and what it might be," he said.

I perked right up. "Oh yeah. Thoughts?"

He held up a finger. "I'll be back in a minute."

As it turned out, he spent well over a minute mixing Moscow mules for a pair of coquettish twenty-somethings. I told myself he *had* to respond in kind, that flirting with female customers was, if not a job requirement, then a way to rake in the big tips. He couldn't possibly *want* to compliment the blonde's sparkly, cleavage-baring sweater or ask the redhead where she'd been keeping herself. Right?

When he rejoined me, he grabbed a rag and started wiping down the bar. So much for tickling the inside of my wrist. "There are literally dozens of red or pink cocktails, Jane. Most of those fancy drinks have a garnish, often a lemon twist. Some are traditionally served in martini glasses, others in a DOF or some other kind of glass."

"DOF?"

"Double old-fashioned. So to answer your question, it would have taken a few minutes for Stu to locate the ingredients in an unfamiliar kitchen, mix them in a shaker, and cut a lemon twist. Even for something as simple as a Cape Cod." At my questioning look, he added, "Vodka and cranberry juice. It's usually served in a highball glass, if that matters."

"You knew Stu," I said. "You tell me. Was he bold enough to waltz into the kitchen belonging to his, for all intents and purposes, blood enemy and calmly mix a cocktail while there's all that activity going on in the front room?"

"Stu Ruskin," Martin said, "like most criminals, was a coward at heart. The kind of guy who'd refer to a simple fistfight as an attempt on his life."

"The kind of guy who'd hire a bodyguard to protect him from the mean man who punched him," I said.

"The kind of guy who, after the bodyguard quits in disgust,

buys a big gun for self-protection."

I didn't bother suggesting that Stu might've bought the gun to do himself in. At that point, it was clear neither of us thought it was suicide.

"So the cops don't yet know what kind of drink was in that glass," I said.

"Not yet, but it's looking like Stu didn't have anything to do with it."

"Wait, what?" I sat up straight as Martin gave me a little smile that said, *Think about it.*

I'm happy to report it took me only a few seconds before the obvious answer smacked me in the head. "They lifted fingerprints from the glass," I said, "and they didn't belong to Stu."

"Correct on both counts," he said. "And before you ask, they don't know whose prints they are. They're not in the database."

"What about DNA?" I asked.

"That takes a lot longer. I'm assuming that if they get DNA off that glass, it won't be Stu's."

I nodded. "It'll belong to whoever left their prints on it."

"Bottom line is, someone else was out there with Stu."

"Or someone else was out there *before* Stu," I said, "and they just left the glass there. Of course, Shelley swears she would've known if anyone else had made use of the hot tub, though I don't see how, since she didn't even know Stu was there."

"For what it's worth, none of the paying guests noticed anyone out there, either. It was pretty chilly that night, so I'm not surprised everyone stayed inside."

Someone apparently signaled to Martin from one of the tables, because he nodded in response, moved to the beer taps, and filled a pitcher. After delivering it, he returned to his place behind the bar, uncorked the tequila bottle again, and topped off my snifter. "Did you happen to notice that Stu left his clothes in a little pile near the hot tub, along with a small leather backpack?"

"No," I said, "but it was dark, and the stiff in the tub was a real attention grabber."

"Well, did you wonder what he was wearing in the hot tub?" the padre asked.

"Is this one of those trick questions Cheyenne is so fond of?" I took a sip of tequila and thought back on the moment I first laid eyes on Stu Ruskin. The churning water of the spa had concealed most of his body. "I just assumed he was wearing swim trunks, but I realize now that would mean he *planned* to end up in the tub. So tell me. What was he wearing?"

"Not a blessed thing," he said.

"Which would seem to indicate it was a spontaneous decision," I said, "taking a dip in that spa."

"Which brings us to the question of why," Martin said. "Was he just driving by and decided it would be great fun to sneak onto Collingwood property and make use of the facilities? Kind of a childish prank for a middle-aged guy to pull."

"Who knows?" I said. "Maybe he'd been getting away with it his whole life."

"Aren't you going to ask what was in the leather backpack?"

"I think I can guess what it held when Stu arrived there," I said. "His gun and silencer. He or someone else took it out at some point."

The padre nodded. "It still contained a spare magazine. The interior was fitted with straps and pouches specifically designed for gun gear. I'm assuming he took it everywhere with him."

"Only to have his own weapon turned on him in the end." Automatically I glanced toward the pub's door as it opened. "Oh my Gawd."

10
No, No, a Thousand Times No

"OH MY GAWD! It's Martin!" Georgia Chen practically leapt across the bar in her zeal to hug him. She managed to give him a big, smacking kiss on the lips. For his part, the padre didn't appear the least bit embarrassed that Jane Delaney, the woman he was pursuing—well, he *was* kind of pursuing me, right? I wasn't imagining it?—had witnessed this lovey-dovey display.

Except it wasn't necessarily lovey-dovey, not if you knew Georgia. It was more like Georgia being Georgia. I tried, without success, to hold on to my pique. Yes, this was the woman who'd told me very enthusiastically how sexy Stu's former bodyguard was, with that killer booty and all.

But, I mean, was she lying? It's no crime to appreciate a hot guy.

Unless she'd done, and perhaps was still doing, naughty things with my hot guy.

Okay, that *my* just kind of slipped out. Martin wasn't *my* guy and might never be *my* guy, so Georgia was welcome to him, right?

Don't answer that!

She grabbed Martin's hands. "I know you told me you tend bar here, but I totally forgot. It is *so good* to see you."

She slid onto the barstool next to mine, still unaware of my presence, having had eyes only for the padre since entering the pub. In the course of comparing notes with him, I'd told him about my encounters with Henry's ex.

"Hi, Georgia," I said.

"Jane! Oh my Gawd!" She leapt off her seat to give me a rib-cracking hug that left me gasping for oxygen. To Martin she said, "Have you met my friend Jane Delaney? They call her the Death Diva. Isn't that the cutest thing ever?"

He gave me a warm smile. "Jane and I go way back."

Good move, grumped Cynical Jane.

Will you just cut it out? responded Sensible Jane. All he did was let an attractive, overly dramatic acquaintance give him a smooch. And face it, nothing would have stopped her short of a suit of armor and bear spray.

She gave my shoulder a playful smack. "You didn't tell me you knew this hunkalicious stud!"

For his part, the hunkalicious stud shook his head with an embarrassed little smile. *Oh, that Georgia.* Not that he didn't concur with her assessment, but he had the grace to pretend otherwise, the smooth operator.

Yeah, I was still a little bit irked. I shoved my snifter across the bar, a wordless demand for more free (yes, I am special) superpremium tequila.

Georgia said, "Did I ever tell you I worked as a bartender when I was young? It's how I put myself through baking school. I still enjoy inventing drinks. I'm a *fab* mixologist if I do say so myself." She laughed.

"Well, if you're ever in the market for a side gig," Martin said, "Max can always use good people behind the bar."

Maxine Baumgartner—"Max" to, well, everyone who knew

her—was the owner of Murray's Pub.

"Who knows?" she said. "Susanne might can me for real one of these days and I'll need the job." She placed her purse on the next barstool over, to hold it. "Amy's meeting me here. I don't think you've met her," she told Martin.

"Amy Collingwood," I clarified. "Ty's daughter."

He said, "No, I haven't—"

"There she is!" Georgia sprang off her seat and waved both arms, as if the woman entering the mostly empty pub might not spot her otherwise. "Amy! Over here!"

Drinks with a Girlfriend Amy appeared a bit more polished than Conservation Scientist Amy, the version I'd met two days earlier. She'd ditched the ponytail, done a bit of a smoky eye, and donned a lavender silk blouse, slim-fitting black jeans, and high-heeled boots. Well, Amy was now single, after all, and it made sense to be prepared. You never knew when you might cross paths with some hunkalicious stud.

Stop it, Jane! I reminded myself that not every female who walked through that door had designs on the handsome gentleman who mixed their silly girly drinks. Probably just fifty to sixty percent of them. Okay, maybe closer to seventy. Whatever.

Once introductions had been made, Martin asked the ladies what he could get them.

Georgia didn't have to think about it. "I'll have a Cosmo. With a lemon twist, please, not orange."

"Coming right up." His gaze locked on mine for a nanosecond, long enough for me to get the message. Even I, who eschewed girly drinks, knew that a Cosmopolitan was made with cranberry juice, and consequently resided somewhere in the reddish spectrum.

As he combined the ingredients in an ice-filled shaker—cranberry juice, fresh lime juice, orange liqueur, lemon vodka—he turned to her companion. "Amy?"

She looked sweetly dubious. "Do you know how to make a Twelve Mile Limit?"

His eyebrows jerked up. "That's an esoteric one. It's been a while. I'll have to refresh my memory."

He shook, poured, and garnished Georgia's Cosmo, then produced a small, well-thumbed bartender's guide from behind the bar and briefly consulted it.

"I prefer a martini glass, if that's okay." Amy nodded toward the martini glass he'd placed on a cocktail napkin in front of Georgia. "Some bars serve it in a regular cocktail glass."

"You got it." He poured white rum into a shaker, followed by rye whiskey and brandy.

"Holy cow!" Georgia said. "That's some bodacious beverage."

"I'm not driving," Amy said. "I took a Lyft."

"Oh my Gawd! Me, too!"

"And anyway," Amy added, "I never have more than one."

As I watched Martin add lemon juice and grenadine, I said, "That's a funny name for a cocktail. Twelve Mile Limit."

"It originated during Prohibition," he said, "when it was illegal to drink booze less than twelve miles off US shores."

"Well then," I said, "it's an appropriate drink for Crystal Harbor. This town was a rumrunner's paradise during Prohibition."

Martin decanted the concoction into a chilled martini glass, propped a lemon twist on the rim, and set it before Amy.

Guess what color this cocktail was. Oh, come on, guess.

Bingo!

It owed its rosy hue to grenadine, a syrup as deeply red as the pomegranate juice it was made from. As it happened, the two drinks differed slightly in color. Georgia's Cosmo was a deep pink with aspirations of red, while Amy's Twelve Mile Limit had undertones of orange.

But they were close enough for Georgia to squeal, "Ooh! Twinsies! We have to toast. To, um…" She lifted her glass, and hesitated.

The women exchanged a look, and somehow I knew they were both thinking of Stu, the dead ex-lover whose charismatic charm had blinded them to his contemptible nature.

Amy's face fell for the briefest instant, before she straightened, pasted on a grim smile, and said, "To worthy men."

"You said it, sister!" Georgia clinked her glass with Amy's. "They're out there somewhere. We just have to find 'em and wrestle 'em into submission."

It might have been my imagination, but Georgia's jolly demeanor appeared more than a little forced, for once. It might have had something to do with the fact that she'd already bagged her "worthy man" years earlier, only to throw him over for a smooth-talking sociopath, as she referred to Stu. She'd have to live with the regret for the rest of her life.

"Here, lemme try that twelve-mile thing." Georgia declared Amy's bodacious beverage to be delish, then set about making all gone with her Cosmo before ordering another. Amy, meanwhile, nursed her strong cocktail with the funny name, taking small sips to make it last.

The four of us engaged in lively conversation, touching on almost every subject except the one thing that was on all our minds: Stu Ruskin's mysterious demise. The padre held up his end of the conversation, with occasional breaks to serve customers, close out tabs, and flirt with every estrogen-based lifeform in the joint.

Georgia and Amy had known each other a mere eight days, yet already appeared to be fast friends—despite, or perhaps because of, their concurrent relationships with Stu Ruskin.

A dark thought squirmed at the edge of my consciousness, demanding attention. Stu had been forty-four years old and reasonably fit, based on what I could see of his arms and chest above the swirling water of the hot tub.

Not for the first time, I imagined a scenario in which another individual forced Stu's gun—or more accurately, the gun's attached silencer—into his mouth and pulled the trigger. Wouldn't Stu have struggled? How had his killer managed to immobilize him? How strong would someone have to be to accomplish that terrible deed?

Which led to the inevitable follow-up question: Could *two* someones of lesser strength have accomplished it, working together?

After about an hour, Amy leaned toward Georgia and said, "That guy's staring at you. The one who just walked in."

"Really?" Georgia looked toward the entrance and gave a small gasp.

Henry Noyer stood just inside the doorway, clearly debating whether to stay or leave, now that he'd spied his ex-wife. She waved him over, and after a momentary hesitation, he crossed the room to join us.

Introductions were made, and Martin asked what he was drinking.

"Beer." Henry peered at the labeled taps and added, in his agreeably raspy voice, "Blue Point Toasted Lager."

I moved one seat over, leaving an opening for Henry to sit next to Georgia. He couldn't refuse without looking like a jerk, so he sat. I assumed these two onetime lovebirds hadn't been together in a bar or restaurant for nearly a year, since Stu came between them.

Henry seemed stiff and ill at ease at first, but gradually relaxed over the course of the next half hour. Conversation turned to safe topics. The mild spring we'd been enjoying. The new Netflix series about the royals. The Ethiopian restaurant that just opened on Main Street ("Oh my Gawd, I discovered I *love* eating with my hands!").

At last, Henry addressed his ex-wife directly. "I was surprised to see you here. Your car's in the garage. I thought you were still home."

"I took a Lyft." She tapped her empty glass to indicate the reason.

He nodded. "How many of those have you had?"

She held up two fingers.

Henry lifted his beer. Took a sip. Set it down. Still staring into the half-filled glass, he said, "You don't have to take a Lyft back, Georgia. I've got my car here."

She gave him a fragile smile before averting her gaze to compose herself. The two of them probably hadn't been in a car together during the past year, either.

When she turned back to him, she stroked strands of hair off his forehead. "You're getting a little shaggy there, Henry. Why don't you let me give you a haircut."

"It's fine," he said. "I'll get to the barbershop soon."

"Yeah, but I'm free and convenient," she said. "And I've been cutting your hair forever. I know how you like it."

Another sip of beer. He glanced at her. "Maybe. I'll see."

"Listen, do you think we could give Amy a ride?" Georgia asked. "She lives at the Americana."

Amy flapped her hand. "Oh no, really. I don't mind taking a—"

"No problem." Henry leaned around Georgia to give the other woman a reassuring nod. "It's practically on the way."

"This is on me." Georgia handed her credit card to Martin. When Amy and Henry started to object, she said, "Oh my Gawd, let me buy your drinks. Jane's, too," she added.

"Thanks," I said, "but mine's taken care of."

Georgia's knowing gaze flicked between the padre and me. I liked to think we'd been pretty discreet about whatever the heck was going on between us, but clearly she'd picked up on the fact that, well, something was going on between us. The corners of her eyes crinkled, and unless I imagined it—always a possibility after a shot of my beloved añejo tequila—Georgia gave off an approving vibe.

Which she wouldn't have done if she and Martin had a thing going, right?

After the three of them said their goodbyes and left, I said, "I guess I should get home, too."

Martin nodded at my snifter. "You haven't finished your drink."

"Someone poured me a little too much. I don't want to be pulled over for DWI."

He lifted my glass and tossed back the rest of my tequila. Holding my gaze, he said, "I know a convenient place where you can sleep it off."

Meaning right upstairs in his apartment over the bar. I had an almost overpowering urge to take him up on the offer. I gave him a wry smile. "'Sleep it off,' huh?"

"Hey, I'm only thinking of your welfare." He pressed a hand to his heart, his expression guileless. "That's just the kind of guy I am."

"Don't I know it," I said, before adding, "Not tonight, Padre."

His smile morphed from teasing to intimate. "Well, that beats 'No, no, a thousand times no.'"

What was I doing? A week ago I'd told him I wasn't ready to take things further, that his secretiveness was a roadblock in our relationship. My *Not tonight* could be interpreted as *Maybe tomorrow*. I was sending mixed signals, which wasn't fair to either of us.

A customer gestured that he was ready to settle his bar tab. Before stepping away, Martin pointed to Georgia's and Amy's empty martini glasses and said, "Don't touch those."

So I wasn't the only one wondering what, if anything, we should do with them. I sat staring at the glasses, prepared to karate-chop anyone who came near them, for the two or three minutes it took Martin to return.

"So, what do you think?" I waved my hand in front of the glasses. "Not one, but two possible matches to the cocktail our mystery person drank out by the hot tub. I've decided to give that drink a fun name, by the way. It's the Hot Tub Homicide."

"Catchy," he said. "You know, the authorities are about ready to close the book on this one."

"With a finding of suicide. So you told me. And yet here we have the victim's ex-girlfriend and his other ex-girlfriend sucking down their favorite adult beverages, both of which happen to be red."

"And both of which happen to be served in martini glasses garnished with lemon twists," he said. "Practically identical to the Hot Tub Homicide."

"Could you put these glasses in a couple of plastic bags and label them?" I asked. "Maybe I can persuade Howie and Cookie to process them, see what they can find."

"As in, do the fingerprints on either of these glasses match the prints lifted from the glass taken from the hot tub?"

"That," I said, "and maybe to analyze the little bit of liquid left in them, see if one of them is the same sort of cocktail."

"Well, one thing I can tell you," he said, "is that you don't want plastic bags, not for fingerprint evidence. The condensation could destroy it. What you need is paper."

"Oh." I didn't ask how he knew that. "Do you have any paper bags?"

"I think I could dig some up," he said, "but I wouldn't want to be the one to hand some random martini glasses to Howie Werker and try to persuade him to take them seriously."

"Not Howie," I said, retrieving my phone from my purse. "I'm calling Cookie. She's more, shall we say, open-minded than her partner. And forget about bagging them. We're not going to touch these glasses until I find out how she wants to handle it."

11
You'll Never Believe What Happened!

"LOOKS LIKE FLOWER is the belle of the ball," I told Dom as I watched his new pet gallop around the section of the local dog park reserved for medium-sized and large dogs, filling up her dance card. Sexy Beast and I were, alas, relegated to the small-dog section on the other side of the chain-link fence.

As recently as a year ago, SB had wanted nothing to do with others of his species. His original owner, Irene McAuliffe, hadn't believed in canine socialization—or canine grooming, but that was another story. Since becoming SB's guardian, I'd made a point of regularly exposing him to other dogs, and he'd made admirable progress.

Four other pint-size pooches and their humans occupied the small-dog section on this Saturday morning, and I'm proud to say Sexy Beast was on chummy, butt-sniffing terms with all of them—the dogs, that is, not the humans, whose butts, sadly for him, were out of reach. The weather was still mild, and the sky was overcast.

My ex stood on his side of the fence, his anxious gaze never leaving his newest family member, now cavorting with a chocolate Lab, a Weimaraner, and a Saint Berdoodle. Yeah, that's right, someone had the bright idea of crossing a standard poodle with a Saint Bernard, and I have to say, it was the sweetest thing ever, a hundred-pound brown-and-white fluffball with thick, curly fur and a lovable personality.

"What do I do if she bites another dog?" he said. "Or a person? Maybe a *child*?"

"She's not going to bite anyone," I assured him. "Look at her. She's having a blast. The folks at the animal shelter tested her temperament, remember? There were no issues."

Dominic Faso, at thirty-nine years of age—that's right, he's a few months younger than I—had never before owned a dog. He'd never felt the lack of one until his recent breakup with Bonnie Hernandez, which meant he was also breaking up with her magnificent reddish-blond standard poodle, Frederick. Frederick was everything my own poodle wasn't. Not only was he big, but he was a champion, in both agility and retrieving. He'd even saved some kid's life once, so the story went.

My ex-husband was a notorious serial bridegroom. He didn't know how to be alone. If adopting a canine companion meant he might not be so quick to turn his next swipe-right date into Mrs. Faso the Fourth, then Flower will have helped him as much as he was helping her by providing a loving forever home.

I was Flower's number-one fan, and had been since the moment I'd spied her curled up in the rear of her kennel at the noisy animal shelter. Dom had insisted I accompany him yesterday to help him select his new pet, because I "know so much about dogs." I suspected the real reason was that I'd steadfastly declined all his invitations to dinners, plays, concerts, and what have you. The clever man knew me well enough to know I wouldn't refuse to help him adopt a rescue animal.

I know you want to know about Flower. She's a one-year-old mix of several breeds, two of which are unmistakable. Right off the bat, this young lady's spooky blue eyes stamp her as part Siberian husky. The short hair and tricolor body—black saddle, white chest and belly, and floppy tan ears—scream *beagle*. She probably owes her long legs and white face to her husky mom or dad, but without knowing who else contributed their doggie genes to the mix, it's hard to say for sure.

Flower has a distinctive appearance and, more important, a sweet, frisky disposition. Dom welcomed her into his life with the same full-hearted joy, tinged with a dose of nerves, with which he'd greeted the births of his three children. I knew the nerves would dissipate in short order and that these two would be good for each other.

Enough about Flower. What you *really* want to know is what happened when I phoned Detective Cookie Kaplan from the pub Thursday night. Well, she'd tried to put me off at first, not wanting to encourage my unproductive meddling, until I finally got it through her thick skull that this was an example of *productive* meddling. "Don't touch those martini glasses," she'd said. "I'll be right there." Fifteen minutes later the evidence had been bagged (paper, not plastic, thank you very much), labeled, and spirited away for crime-lab voodoo. Cookie had promised an update, but I figured I'd have to chase her for it. If I didn't hear anything by Monday morning, I'd start nagging her.

Sexy Beast ran over to me for reassuring scritches and good-boy praise, before racing off to rejoin his tribe of itty-bitty lapdogs with delusions of Rottweiler. Meanwhile, Dom was frowning worriedly at his new pet while she play-wrestled with the Saint Berdoodle.

I reached across the fence to massage his stiff shoulders. "Relax, Daddy. She's doing just fine."

He offered a lopsided smile. "This is all new to me, this dog stuff."

"I know, but you've got to chill or Flower will pick up on your tension and rip out your throat while you sleep."

"Oh, is that how it works?" he asked.

"Trust me," I said. "I'm the one who knows all about dogs. You said so yourself."

He watched Flower for another few moments before turning to look me in the eye. "I've been going for counseling, Janey."

My surprise must have shown. In all the years I'd known Dom, he'd never been the type to seek help in figuring himself out. Not that he was a stranger to self-reflection, he'd just never seen the need to involve a professional.

"What prompted that?" I asked. I figured if he didn't want to talk about it, he wouldn't have brought it up.

"You and me," he said.

"Oh." I'd expected it to have something to do with Bonnie. After all, they'd been engaged for more than a year, if you didn't count a two-month hiatus last summer.

"I messed up so badly with you," he said. "I was so young and so damn sure of myself. I didn't realize what I was giving up. All those years we could've had..." He closed his eyes briefly, shook his head.

"It wasn't just you, Dom," I said. "We were both to blame."

"No," he said, firmly. "I was the one who insisted I didn't want children. What did I know? A stupid twenty-one-year-old kid."

All these years later, our painful arguments were still fresh in my mind. We had plenty of time to start a family, I'd told him. I was happy to wait, but I needed some assurance that eventually we'd have at least one child. His response was a flat refusal: Fatherhood was not for him.

And if you're thinking this was a conversation we should

have had before saying *I do*, you're not wrong. I guess I'd just assumed Dom and I were on the same page about this, as we'd been about nearly everything else up to that point.

Couldn't I compromise, he'd asked back then, for the sake of our marriage? If compromising meant I could never satisfy my all-consuming desire to become a mother, I'd said, then no, I didn't have it in me to live with that kind of so-called compromise.

"And the rest is history," Dom said, with a smirk at his own stubborn, youthful self. "As soon as our divorce was final, I had three kids by two wives, all while I was still in my twenties."

"They're wonderful kids," I said.

"No doubt about it. I'm ashamed to say that if Lana and Meryl hadn't taken the decision out of my hands, then Kari, Ivan, and Jon would never have been born."

"Then maybe it was meant to be," I said, "our breaking up so you could bring them into the world."

"I refuse to think that way." His expression turned to one of excruciating longing. "I will never stop loving you, Janey, never stop wanting to marry you again, to make those babies we should've had back then. I can't put it any plainer."

I swallowed hard, forcing myself to meet his intense gaze. Ever since our divorce, I'd fantasized about hearing those words. No, that's not accurate. During most of that time, I'd have loved nothing more than to undo what I'd considered to be the biggest mistake of my life. The past year, however, had been instructive, a time of personal growth, as hokey as that sounds. I hadn't lied when I'd told Martin it was over with Dom. That didn't mean it was always easy to sort out my emotions.

When I didn't respond, he cleared his throat. "Anyway, it's been good, talking to this counselor. He's helping me to see everything more clearly, to identify things in my life I might want to work on."

"Such as…?" Over Dom's shoulder I watched Flower and the chocolate Lab play tug-of-war with a rope toy.

"I know it seems like I rush into relationships," he said. "That's because, well, I rush into relationships. I get antsy without a significant other."

I didn't want to think about all the years I'd avoided meaningful relationships while yearning for a second chance with my ex. I forced myself to say, "You know I was always hoping we'd get together again. I wasn't very good at hiding it."

"I know." He looked away, then back at me. His voice was thick with self-reproach when he said, "I guess I figured you'd always be there."

Humiliation clogged my throat. "Conveniently waiting, in the unlikely event you failed to find someone better. Younger. Prettier. With a respectable career and a sense of style."

"Janey—"

I held up my hand. "No, I get it. I was the fool for sticking it out for so long, with no encouragement from you." Well, not *no* encouragement. Dom had doled out just enough positive reinforcement to keep my hopes up. Did he realize he was doing it? I didn't know, and at this point, I could honestly say I didn't care.

It was over.

He reached across the chain-link to take hold of my hands. "I'm not proud of how I treated you. I'm working on it, working on myself. I want to be the man you need me to be."

I pulled one of my hands free to stroke his smooth-shaven cheek. That was one of the things I'd missed the most—simply touching him. "I want you to do that work, Dom. I'm glad you're sorting through your issues."

He saw it coming. "Don't, Janey." He squeezed my other hand.

"It's too late for us." My eyes stung. I refused to let one tear fall. "You know I'll always care about you, but it's too late for us."

Sexy Beast, like most dogs, is downright telepathic when it comes to his human's feelings. I felt his little feet on my leg and welcomed the interruption. I picked him up and dried my eyes in his warm, curly fur.

Dom took a step back from the fence and stood watching Flower, his gaze so unfocused I wondered if he actually saw her running in circles with her new packmates.

A newcomer, a handsome brindle-coated boxer, streaked past Dom, eager to join in the fun. A female voice I recognized called out, "Be a good boy, Jackson. Don't hump everyone else this time. That's not the way to make friends."

In the next instant, Georgia Chen spotted me and sprinted over to the fence. "Jane! Oh my Gawd, you'll never believe what happened! They arrested Amy!"

12
A Whole Big Brouhaha Over Nothing

"WHO TOLD YOU we arrested Amy?" Cookie asked. I'd called her as soon as I got home.

"Georgia Chen."

"Well, that explains it," she said. "Someone's gotta introduce that woman to decaf."

"Does that mean Amy's not under arrest?" I shifted the phone to my other ear so I could shrug off my fleece vest and toss it onto a chair in my breakfast room.

"Not yet," she said. "We brought her in for questioning yesterday. We don't have enough to arrest her."

"I know you interviewed her the day after Stu died." I opened the refrigerator and pulled out a jar of Vienna sausages. Sexy Beast had been so good at the dog park, he deserved his favorite treat. "So, what's different now?"

"I think you can guess what's different now," Cookie said, "seeing as you're the one who handed over those martini glasses at the pub Thursday night."

"Fingerprints." I offered Sexy Beast a Vienna sausage and watched him run with it to the sink mat, his preferred snacking spot.

"The prints on Amy's glass from the pub match the ones we lifted from the glass by the hot tub," she said, "and the only reason I'm telling you this is that you'd have figured it out soon enough anyway."

"I *knew* you didn't believe Stu killed himself." I opened the fridge again to see if there were any lunch-worthy leftovers lying around. I pulled out all the takeout containers I could find and started taking inventory. The first one housed half a chicken enchilada and a few forkfuls of rice. I set it aside for consideration, but figured I could probably do better.

"We haven't ruled out suicide," she said, because she had to.

"Yeah, yeah. So tell me," I said, "did Amy and Stu hang out in the hot tub together that night? She told me she'd broken it off with him over the phone that morning and refused to see him again."

"I'm not getting into this, Jane," she said. "I shouldn't even be discussing the case with you."

"You didn't tell Amy that I gave you her glass from Murray's, did you?" The next takeout box contained a little lamb vindaloo and half a piece of dried-out naan bread from the local Indian restaurant. I gave it a tentative sniff and tried to recall when I'd shoved it into the fridge.

"I promised you I wouldn't tell her about your involvement," Cookie said, "and I didn't. When we told her she left her prints on the glass by the hot tub, she didn't question how we made the match, she just admitted she'd been there."

"As opposed to the first time around," I said, "when she told you she hadn't been near the place that night. Did they test the residue in both glasses, to see whether it was the same concoction?"

"They don't really need to since the prints match," Cookie

said, "but yeah, preliminary testing would indicate it's the same or a similar cocktail."

"The Hot Tub Homicide."

"No, it's got another weird name," she said, "but that homicide thing sounds like a drink I'd like to try."

"I, um, meant Twelve Mile Limit," I said. "That's what she was drinking at Murray's. So tell me—"

"Jane, I'm going to hang up—"

"Who else did you interview a second time?" I opened a Styrofoam takeout box I'd found way in the back of the fridge, closed it immediately, and consigned that furry science experiment to the garbage bin. "I mean, if Amy was at The Gabbling Goose that night, then Shelley and/or Woody must've known about it. And yet, both of them said she wasn't there. So I know you would've talked to them again."

"Well, you have to take anything Woody says with a grain of salt," she said. "Not that he intentionally lies, but he's not the most reliable witness."

Her tone told me she assumed I knew Woody better than I did. I thought back to the last time I'd spoken with Shelley. She'd described her husband as "forgetful and confused."

I said, "So you're saying you think Woody… misremembered something?"

"Maybe," she said, "but how to know? When we first spoke with him, the night of the murder—I mean, the probable suicide—"

"Give it a rest, Cookie. It was murder. You know it. I know it." I lifted the lid of the last takeout box. Sushi from three days earlier. What had possessed me to save leftover raw fish? Okay, that one was a hard no. It looked like lunch was going to be a jolly mélange of days-old Mexican and Indian, with a slug of

Pepto-Bismol for dessert. "What did Woody tell you the night of the murder? Did he see Amy at the inn?"

"No," she said. "Both times we spoke with him, he said he had no idea she was there."

"But..." I prompted.

"Well, when we questioned him the night of the murder, he told us he hadn't seen Stu, either. Which made sense to us at the time. Shelley hadn't seen Stu. The guests hadn't seen Stu. No one had seen Stu, the sneaky SOB."

Except Amy? I wondered. Cookie had already shut down that line of questioning, so I didn't bother bringing it up again. Instead I asked, "What did Woody say when you reinterviewed him yesterday?"

"Now he's saying he *did* see Stu in the hot tub—very much alive—when he went out to the deck that night to look for dirty dishes and whatnot. He insists he told us this before, but of course, he didn't."

"Is that significant?" I asked.

"Not really," she said. "I mean, we know Stu was out there, whether or not anyone saw him. Woody's inconsistent recollection just means we can't rely on anything he tells us."

"I doubt he could offer much usable information, anyway," I said. "Shelley's the one who runs The Gabbling Goose, and she's Amy's confidante—they're really tight. I mean, I'm sure Amy loves Woody too, but she didn't even tell him she and Stu were engaged. No one knew except Shelley. It was this big secret."

"Well, somehow he found out," Cookie said, "because when he told us about seeing Stu in the hot tub, he referred to him as 'Amy's fiancé.' He said he's known about the engagement for months."

AN HOUR LATER, Sexy Beast and I found ourselves at The Gabbling Goose for the third time in ten days. I'd checked in with Shelley, who told me Amy had gone across the street to walk on the beach. The earlier overcast had turned into serious cloud cover, with a fine mist that made me zip up my vest and snug it around my throat as I followed in her footsteps.

As SB and I traversed the parking strip and stepped onto the sand, it occurred to me to wonder whether dogs were banned from the beach. I saw no posted signs to that effect, and the sand was nearly deserted on this damp afternoon, so I doubted it would become an issue.

I say *nearly* deserted because I did indeed spy Amy at the shoreline, squatting to examine something crawling among the pebbles and shells. It occurred to me that a conservation scientist was probably never bored when out in nature.

Neither was Sexy Beast, who let his nose lead him in a random pattern I couldn't hope to decipher.

Amy looked up as I approached, then stood, dusting her hands on her jeans.

I'd assumed I'd have better luck tracking her down at her family's B&B rather than her lonely apartment, and I'd been right. I smiled in greeting and said, "Not really my idea of a beach day."

She leaned down to give SB a couple of pats. Her expression was sober. "I've always found natural bodies of water to be soothing."

I didn't need to ask why she needed soothing today, after her unpleasant police interview yesterday. I almost felt contrite over the role I'd played in bringing her to Cookie's attention.

Almost. The fact remained that Amy had lied to police detectives investigating a violent death. Even if she had nothing to do with that death—and I had yet to decide how big an *if* that was—I couldn't think of any excuse that would justify what she'd done.

The mist was turning into a light rain. Amy glanced up at the sky and said, "I guess there's no point in staying out here and getting soaked. Come on."

We retraced our steps back to The Gabbling Goose. By unspoken agreement, we remained on the broad covered porch that extended the length of the building. The porch was furnished with a half dozen rocking chairs, painted Colonial blue, along with several small round tables and a couple of wicker loveseats. Flowering plants hung from the eaves between the support columns.

We parked ourselves on a couple of rockers and watched the rain intensify over the bay, blurring the horizon. After reconnoitering to his satisfaction, Sexy Beast jumped onto the cushioned seat of another rocker and went right to sleep.

Amy apparently decided the time for small talk was over. "Why did you come looking for me, Jane?"

"Georgia told me the detectives brought you back in for questioning," I said. "Well, to hear her tell it, you'd been arrested."

That earned a small smile. "I like Georgia, but she takes a little getting used to. It wasn't just me. They also talked to Shelley, Woody, and Dad again."

"I wanted to see how you're doing," I said. It wasn't a lie, even if it wasn't my only reason for being there. The question of guilt or innocence aside, Amy possessed a tender vulnerability that made me want to look out for her. Perhaps it was my frustrated mothering instinct, though she was only eight years younger than I.

"I'm not doing so great, since you ask. These last ten days have been…" Her sigh sounded inexpressibly weary. "You know why they wanted to talk to me again? Werker and Kaplan?"

"I think I heard something about it. You know how folks in this town talk." I shifted uncomfortably and reached over to pet Sexy Beast, unwilling to meet Amy's gaze. "Something about fingerprints?"

"They found my prints on a glass near Stu's body," she said. "Just to be clear, I didn't want to lie to them. It wasn't my idea."

I did look at her then. "Someone else told you to tell the cops you weren't here that night?"

She nodded miserably and glanced at the closed door to the inn, before lowering her voice. "Shelley meant well. She was just trying to keep things from getting messy."

"Messy how?"

"Well, she said it was obvious to anyone with half a brain that Stu killed himself, and it would just raise doubts, and start a whole big brouhaha over nothing—that's how she put it, a brouhaha—if they found out we were together back there."

Her words zapped me like a cattle prod. So Amy and Stu *had* been back there at the same time. Before I could formulate a response, she added, "Needless to say, any hint of a murder on the premises would cause a lot of negative publicity for The Gabbling Goose."

I was reminded of something Shelley had said the night of Stu's death. *Let's hope he left a suicide note. As terrible as that is, how much worse would it be if it turned out someone else did him in?* It was clear she'd been thinking of the inn's reputation.

Which might be a backwards way of looking at it, considering that part of The Gabbling Goose's enduring allure was the dark doings in its history, most notably Oswald Collingwood being shot by the king's men behind the house, and Percival Ruskin being poisoned to death by Sybille right in the front parlor, just a few feet from where we sat on the porch.

Amy wasn't finished. "Mostly, though, I think it just comes down to Shelley being overprotective, as always. She figured it would turn into this big, unnecessary investigation, with me at the center of it, and for nothing."

"Because it was obvious Stu committed suicide," I said.

"Right. Now, of course, I wish I'd come clean from the start, but Shelley and Dad insisted the cops didn't need to know I was here."

"So wait, it wasn't just Shelley?" I said. "Your dad also told you to lie to the detectives?"

Amy gave an unhappy nod. "He agreed with her that this was the way to handle it. It didn't seem right, but I was kind of in shock when I learned Stu shot himself, so I just did what they told me to."

We sat quietly for a minute, listening to the staccato drumbeat of rain on the porch roof, inhaling that fresh-scrubbed spring-rain smell. I watched a white SUV turn onto the brick driveway and pull into the parking area next to the house. A young couple emerged, grabbed a suitcase from the trunk, and hurried across the lawn in the rain. They leapt up the wooden steps to the porch, laughing at how soaked they'd gotten in just a few seconds. Ah, youth.

Sexy Beast yawned, stretched, and propped his front feet on the arm of his rocker to demand scritches, which were happily bestowed as Amy and I exchanged greetings with The Gabbling Goose's newest guests.

After the front door had closed behind them, I said, "The thing I'm a little confused about, Amy… you told me that when you broke up with Stu, he wanted to talk it over in person, but you said no."

"You want to know how we both ended up back there that night," she said. "That wasn't my plan, believe me. I would've been happy never to see Stu Ruskin again. I came here for a nice, solitary soak in the hot tub. I figured none of the guests would be using it, and I was right. It was kind of nippy, but that didn't bother me. The water was plenty warm."

"Do you do that a lot? Come here to use the spa?" When she nodded, I added, "So it isn't just *natural* bodies of water you find soothing."

That earned a half smile. "Anyway, I was in no mood to be sociable, as I'm sure you can appreciate, so I slipped in through the back door, had a good cry on Shelley's shoulder in the kitchen, grabbed a towel, and went back out to the spa."

I was glad to see the rain was letting up. "That explains why none of the guests saw you that night," I said.

"I had my swimsuit on under my clothes. Shelley made me a cocktail and brought it out a couple of minutes later."

"What kind of cocktail?" I asked, all innocence.

"Twelve Mile Limit," she said. "The same thing I had at Murray's on Thursday."

"So did you take a Lyft from your apartment, like you did then? I mean, since you probably knew you'd be drinking." I was thinking the ride-share company could verify precisely when she arrived and left.

"No, I walked," she said. "It's only about a mile from here to the Americana apartments, and I like to walk."

"What time did you get here?" I asked.

"About nine."

"I assume Stu wasn't out there in the hot tub when you arrived."

"You assume correctly," she said. "I wasn't there fifteen minutes before he slipped around the side of the house and started stripping down."

"How did he know you'd be there?"

"Like I said, it was a pretty regular habit of mine. Plus, well..." She gave an embarrassed shrug. "We used to meet here sometimes and enjoy the spa together."

"Stu had to be persona non grata at The Gabbling Goose," I said.

"Was he ever. But somehow, he never got caught. And I guess it gave me kind of a naughty thrill, sneaking a Ruskin onto the ancestral Collingwood property. It all seems so juvenile now."

The sky brightened as the sun peeked out through a few lingering clouds. A dark blue van labeled Jankovic Brothers Electric pulled into the inn's parking area. Two dishy men about Amy's age jumped out and hauled their toolboxes across the lawn and up the porch steps. The brothers engaged in the obligatory adoration of the pup while the four of us swapped polite greetings and appreciative once-overs.

Well, what can I tell you? These guys were seriously cute. After watching with rapt attention as they disappeared into the house, I tried to remember what Amy and I had been talking about.

Oh yeah.

"So how long did you and Stu share the hot tub that night?" I said.

"About a nanosecond." Amy grimaced. "The whole time he was shucking off his clothes, he kept telling me why we belong together, and I kept telling him to leave. Instead he stepped into the tub with me. I was out of it before his bare tush hit the seat."

"What did you do then?" I asked.

"Normally I would've gone into the house to change out of my wet swimsuit and back into dry clothes, but I was so upset, I just toweled off, threw on my things, and bolted out of there." An impish smile tugged at her mouth. "I considered stealing his clothes. And the towel."

"See, the difference between you and me," I said, "is that I would've done more than just consider it."

"Oh, he deserved it, for sure," she said, "but after the immature stunt he'd pulled that night, it would've meant lowering myself to his level. So I just left."

"What time was that?"

"Around nine-thirty," she said. "I jogged all the way home. I assumed Stu left right after I did, but apparently he stayed out there in the hot tub. Pushing his luck."

I know she meant "pushing his luck" in the sense that at any moment Shelley could have discovered him out there and, what, called the cops? Accused him of trespassing? But the fact was, Stu had pushed his luck so far that night, he'd ended up dead.

Martin and I got to The Gabbling Goose just before eleven that night, for the sexy-time date that was not meant to be. That left a window of nearly ninety minutes during which Stu had been murdered. Either Amy Collingwood killed him before she left or someone else went out there later and turned Stu's own gun on him.

And made it look like suicide. Presumably it would have been easier to shoot Stu in the back of the head, but who does himself in that way? And then, after killing him, the murderer dropped the gun into the tub, where it would naturally have landed after falling from Stu's lifeless hand.

I couldn't ignore the fact that Amy had initially lied to the police, for whatever reason. Also, she'd had more than a week to refine her story. I tried not to let her vulnerability and my protective instinct cloud my judgment. This young woman had the means, motive, and opportunity to eliminate her detested ex-fiancé: the murder trifecta.

13
Déjà vu

AMY ROSE. "I'm going to see if Shelley needs help with the guests."

I lifted a sleepy Sexy Beast and followed Amy into the house. "I'd like to say hi to Woody. I didn't see him when I got here."

The young couple had already changed into dry duds. They were enjoying a leisurely tour of the main floor and peppering Shelley with questions about Oswald Collingwood's ignominious demise and Percival Ruskin's got-what-was coming-to-him poisoning death.

In case you thought I was, you know, exaggerating the appeal of the grisly goings-on in the B&B's history.

The little group was in the front parlor, examining Oswald's portrait. It turned out Cherry Tagliaferro and her husband, Alex, were both history buffs. They were also both blond, both middle-school art teachers, and both just so darn *adorable*. They found every detail of this historic inn, no matter how insignificant, of absorbing interest.

Since Shelley seemed to have everything under control, Amy excused herself to check out the installation of the new hot tub on the deck.

"So that's what's going on back there," I said. As soon as I'd stepped inside, I'd heard muted male voices, along with some banging and clanging, coming from behind the house. "I'm guessing that's where I'll find Woody."

"You know men," Shelley said. "Construction projects are like catnip to them."

"Come on, SB. Let's go say hi."

I followed the sounds of activity to the back door and stepped onto the rain-damp wooden deck, taking care not to get in the way of the beauteous Jankovic brothers as they prepared to supply power to The Gabbling Goose's new spa. The brothers wore snug T-shirts, snugger jeans, and those big leather tool belts that I've decided look sexy as all get-out, don't ask me why. One of the brothers was installing an electrical panel on the back wall of the house, while the other took precise measurements to determine where to run the conduit from the main circuit breaker inside.

Earlier in the week, a large, square opening had been carved into the deck, and the brand-spanking-new spa sunk into it. A section of decking next to the tub had been turned into a removable access panel to expose the working guts of the spa.

I joined Woody Bernstein, Ty Collingwood, and Amy, who were observing the process from several feet away. Woody and Ty, standing with arms crossed, provided play-by-play commentary. I doubted either of these electrical geniuses had so much as replaced a switch plate cover.

Even the presence of the beauteous Jankovics wasn't enough to keep boredom at bay, and I was mentally debating how to get Woody alone for a little chat when he said, "Well, I'd better go put away the stuff they delivered from Costco."

"I'll help you!" I said.

Back inside the house, he opened a heavy door off the

kitchen, and we descended a set of scarred wooden stairs to the cool, dark basement. Woody flipped light switches, illuminating the huge room.

I gazed in awe at our surroundings, from the low, timbered ceiling to the massive brick support columns to the humongous, soot-stained fireplace which dominated one of the ancient brick walls. Three adults could have stood inside that fireplace, though they'd have to make room for the large black kettle that hung from an iron crane bolted to the bricks. A domed baking oven was built into the wall next to the fireplace.

"I'm guessing this was the original kitchen," I said.

He nodded. "Back then they wanted to keep the smoke and odors and all that away from the main part of the house. You can take that little fella off the leash if you want. There's not much trouble he can get into down here."

He had a point. This room was fairly clean and free of clutter, and SB was squirming in my arms, eager to explore. The instant I set him on the cement floor—long ago poured on top of the original dirt floor, I assumed—he began to patrol the perimeter, and I could only wonder at the wealth of information imparted by his superpowered schnoz.

A large, rough-hewn farm table occupied the middle of the room, piled high with cases of paper towels, toilet paper, soda, and assorted nonperishable foodstuffs Woody had purchased in bulk from the no-frills retail warehouse. Against one long wall were several heavy-duty plastic shelving units, partially filled with canned goods and other supplies.

I heard a trilling purr and saw that Toby had decided to join us. The big cat and SB lost no time renewing their acquaintance and chasing each other around the room.

Woody transferred a couple of supersize tubs of mixed nuts

from the table to a shelf. "Toby keeps the place free of vermin, but I still wouldn't keep any food down here that wasn't sealed up tight."

"Don't blame you." I moved a jumbo bottle of laundry detergent onto a shelf. I knew it would take no more than a couple of minutes to accomplish our chore, so I didn't waste time on small talk. "So, Woody. I understand Werker and Kaplan interviewed you again." When he frowned in confusion, I added, "The police detectives."

"Oh. Yes, they talked to all of us right after Amy's fella did himself in out there." He shook his head and picked up a box of double-A batteries. "Terrible business. Do you know about that?"

"I do. Terrible." Obviously he didn't recall that I was the one who discovered Stu's body. "They also spoke with you again yesterday. The detectives."

He paused, thought about it, and nodded. "We went to the police station. I'd never been there. It's not like on TV. Those detectives are all right, especially the lady. Candy, I believe her name was."

"Cookie," I said. "Cookie Kaplan." Well, anyone can make a mistake like that, right? I'd had a hard time recalling her name at first myself. I lifted a plastic-wrapped case of toilet paper, thirty-six rolls, and found a spot for it on a high shelf. "You know what seems strange? No one saw Stu Ruskin out there in the hot tub the night he died. I mean, you know, while he was still alive."

"Not true." Woody grabbed a bundle of a dozen paper towel rolls, huge but lightweight, and shoved it next to the toilet paper. "I saw him with my own two eyes, and he was alive then."

"How do you know?" I asked. "Was he moving?"

"No, he was just relaxing. Maybe dozing."

"So then, um, couldn't he have already been, you know…?"

"Well, the way he went, shot in the face like that…" Woody shook his head. "What I mean to say is, his face looked normal. Sorry, young lady. I shouldn't have been so graphic."

I waved away his concern. You want graphic, come along on some of my Death Diva jobs. I didn't know what Woody had been told, but Stu had not, in fact, been shot in the face. His face appeared normal when I discovered his corpse that night. From where Woody had stood on the deck, the bloody stone coping under Stu's head would not have been visible. Plus, of course, Woody had been viewing the scene at a distance by moonlight.

He could very well have been looking at a dead man. Or not. There was simply no way to know.

"What time was that?" I asked.

"About ten o'clock," he said. "I always go out back around that time, to check for anything the guests might've left, especially dirty dishes. Those raccoons are always on the prowl for leftovers. No sense encouraging them. Do you have a raccoon problem where you live? I swear, those critters get bolder every year."

"Um, to get back to Stu in the hot tub," I said, "you must've been surprised to see him there."

"Well, I'd noticed him out there with Amy once or twice during the past few months," he said. "They never knew I saw them, and I never mentioned it to Shelley because I figured it was Amy's business. She's an adult now and can make her own decisions."

I was about to offer some inane platitude about his wise reasoning when he picked up a case of chocolate chip cookies and added, "But this time I did tell Shelley, because it was just

Stu out there, alone. Amy wasn't with him. That didn't seem right to me."

"Wait," I said, "Shelley knew he was out there that night?"

"Yep." He shoved the cookies onto one of the middle shelves. "She stormed out there to give him what for."

"And how did that go?" I asked.

"I didn't stay for the show," he said. "I was in the front parlor taking care of the guests. I imagine she fussed and fumed at Stu, not that it did her any good, because we all know what he did after she went back inside."

Meaning he didn't leave the premises, as Shelley would no doubt have demanded. Instead, he removed his gun from his leather backpack, attached the silencer to the muzzle, and committed suicide. That was what Woody, Shelley, and Amy believed—or claimed to believe.

Assuming Woody's version of events is accurate, his wife went outside that night around ten o'clock to confront the trespasser. Not just any trespasser, mind you, but a Ruskin. And not just any Ruskin, but the detestable Ruskin who'd managed to turn her darling Amy's head until she'd lost all sense of reason.

Assuming Stu was still alive at that point, would Shelley have restricted herself to "fussing and fuming"? And if their encounter had left her mad enough to kill, how could a lone eighty-year-old woman have accomplished the deed?

Of course, there was always the possibility we weren't dealing with a lone murderer. Not for the first time, several potential pairings presented themselves to my overstimulated imagination.

"Did you happen to mention it to anyone else besides Shelley?" I asked. "You know, that you saw Stu out there in the hot tub?"

He took his time thinking about his answer as he wedged a box of kitchen sponges between the laundry detergent and a tub of chocolate-covered almonds I'd been trying to ignore. There must have been three pounds there. They wouldn't miss a handful, right?

Finally he said, "You know, I think I might've told someone else, but I can't be sure. My memory's not what it used to be. One thing I *do* remember is what that great lady Bette Davis once said—that old age ain't for sissies. She got that one right."

"I noticed that you called Stu 'Amy's fella.' How serious were they?"

"Well, they were going to get married," Woody said. "I'd call that pretty darn serious."

"Amy told you they were engaged?"

"I overheard Amy and Shelley talking about it in the kitchen back in... well, I know it had to be close to Thanksgiving because I'd just bought the turkey, and I was in the pantry, trying to find room for it in the freezer."

"They didn't know you were in there?" I asked.

"Nope. The door was open, but it's a big pantry and I was all the way in the back. I heard Amy and Shelley talking about the engagement. Well, it was more of an argument. I distinctly heard Shelley say, 'Mark my words, that man is using you.'"

Woody's recollection had enough detail to convince me it was a legitimate memory. But so what? In the end, did it matter that he knew about the engagement? That it wasn't the well-kept secret Amy and Shelley seemed to think it was?

A little voice in the back of my mind told me it very well might be significant, but for the life of me, I couldn't figure out how.

I grabbed a heavy case of soda cans before Woody could get

to it. He seemed fit enough, but let's face it, I was half his age. "If you could just make a little room on the bottom there," I said, "I think this will just about fit."

He did so, while grumbling, "What kind of gentleman lets a lady do the heavy lifting?"

I positioned the case of soda on the shelf as someone's heavy work boots thundered down the staircase. "Trust me," I said, "I can use the exercise."

One of the beauteous Jankovics entered, carrying a big toolbox. "Oh, I don't know," he said, with a dazzling smile. "You look like you're in pretty good shape already."

And yes, I admit it, I giggled.

Do not judge me. You never saw the beauteous Jankovics. You don't know.

He strode across the room and set his toolbox down next to the back wall, the one closest to the deck. The main circuit breaker, sprouting multiple wires leading to the rest of the house, was located on the adjacent wall.

Flipping open the toolbox, he produced a cordless, caged work light and hung it on one of the scary wrought-iron hooks protruding from the ceiling timbers. He switched it on, retrieved a steel measuring tape and a permanent marker from his tool belt, and turned to Woody. "Sir, would you happen to have some sort of stepstool or something I can stand on? It would save me a trip out to the van."

Thrilled to be part of this manly endeavor, Woody said, "Sure thing," and opened a heavy door that led to what I could only assume was a storage room. He emerged seconds later with a paint-spattered stepstool. "Will this do?"

"That's perfect. Thank you, sir."

I scooped up Sexy Beast so he wouldn't get in the

electrician's way. I tried to steer Toby to the front of the room, but you know what they say about herding cats. I did manage to annoy her enough to send her racing upstairs with an indignant chirp, so it was all good.

We watched as Jankovic took careful measurements and marked a spot high up on the wall. Woody crept closer to the action as the electrician donned leather gloves and safety glasses, and inserted a long drill bit into the biggest cordless drill I'd ever seen.

And if you're waiting for me to make a rude comment about that, you can keep waiting, because I'm a lady.

Stop snickering.

Jankovic mounted the stepstool and began to drill. The noise made SB yip in alarm, and I tightened my hold on him.

Woody crossed his arms and announced with authority, "That's a special masonry drill bit. It's for drilling into brick."

I actually knew that, believe it or not. The skills one picks up as a Death Diva. Don't even ask.

"Right now he's drilling a pilot hole," he added. "He'll need to enlarge it for the conduit."

Okay, knew that, too.

I watched the muscles in Jankovic's arms and shoulders flex in the most distracting way as he wielded the drill. Finally he turned it off, shoved the safety glasses up on his head, and gave the wall a couple of hard thumps. "Yo!" he hollered. "How's it look out there?"

No response.

"Yo! Bro! Is the hole in the right spot?"

When he still received no response, he huffed in frustration, said, "'Scuse me, folks," and took the steps three at a time to go back upstairs.

Woody and I looked at each other and shrugged. I set Sexy Beast back down on the floor. We hadn't quite finished putting away the purchases. Working together, the two of us managed to shoehorn a case of microwave popcorn, a pretzel variety pack, a bag of turkey jerky, and about a thousand cans of premium cat food onto the shelves.

As we were finishing up, the beauteous Jankovics appeared, as well as Ty and Amy.

"I'm not making it up, bro." The drill-wielding Jankovic—let's call him Jankovic Number One—marched over to the back wall and pointed to his handiwork. "Same exact measurements as outside."

"You measured wrong, bro," his brother said.

"I did *not* measure wrong. I know how to measure, bro." Jankovic Number One was getting red in the face. On him it looked good.

I turned to Amy and murmured, "What's going on?"

"There's no hole on the outside," she said. "The drill didn't go through."

Jankovic Number Two produced his own steel tape and remeasured, ending up at the exact spot where the hole had been drilled. He scowled. "You didn't go all the way through," he said.

"I *did* go all the way through." Jankovic Number One shoved the drill at his brother, who stepped onto the stepstool and inserted the long drill bit into the hole, up to the hilt.

"See? Do not question my measuring or my drilling, bro. That's disrespectful."

Jankovic Number Two hopped off the stepstool and turned to Ty, who was watching the proceedings with a perplexed frown. "Could there be something behind this wall, Mr.

Collingwood? Some kind of crawlspace maybe?"

Ty started to shake his head, then turned to Woody. "You know this place better than anyone, Woody. You ever hear of a space that got bricked up?"

"No, and the brick on that wall is as old as the rest of this place." He spread his arms to indicate the rustic seventeenth-century brickwork surrounding us. It all matched.

Woody went to the bottom of the stairs and called up to Shelley, who came downstairs with Cherry and Alex Tagliaferro in tow. It was starting to get pretty crowded down there. Amy quickly got Shelley up to speed.

"So that's what all the yelling was about," Shelley said. "I don't know anything about any space behind that wall."

"Ooh." Cherry's eyes shone. "A secret room."

Alex grinned. "I'd say we're getting our money's worth. Do you do this for all the guests or are we special?"

"We have an inspection camera in the van." Jankovic Number Two started toward the stairs. "It's got this skinny scope. I'll just shove it in that hole and we can see—"

"No." Ty's expression had turned obdurate. "Break it down."

"What?" Amy turned her startled gaze on her father. "There's no need for that, Dad. Let them look in there first, see what we're dealing with."

But Ty was already striding toward the storage room. "Do we have a sledgehammer, Woody?"

"Uh, yeah, but…" He watched his boss disappear through the doorway, then gave an elaborate shrug.

Ty reappeared carrying a massive sledgehammer with a three-foot-long handle, which he carried to the back wall.

"Dad!" Amy rushed toward him. "Let someone else do that."

But he'd already taken the first swing. Fragments of brick and mortar flew as he hauled back for a second blow.

Amy grabbed his arm. "Dad, please!" She sent the electricians a pleading look, wordlessly asking them to take over. Obviously she was concerned about her father's heart condition.

Sexy Beast decided that what this situation required was a seven-pound poodle running up to the man with the enormous sledgehammer and scolding him with rapid-fire barking. Amy got to the little troublemaker before I did, and handed him to me.

Jankovic Number One addressed Ty. "You sure about this, Mr. Collingwood?"

"I'm sure." He was immovable. "This wall has to go. There's something back there, something… important. I just know it."

Ah, so that was it. Ty Collingwood had spent his entire life searching for his ancestor Sybille's punch recipe. His quest had turned into a fixation. He'd looked everywhere—except in a bricked-up space he never knew existed.

"You're the boss." The electrician took the hammer from him. He put his leather gloves and safety glasses back on. "Please stand back, sir, ma'am."

Ty and Amy retreated as he took his first swing. Within a few minutes he'd created a small opening and began to chip away at its edges. Jankovic Number Two offered to spell him. "Nope, I'm good." He wiped the sweat from his face with a bandana and gave his brother a pointed look. "Something else I know how to do, bro. Demolish walls."

When the opening was about eighteen inches in diameter, Jankovic took a break and stepped back. We all rushed forward as one, half stumbling on the rubble under our feet, eager to check it out. I was at the front of the group with Ty, and the first thing that struck me was the musty smell wafting from the dark space behind the bricks.

Ty snatched the work light from its hook and thrust it into the opening, leaning in as far as he could manage. After a few seconds he jerked back, slamming his head on the ragged opening and losing his grip on the light, which fell into the space.

"Dad!" Amy cried. "Are you okay?"

He stumbled back a step. I don't think I'd ever seen anyone look so pale. Amy and Shelley were all over him, making him sit on the stepstool while they ascertained that his head wasn't bleeding. They barraged him with questions. Did he feel faint? Was he having chest pains? He kept shaking his head no, unable, or unwilling, to speak.

The rest of us looked at one another, and at the opening in the bricks, eerily illuminated now by the work light Ty had dropped inside. Then we looked at one another again.

Sexy Beast, picking up on the collective mood, whined something that sounded an awful lot like, *Now would be a good time to run away from this scary place and never look back.*

I made an impulsive decision, based on my assumption that whatever was behind that wall was less likely to freak *me* out than these other folks. I mean, think about it. I make my living doing stuff that would freak out the average person. It's how I keep the lights on and pay for Sexy Beast's Vienna sausages.

And really, how bad could it be?

"Would you take him for a minute?" I handed SB to a wide-eyed Cherry Tagliaferro, who clutched him to her like a life preserver.

Without giving myself time to reconsider, I stuck my head into the musty space and looked around. There wasn't much to see at first, just a small, cobwebby room constructed of the same antiquated brickwork as the rest of the house.

Then I looked down.

A human skeleton lay curled on its side on the dirt floor, facing the wall we'd just breached. The bones of its right hand rested near a metal cup, which appeared to be pewter. A large bowl of the same material sat in a corner. Most disconcertingly—

What's that? Yes, I know this is already disconcerting enough, but it gets better. By which I mean worse. If I may continue?

Most disconcertingly, there was a significant depression in the dirt floor at the edge of the wall. The pewter cup lay in that depression. This poor fellow had been trying to dig himself out of his crypt.

He'd been walled up alive.

How did I know it was a *he*? The skeleton appeared complete, with one notable exception. In lieu of lower leg and foot bones on his left side, there was a carved wooden peg leg, complete with a rounded socket at the top for the stump. I saw no sign of a crutch, but what use did Percival Ruskin have for one at that point, anyway? His tomb was the size of your average powder room.

Well, of course it had to be Percy. Do the math.

"Jane?" It was Shelley. "What do you see?"

The work light had bounced off Percy's cranium and rolled away, a bit too far for me to reach. I glanced behind me and caught the eye of Jankovic Number One. "Can you make sure I don't tumble inside?"

"No problem, ma'am. I got you." He positioned himself right up against me and got a good grip on my hips as I wriggled half my body through the opening. By some miracle, I managed not to giggle again, which, let's face it, would have been a tasteless thing to do as I reached across the mortal remains of poor Percy to curl my fingers through the work light's cage.

"Okay," I said, and Jankovic hauled me back, and this time I giggled just a little bit.

Woody and the beauteous Jankovics craned their necks for a glimpse inside the space, now that a mere female had taken a good long gander and hadn't expired of fright, but the dark interior revealed nothing. I held on to the work light for the time being.

Ty came to his feet, brushing off his daughter and Shelley as they continued to fuss over him. "I'm fine, I was just a little… surprised." He looked at me then, his blue-gray eyes haunted. "Poor devil."

I nodded in grim agreement.

"What…" Amy swallowed hard. "What's in there, Jane?"

I took a deep breath and addressed the group. "I don't suppose anyone believed Sybille Collingwood back in 1668 when she claimed Percival Ruskin ran off. Most folks probably thought he ended up in a shallow grave or the nearest lake. In fact, he never left The Gabbling Goose."

It took a moment, then Shelley stifled a gasp with her hand. Her husband put his arm around her shoulders and pulled her close. Cherry and Alex gaped at each other as my meaning sunk in.

Jankovic Number One said, "Not sure who this Percival guy is, but do you want us to finish demolishing the wall, Mr. Collingwood?"

"Why don't you hold off for the time being," Ty said.

Just then, from the farthest reaches of the house, came three hollow, metallic sounds.

Clang. Clang. Clang.

Shelley brightened. "It's Percy! He's thanking us for freeing his spirit."

I didn't remind her that she held a low opinion of Percy and that, according to her, his spirit was just waiting for an opportunity to exact vengeance on the Collingwoods. Nor did I point out that Percy's preferred method of communication sounded suspiciously like the banging of air in geriatric plumbing.

Then I recalled her explanation for how Percy produced those metallic sounds. He banged his pewter cup on the punch bowl. And what two items had accompanied him in death?

I admit it. I shivered.

Now that I'd prepared the others for the sight, I handed the work light to the Jankovics and the Tagliaferros, who took turns exclaiming over our grisly find.

Ty said, "I guess we have to report this."

I was already tapping my cell phone. When Detective Cookie Kaplan answered, I said, "Déjà vu, Cookie. There's a dead body at The Gabbling Goose."

14
Corpse-Obsessed Weirdo

"CAN YOU IMAGINE anything more *gruesome* than finding out you've been living in a house with a *corpse?*" Miranda Daniels's snarling face dominated the enormous television screen in my family room. As usual, her platinum-blonde hair had been shellacked to a fare-thee-well, and she wore enough makeup to supply a clown convention. "I'm about to lose my lunch just *thinking* about it."

"You're not going to make me watch the whole show, are you?" Martin groaned. Well, it might've been more of a whine. He leaned toward the coffee table, speared a savory spinach ball with a bamboo hors d'oeuvre pick, and gave it a good dunking in spicy mustard sauce.

"Don't worry," I said. "I just want to see what kind of spin she's giving the case. I'll turn it off in a few minutes."

Sexy Beast, lounging between us on the horseshoe-shaped ivory leather sofa, seconded that plan with a poodley snort that can only be described as judgmental.

I don't normally tune in to Miranda's sensationalist nightly program, *Ramrod News*, but there was no denying it had a large and loyal viewership, and I couldn't help but wonder what she'd have to say about the latest development in the Stu Ruskin "suicide versus homicide" question.

Not that Percival Ruskin's long-ago demise was directly related to Stu's more recent one, but the discovery of Percy's skeletal remains on the same property two days earlier was juicy enough to keep Stu's case front and center in the public's imagination, and to help the network's sponsors sell more car insurance and diabetes medication.

Miranda had already introduced her guests, Cherry and Alex Tagliaferro, the "brave young couple who just spent an *entire weekend* in the house of horrors where guests are dropping like *flies!*"

"Okay, first of all?" The padre gesticulated with his empty hors d'oeuvre pick. "Stu Ruskin was not a guest of The Gabbling Goose. He was a trespasser."

"I suppose a case could be made that Percival Ruskin was a guest of the inn," I said, "if it's true that Sybille invited him over for a nice, bracing cup of Sybbie's Punch. But that would be a stretch."

"It would also be ancient history," he said. "Do you think her viewers are buying this nonsense?"

"Probably." I offered a tiny bit of spinach ball to SB, who gave it a skeptical sniff, accepted it just to be polite, then daintily deposited the half-chewed wad back onto my palm. I said, "Who was it who said you'll never go broke underestimating the intelligence of the American public?"

"The journalist H. L. Mencken," Martin said, "and that's not exactly what he said—or rather, wrote—but it's close enough."

"How do you know that?" I asked.

He shrugged. "I read."

Martin had shown up a short while earlier bearing the

platter of homemade spinach balls: scrumptious baked tidbits that combined the healthy green stuff with enough unhealthy tasty stuff to make them irresistible, particularly when slathered with the zingy mustard sauce he'd whipped up to accompany them.

And if you're thinking that the men in my life seem determined to feed me, you wouldn't be wrong—although now it was the *man* in my life. Singular. I'd thought a lot about my conversation with Dom two days earlier, when I'd ended our romantic connection for good. I had yet to regret that decision, and somehow knew I never would.

Onscreen, Miranda turned to the Tagliaferros, who'd joined her at the show's studio in Manhattan. Whoever designed the set had apparently decided that a scary-looking frosted-glass table with jagged edges would convey the appropriate tone for *Ramrod News*.

Actually, I have to say, they nailed it.

"So how *terrible* was it," Miranda asked the couple, "going into that secret room and finding a *disgusting, rotting corpse*? How do you *recover* from something like that?"

"Well, first of all," Cherry said, "we didn't actually go into the room, we just looked through an opening. And the body was completely skeletonized, it wasn't a, um… that is to say, the soft tissues had thoroughly decomp—"

"What about *you*, Alex?" Miranda said. "Was it just the most *horrifying* thing you've ever seen? The *smell* must have made you *gag*! Don't leave *anything* out. Our audience can take it."

"It wasn't so bad," he said. "We kind of knew what to expect because Jane had basically told all of us what was in there."

"Ah, yes." Miranda glared right into the camera. "That would be Jane Delaney, the corpse-obsessed *weirdo* they call the

Death Diva. We invited Ms. Delaney onto the show. She *declined*." Her raised eyebrows invited her audience to draw their own conclusions.

I saluted her with my beer bottle. "Love you, too, Miranda." Which, as you've probably guessed, was a big fat lie. Miranda Daniels and I had had our run-ins.

In truth, I welcomed her over-the-top characterization of me. It was free publicity. I had no doubt some of her viewers were even now looking me up online, and that a few of them would, at some point in the future, decide they required the services of a corpse-obsessed weirdo to handle whatever icky death-related chore had fallen into their lap.

"Why did she want this young couple on her show?" Martin asked. "It's not like they're experts or anything."

"The Tagliaferros were her last choice," I said. "Everyone else who was in that basement had the good sense to decline. Even the beauteous Jankovics."

His brows pulled together. "The who?"

"Oh, just…" I flapped my hand. "It's not important. As for having a bona fide expert on the show, Miranda tried hard to get Carmen Hidalgo, the forensic anthropologist who examined Percy's skeleton. Dr. Hidalgo offered statements to legitimate news outlets but gave *Ramrod News* a wide berth."

The padre lifted Sexy Beast and settled him on his other side so he could move closer to me. I did not mind one little bit.

He said, "Obviously, Percy's death isn't a police matter."

"Gee, I don't know," I deadpanned. "There's no statute of limitations on murder."

"I'd say his killer is beyond the clutches of the law. About three hundred fifty years beyond." He stabbed a spinach ball, dipped it in mustard sauce, and brought it to my mouth. Those things were downright decadent.

Onscreen, Miranda had given up on her attempt to extract disgusting descriptions from her guests and was yowling about the unmitigated horror of the crime. "Walled up in the *kitchen*, if you can imagine that. Where generations of the Collingwood family prepared their *meals*! I personally can't think of anything more *stomach-churning*."

Cherry and Alex exchanged anxious glances, clearly wondering what they'd gotten themselves into.

The camera zoomed in on Miranda's glowering mug. "And what did that poor man do to *deserve* a lingering death like that?" she asked. "Like something Edgar Allan *Poe* would've cooked up? *Nothing*, that's what! Percival Ruskin was an innocent *victim*. His only crime was falling in love with the wrong woman. He was too *trusting*."

"Executive decision." Martin commandeered the remote and turned off the program.

"It's my house," I said. "I get to make the executive decisions."

"Not when it comes to TV shows that make my brain hurt. I can't sit here and listen to that loathsome woman rewrite history. For one thing, I wouldn't call Percival Ruskin innocent."

"His only crime was falling in love with Sybille Collingwood?" I scoffed. "How about setting up her husband to be killed so he could get his hands on the recipe for Sybbie's Punch?"

"The Edgar Allan Poe reference is on target, though," he said. "That's how Fortunato meets his end in 'The Cask of Amontillado.' Montresor walls him up in his family's crypt."

"Gee, thanks for the spoiler," I teased. I'd first read that old story back in junior high school. Like most of Poe's work, it was calculated to impart a macabre thrill.

"You have to admit," he said, "that's a horrible way to go. You said it looked like Percy was trying to dig his way out?"

I nodded. "Shelley speculates that the little room back there was the larder, where they stored salted meats and other perishable foods. Can you imagine what Percy's last hours must've been like?"

"More like days," the padre said. "That's not a quick way to go."

"It must have been pitch-black in there, and all he had with him was that cup and punch bowl."

"Didn't Shelley say the constable was Sybille's cousin," he asked, "and that's why she was never brought to justice?"

I nodded. "Also it was assumed he helped her dispose of the body. Here's how I think it might've played out. Sybille Collingwood is devastated by her husband, Oswald's, death."

"Even though he's a lazy good-for-nothing?"

"Yeah, but he's *her* lazy good-for-nothing," I said. "After he was gunned down by the king's men, Sybille planted an oak tree on the very spot where he died and put a curse on anyone who might cut it down. The tree's still there. It's ginormous."

"Once Oswald is dead," Martin said, "Percy romances her to steal her secret recipe."

"Which he probably accomplished the same way his descendant Stu did generations later," I said. "By watching her make a batch. Whereupon he starts selling Peg Leg Punch, which is when Sybille finally puts two and two together."

"And realizes Percy was involved in Oswald's death," the padre said. "That's when she decides to get even by luring him to The Gabbling Goose and serving him poisoned punch. But obviously he survives—at least long enough to try and dig his way out of his tomb."

"I think I have that part figured out." I took a swig of beer. "Sybille gives Percy just enough poison to knock him out, maybe put him into a temporary coma, but not enough to kill him. That's when she gets her cousin the constable involved."

"They toss Percy into the larder," he said, "and brick up the doorway while he's still unconscious. But the thing I don't get is, why leave him with the punch bowl and cup?"

"Think about it," I said.

"I am thinking about it, but obviously not as hard as you are. Why don't you explain it to me."

"That punch bowl isn't empty when she puts it in his makeshift tomb," I said. "It contains the rest of the poisoned punch. She knows that when he wakes up in that tiny dark space, he'll figure out what she's done."

Martin was getting it. "And he'll know that the punch in the bowl will likely kill him. But eventually he'll be so crazed by thirst, he'll have no choice but to give in and drink it."

"Just one more way to torment him while he dies," I said.

He gave a low whistle. "That Sybille, I've gotta hand it to her, she didn't mess around."

"I wouldn't be surprised if she sat on the other side of that brick wall, calmly embroidering tea towels and listening to Percy's desperate pleas for mercy."

Sexy Beast roused himself from his nap, stretched, and climbed onto Martin's lap, where he received all the scritches a little poodle could want.

"There seems to be a weird connection," the padre said, "between dead Ruskins and The Gabbling Goose's hot tubs. First Stu and now Percy."

"Ty was really shaken when he saw that skeleton. 'Poor

devil,' I said. Like he felt real sympathy for old Percy."

"You'd have to be pretty heartless not to."

"Ty has always blamed Percy for starting the feud way back when," I said, "but there's no denying he was shocked at the punishment Sybille devised. The fact that she was capable of that level of cruelty, well… I have to wonder if it's altered Ty's preconceived notions of his Collingwood ancestors and their supposed moral superiority to the Ruskins."

"Good question," he said. "It would be hard to argue there's anything morally superior about what Ty's ancestor did to Stu's ancestor."

"I know Ty was expecting to find the recipe for Sybbie's Punch behind that brick wall," I said. "Of course, it wasn't there. I doubt it'll ever be found. Both families probably committed it to memory way back when and never saw a need to write it down."

"Yeah, probably," Martin said, distractedly. He settled back against the sofa, staring straight ahead. He took a long swig from his beer bottle. To the casual observer, he would have looked totally at ease. The tension I felt radiating from him told a different story.

Finally he set down the bottle and said, in a serious tone, "There's something I need to tell you, Jane."

My heart banged. This was it. Whatever had been happening between us was over. Martin felt I was stringing him along and wanted no more of it. Not that he would put it that way. He'd think of some horribly kind way to say it.

So then, what was the point of plying me with those delicious spinach balls if he was just going to dump me? Was it his way of letting me down easy? If so, he could shove those darn things, *and* the hot mustard sauce—

"You okay?" He was frowning at me. "You look like someone just died."

Sexy Beast deserted Martin to give me a doggie hug, leaning on my chest and staring into my eyes while fretting about the emotional stability of his alpha female.

I cleared my throat. "I'm fine, I just… What do you want to tell me, Padre?"

He took a deep breath. "You accused me of being secretive. Remember?"

I nodded, recalling the talk we had at The Gabbling Goose the night Stu died. "You told me there are some things you don't share with anyone," I said, "and that you're not one of the bad guys. You asked me to trust you."

"I've thought about that conversation a lot since then," he said. "I might've been asking too much of you."

"What do you mean?"

"I mean I've given you little reason to trust me." After a moment, he added, "I'm not used to opening up about myself."

"You mean to women you're, um, involved with?" I asked.

"To anyone," he said.

"Why?"

"I have what you might call a checkered past, Jane."

Suddenly I dreaded hearing whatever he had to say. But I knew I had to. For better or worse, I needed to know who I'd fallen in love with.

Yeah, I said it.

Oh, you figured it out long before I did, huh? Well, give yourself a gold star.

"Okay," I said, as SB curled up on my lap, "first just tell me this. Have you ever gone to prison?"

"No," he said.

I breathed a sigh of relief.

"Because I never got caught," he added.

"Oh."

"Well, except for one time." He paused to collect his thoughts. "Do you remember last year when I told you about my grandparents?"

"Yes," I said. "Arthur and Anne McAuliffe. I also remember you telling me about their middle son, Hugh. Your father."

"The fine, upstanding, married deacon who was getting some on the side forty-something years ago with a teenage exotic dancer."

"Your mom." I'd met Martin's mother, Stephanie Borden, and I liked her a lot. "Hugh kept you a secret from his family, as I recall."

"God forbid the world should learn he sired a bastard."

"But your grandparents eventually found out about you," I said. "I think you said you were eleven then? And you became very close with them."

Martin's expression softened with the memory. "Yeah, we became close. Grandma and Grandpa were appalled when they found out their son had been treating *his* son like some kind of shameful secret. Those few years I got with them were... well, they were special." He grimaced. "Then Irene came along."

"And broke up their marriage." Which is how Irene Hardy McAuliffe, the high-maintenance homewrecker who gave me my start as the one and only Death Diva, ended up owning Anne's dream house after Arthur's death. Irene, in turn, bequeathed the house to her little poodle, Sexy Beast. Okay, technically, she bequeathed it to me, but SB holds what's called a life estate, which means it belongs to him during his lifetime. And of course, I get to live there with him as his guardian.

"Grandpa divorced Grandma," the padre said, "and married Irene right away. Eight months later, Grandma was dead. I was fifteen then. It tore me apart, losing her."

I recalled Martin telling me she died of a broken heart. I was trying to figure out what this had to do with his so-called checkered past when he said, "That's when I turned into a little thug. If you ask my mom, she'll say it's when I started 'acting out.' A euphemism if ever there was one."

"What form did this thuggery take?" I asked.

"Rocky Bay didn't have any gangs per se, but it had its share of rough characters, and I sought them out."

Rocky Bay was the working-class town on the South Shore where Martin grew up. His mom still lived there.

"We're talking small stuff at first," he said. "Graffiti, knocking down mailboxes, your basic minor vandalism. I'd cut school and go joyriding, call in fake bomb threats. Before long, I graduated to shoplifting, picking fights, criminal trespass."

"Where did you trespass?" I asked.

"Office buildings in the middle of the night. A catering hall. We tossed stuff around, pilfered a few items. You'd be surprised how lax security is in some of those places." He was watching me closely to gauge my reaction. I managed to keep my expression neutral.

"You were able to get out of the house in the middle of the night without your mom knowing?" I asked.

"That was the easy part," he said. "I also ran away a couple of times. Both times, I took her car."

"You were old enough to drive?"

"Sure I was old enough to drive," he said. "I just wasn't old enough to have a license."

"You said you got caught once," I reminded him.

"My new friends, if you can call them that, introduced me to the fine art of burglary."

"You broke into people's homes?" I didn't like the sound of that.

"For kicks, yeah," he said, "when the owners were away. I never took anything, but I did come away with some useful if not altogether lawful skills."

I was familiar with those useful skills, having witnessed the padre deploy them in the service of goals far loftier than burglary. He'd even coached *me* through my first ever lock-picking session in the inky depths of a tunnel, when every second counted and our survival depended on mutual trust. We very nearly became food for worms that hair-raising day.

"It didn't take long for me to get bored with that new game," he said, "so I decided to up the ante."

I *really* didn't like the sound of that. "What did you do?"

"I broke into my dad's house in the middle of the night."

My jaw dropped. "Hugh McAuliffe? Irene's son? I mean stepson."

He nodded. "The pillar of society who, sixteen years earlier, sicced a squadron of high-priced lawyers on the teenage girl he knocked up, ensuring that he'd never be held accountable, financially or in any other way. *That* Hugh McAuliffe."

"But why?" I asked. "What did you hope to gain by doing something like that?"

"You're assuming I worked it all out beforehand, went in there with a plan." He wore a self-deprecating smile. "I was just this dumb kid harboring a lifetime of resentment and looking to stir up trouble."

"Which I assume you accomplished," I said.

"Hugh had an alarm system for the doors, but not the

windows," he said. "That's how I got in, through the window of what turned out to be his study, or office, or whatever he called it."

"But no one was home, right? You said you chose vacant houses."

"Not this time," Martin said. "I was tired of being ignored, tired of that SOB pretending I didn't exist—living his life as if his son was just one more nuisance he could eradicate by throwing money at it."

"Did you ever meet him?" I asked.

"Not until that night," he said.

"So he caught you."

"I wasn't exactly trying to be stealthy. I ran around on the first floor, throwing things, making a mess."

"You're lucky he didn't have a dog," I said.

"He had a dog." Martin grinned. "Whupper. That's what his tag read."

"You got close enough to read his tag?"

"Oh, Whupper and I were instant buddies," he said. "Friendliest pit bull I ever met. He led me right to the cabinet where they kept the dog treats. Once he had his fill of those, he kept bringing me toys to throw. We had a great old time, until Hugh came downstairs with his twelve-gauge."

A soft gasp escaped me. "He pointed a shotgun at you?"

The padre shrugged. "Beats a handgun for home protection."

"But you're his *son*," I said.

"At that moment I was just some punk who broke into his house," Martin said. "He'd never met me, never even asked my mom for a picture of me. Not that he exchanged two words with her after she told him she was pregnant. He let his lawyers issue the threats."

"Did you tell him who you were?" I asked.

"He figured it out soon enough. I taunted him, cursed him out, belittled his manhood for how he'd treated my mother. And the funny thing? Even after he realized who I was, he never lowered that shotgun. Just kept yelling at Whupper to get out of the line of fire."

I close my eyes briefly, hurting for Martin, for the angry, aggrieved kid he'd been.

"Eventually his wife crept downstairs," he said. "She heard all this hollering and deduced it wasn't a simple break-in. Hugh tried to order her back upstairs, but by then their daughter, Claudia, had joined them, and the women wanted answers."

"How old was Claudia?" I asked.

"A few years older than me," he said. "College age. Later I found out she was enrolled at Harvard. She was home for the summer then."

"I'm assuming Hugh had never told his wife and daughter about you," I said.

"He'd never told *anyone* about me. I lost no time bringing the ladies up to speed. Hugh tried to bluster his way out of it, of course, but anyone looking at the two of us would know instantly that we're related."

"Claudia and her mom were shocked, no doubt," I said.

"Yes and no," he said. "They didn't know about me, but they knew what kind of man Hugh was. I could see it in their eyes."

"So that must've made for a fun family confab," I said, dryly. "All of you getting acquainted in the middle of the night."

"Hugh's wife was sobbing and carrying on," Martin said. "Claudia was screaming at her father to put the damn gun down. I think she was afraid he'd shoot me."

"By accident?" I asked.

"Or not. The man was apoplectic. He was used to being in control. That much was clear. He had no idea what to do about me. Well, he had one idea. He started to call the police to report the break-in."

"*Started* to call?" I said.

"Claudia stopped him," he said. "She told him that reporting it would ensure that everyone would find out about me. It was a family matter and should be handled as such. I have to hand it to her, she knew how to defuse her old man."

"Do you think she actually cared about her dad's reputation?" I asked. "You know, protecting the family name and all that? Or was she trying to protect *you*? Her half brother."

"I've asked myself that question many times," he said. "I'd have liked to ask Claudia herself, but we don't have anything to do with each other. None of the McAuliffes have any use for me. It goes both ways."

I thought that was terribly sad, but I kept it to myself. What I said was, "So did you keep on the same path after that? Hanging with the criminal element? A burglar in training?"

"For a little while," he said, "a few more months. At least the 'criminal element' accepted me for who I was. It was comfortable in a dysfunctional sort of way."

"And you never got into trouble with the law?" I asked.

"I had more luck than brains, as the saying goes."

"What made you stop?" I asked.

A gentle smile curved his mouth. "Lexie." His daughter.

I returned his smile. "When did you find out you were going to be a father?"

"Four days after Christmas," he said, "which happened to be my seventeenth birthday. Erin told me as soon as she found out."

"That's some birthday present."

Erin Davey had been a high-school friend of Martin's. They weren't in a serious relationship back then; it was more like friends with benefits. I'd met Erin and their daughter, Lexie, a year earlier at Lexie's wedding to Dillon Kovac, when Martin had proudly walked his daughter down the aisle. The young couple were expecting their first child in September. Martin was going to be a grandpa. I was still trying to wrap my brain around that.

"It was like a switch flipped inside me," he said. "All the stupid decisions I'd been making, the selfish, self-destructive hole I'd plunged into after Grandma's death, that was all over. I had this precious little life to take care of. I was determined not to let my child down. Or Erin. As scared as I was, I knew it was worse for her. She needed me to be strong."

"That's a lot to take on at seventeen," I said. I knew that Martin had worked hard to be a good dad, to do his part to help support and raise Lexie, even after Erin got married and gave their daughter two siblings.

When it came to paternal commitment and sacrifice, the contrast between Martin and his own father could not have been greater.

"Lexie reordered my priorities." His expression softened. "Grandpa doted on her."

"How old was she when he died?"

"Just two," he said. "She doesn't remember him, unfortunately. He left me some money. Not a fortune, but enough to help pay for college, combined with work study."

"I didn't know you went to college. What school?"

"John Jay College of Criminal Justice in Manhattan." He

smiled at my astonished expression. "After graduation, I became a PI."

"Is that how you got your start as a bodyguard?" I knew that private investigators often take that kind of assignment.

"Yep," he said, "though I prefer 'executive protection.' Sounds so much swankier. I found I enjoyed protection work more than spying on cheating spouses. There's often some overlap, though, so I still do a little investigating on occasion."

"So you have two completely different jobs," I said, "bartender and bodyguard-slash-PI."

"They're not so different," he said. "I've long believed that bartenders make the best investigators. Think about what people tell their bartender. You can get a lot of information out of someone without offering anything in return."

"Except maybe a free beer or two," I said. "I'm thinking of your buddy on the force. The one who blabs about ongoing cases."

"It's actually a couple of buddies," Martin said, "and I've known them forever. There are times when a PI has to coordinate with the local police, so you get to know each other."

"Is that how you met Ben?" Ben Ralston, a local private investigator, helped me out from time to time. He was currently living with Martin's mom. "You once told me you knew him back when he was still a cop."

"Yeah, Ben and I go way back. And then after he set up shop as a PI, we collaborated on a few cases. Most of my bodyguard work involves legit folks with legit reasons to need protection. Often it's high-profile types like celebrities, foreign dignitaries and their families, business leaders, that sort of thing."

I made a mental note to demand names later. For now, though, I was curious about another kind of client. "Mobsters?"

I asked. "Drug dealers? Do they hire you, too?"

"They try," he said. "If a prospective client seems sketchy, I turn down the job. Sometimes, though, you don't know until you're already involved. And it's not cut-and-dried. There are gray areas."

"Like with Stu?"

"Stu Ruskin seemed like easy money at first," he said. "He'd call me for occasional protection, but like I said, he refused to provide the info I needed to do my job right."

"Meaning the name of the person who supposedly tried to kill him," I said.

"Which turned out to be a big yawn." He went all Humphrey Bogart. "A good old-fashioned tussle over a dame."

"You make a fistfight sound downright wholesome."

"A client who doesn't listen to you," he said, "who doesn't accept his bodyguard as the alpha dog, that just spells trouble. I should've walked right then."

"Why didn't you?" I asked.

The padre shrugged. "Stu was paying top dollar, and it seemed like a simple, once-in-a-while gig. I learned my lesson."

"Georgia Chen told me you were very... understanding when things came to a head with Stu. She said she was in a rough place, mentally, and that you really helped her."

He looked me in the eye. "I didn't sleep with Georgia."

"I actually know that," I said. "I mean, I came to that conclusion, though I do admit I wondered at first."

"Taking advantage of a woman who's in a vulnerable emotional state," he said, "is no better than if she were drunk or on drugs or whatever. I don't do that. Plus, I like Georgia well enough, but she's a bit hyper for my taste."

"Not to mention," I said, "she's still hung up on her ex."

"Not that you know what that's like," he said.

"Okay, just so you know," I said, "it's official. Dom and I are history."

"This is news?" he said. "You've been saying that for a while now."

"Yeah, and you never really believed it," I said. "Well, believe it. We're done. For good."

The padre studied me, gauging my sincerity. Finally he said, "Does he know this?"

"He knows," I said. "He's not happy about it, but he knows."

I could see him thinking about it, about the barriers that had fallen away that evening. My ex. Martin's own mysterious past.

When he met my gaze, he looked more contented than I'd ever seen him. The corners of those astonishing blue eyes crinkled as he lifted his hand to cup my cheek. I turned my head to press my lips to his palm.

Martin leaned closer and kissed me, a sweet, deep kiss full of promise. Then he glanced at his wristwatch and groaned.

"I know," I said. "You have to go to work."

He gave me one last, quick kiss and stood up. "This conversation isn't finished, Jane."

I grinned. "You bet your killer booty it isn't."

15
Kooky Instructions

"YOU DIDN'T WASTE any time," I told Ty as a bricklayer named Felix began to lay a second course of bricks across the door-size opening to Percival Ruskin's basement tomb. The hole that had been created by Jankovic Number One three days earlier had subsequently been enlarged to allow for examination and removal of Percy's skeletonized remains.

It was kind of mesmerizing, watching Felix set each brick into a bed of mortar and neatly scrape off the excess before moving on to the next one. The new brickwork was much neater and more uniform than the Colonial-era wall that surrounded it. I preferred the look of the old, irregular bricks, but that's just me.

I said, "I'm glad you're doing this, Ty, but don't be surprised if someone asks why you didn't install a door there and leave the little room intact."

Amy, standing next to me, shuddered. "As what, some kind of sick tourist attraction?"

Ty said, "It was bad enough having those ghouls sneak onto the property to mess around with the hot tub after Stu died in it. The last thing I want is someone getting the bright idea to slip down here and hunt for souvenirs."

"Good point. Is that why you're leaving the punch bowl and cup in there?"

Amy said, "Every time I see them, I'm reminded of what Sybille did to Percival, of his agonizing death. I never want to see those things again."

"Better to leave them where they are," Ty said.

The sound of footfalls on the stairs made us turn. Shelley stopped halfway down and said, "You have visitors, Ty."

"If they're from *Ramrod News*," he said, "get rid of them. Ditto for *The Romano Report*."

A gray eyebrow rose. She said, "Didn't I run those jackals off last time they came sniffing around?"

The Romano Report, hosted by chef-turned-TV-personality Leonora Romano, competed with Miranda Daniels's show in the same time slot and was only marginally less offensive.

Shelley descended two more steps and whispered, "It's Stu Ruskin's brother and his wife. He said it's important."

Amy turned to her father. "What could they want?"

"Only one way to find out." He glanced one last time at the brickwork in progress, then led the way upstairs.

It was about six p.m. on Tuesday. Twenty-four hours had passed since Martin had finally taken the mystery out of his mysterious background, and had been assured, in turn, that my ex-husband was absolutely, positively, one hundred percent *ex*. You can imagine how I'd been obsessing over that conversation, and wondering (okay, fantasizing) about the kind of future we might have together.

I'd decided to take a break from my giddy musings to swing by The Gabbling Goose and see what Ty had decided to do about the little room where Percival Ruskin had died. I'd left SB at home this time. It was my fourth visit in the past three weeks.

One of these days I really ought to rent a room—well, maybe not alone—and have the whole Gabbling Goose experience.

Gilbert and Darla Ruskin stood in the front parlor, looking ill at ease. Gilbert wore a dark suit and tie, just as he had at this brother's funeral. Likewise, his wife wore yet another dumpy jacket dress, identical to the ones I'd previously seen her in, except for the color. This one was a muddy olive green that would have flattered precisely no one. I could only assume she'd gotten a volume discount.

Darla's distracted gaze skittered over the antique furnishings, the portrait of Oswald Collingwood, and the enormous cat grooming itself on the bottom step of the staircase, before coming to rest on yours truly. She blinked in surprise.

"Hi, Darla," I said. "Remember me?" You'll be happy to know I refrained from asking if she'd reconsidered my job offer as an entrails-mopping intern. Oh, but I wanted to so bad.

See? I can be mature when the occasion calls for it. Most of the time, anyway.

Darla's mouth tightened into a thin line. If she wondered what the heck the disgusting Death Demon was doing there, she didn't give voice to the thought. Which meant both of us were doing a good job in the maturity department. I was darn proud of us.

"Sure you folks wouldn't like something to drink?" Shelley asked the couple. "Last call." Disapproval rolled off her in waves. I could tell she chafed at having Ruskins darken The Gabbling Goose's doorstep. I wouldn't be surprised if she sprayed the place down with disinfectant after they left.

"Thanks, but we can't stay." Gilbert turned to Ty. "We just wanted to, uh, discuss something with you, Mr. Collingwood."

"Please, call me Ty." He gestured toward the seating area,

and they chose the love seat Martin and I had occupied the night of Stu's death. Gilbert sat like a normal person, while Darla perched on the edge as if ready to flee at a moment's notice.

I gave a little wave. "I'll say goodbye now."

"Oh, don't rush off, Jane." Amy seized my wrist and steered me to one of the antique armchairs. I got the feeling she was worried about a possible confrontation between her father and the Ruskins, and figured my presence might keep them from going at it. "Mr. Ruskin said this won't take long."

"Uh, you can call me Gil," he said, because it would have been awkward not to. Mrs. Ruskin apparently had nothing against awkwardness, because she remained mute.

Ty sat on the sofa, next to his daughter. "I think I can guess what brought you here, Gil."

The Ruskins exchanged frowns. Darla rested her hand on her husband's arm, wordlessly telling him to let her handle it. "And what would that be, Mr. Collingwood?"

"I should have reached out to you when your ancestor's remains were discovered in the basement," Ty said. "It was wrong of me not to. It honestly didn't occur to me, but of course, that's no excuse. You shouldn't have had to learn about it from the police."

Darla said, "We learned about it from the TV news. And it seems you need to be reminded—" she shook off her husband's warning touch "—that Percival was not the only Ruskin to die on your property."

Okay, I knew for a fact that Gil and Darla hadn't learned about Stu's death on the TV news. The police notified them. And what did she think Ty should have told them at the time? *I'm sorry that your brother, who'd been manipulating and deceiving my daughter for close to a year, and scheming to get his greedy mitts on my ancestral estate, trespassed onto my property and blew his brains out.*

Ty's features hardened fractionally, but he was a gentleman and knew the right words. "Please accept my apologies for that lapse, as well, Mrs. Ruskin. I should have been in touch."

Darla didn't seem to know what to do with that. Finally she gave a curt nod, not meeting Ty's gaze.

"It occurs to me," Ty said, "that you might want to view the location where Percival was found. A bricklayer is down there right now, sealing up that space again, but if you're interested, I can ask him to hold off for a bit."

Gil and Darla shared an unspoken communication. I could almost hear them wondering whether an invitation to view the bloody hot tub would be next on the agenda. "I don't think so," Gil said, "but thanks for the offer."

"Let me ask you, Gil," Ty said. "Have Percival's remains been released to you yet?"

"Well, uh, we can have them anytime we want," he said. "I'm just not sure what to… I mean…"

"Cremation," Darla said. "Simple and respectful."

And cheap, I thought. *Don't forget cheap. We all know you're thinking it.*

Gil studied his shoes. "Or, uh, donation. Of the, uh, bones. We were thinking science might be interested."

Quick! Someone get Science on the phone!

"Well, of course it's up to you," Ty said, "but I believe it would be appropriate for Percival to be laid to rest in Whispering Willows Cemetery, in the older historic section next to his immediate family members."

The Collingwood ancestors were also in the historic section, which was the boneyard's priciest precinct. Darla's nostrils flared, while Gil turned an embarrassed shade of pink as he struggled to come up with a response.

Ty startled me by saying, "I'm glad Jane's here. We can take advantage of her expertise. I feel a responsibility to your family, Gil. I can never make up for the reprehensible actions of my ancestor Sybille Collingwood, but if you'll allow me, I would like to offer Percival a cemetery plot, a casket, and all the expenses associated with a dignified Christian funeral."

The Ruskins were stunned into silence. Amy's face relaxed into a near smile. She gave her father's hand a little squeeze.

"The particulars would be up to you, of course," Ty continued, "and you probably want to handle those yourself—"

How we all managed to keep a straight face, I don't know.

"—but we have the expert sitting right here." Ty gestured in my direction. "This sort of thing is right in Jane's wheelhouse, and she has an outstanding reputation for attention to detail. I'd like to hire her to take care of the arrangements, subject to your approval, of course, Gil."

I could see Darla's parsimonious nature warring with her intense dislike of me. Finally she and Gil exchanged a little nod. It would seem she was kind of okay with letting the disgusting Death Demon arrange Percy's sendoff as long as someone else picked up the tab.

Ty turned to me. "I should ask Jane if this is something she's interested in taking on."

"Of course," I said. "I can begin working on it immediately."

"Well, uh, thank you, Ty," Gil said. "That's very generous of you."

"Please. I'm happy to do it," Ty said, and I believed him. "I just wish… things had turned out differently way back then."

Could this be the beginning of a long-awaited rapprochement between the Collingwoods and the Ruskins?

"Well, I feel good about this." Ty started to rise. "Jane will coordinate with you—"

"We actually, uh, came here about something else," Gil said.

"Oh." Ty resumed his seat. "Whatever it is, I hope I can help."

"It's not like that. It has to do with… well, a few days ago, Jane here mentioned something to my wife. She, uh, didn't think anything of it at the time, right, dear?"

Darla just gestured for him to continue.

"Yeah, so anyway," Gil said, "then that skeleton turns up, and the news stories are all talking about the poisoned punch. You know, the, uh, punch Sybille made Percival drink?"

"They know about the poisoned punch, for crying out loud." Darla jerked her head toward me. "She told me Percival stole Sybille's punch recipe way back when. She wanted to know if anyone in the family still had it."

Amy's brow crinkled. "You were looking for the punch recipe, Jane?"

I addressed Ty. "I was just trying to do you a favor. You were so anxious to find that old recipe, and I just happened to be speaking with Darla, and it seemed like the perfect opportunity to do a little digging. I know you don't believe anyone in the Ruskin family still has it, but I thought, what the heck, it couldn't hurt to ask."

Ty turned to the Ruskins. "I assume the answer is no, that the recipe is long gone."

"Well, uh, here's the thing," Gil said, and Ty went very still. I sensed him holding his breath. "Turns out, Stu had that old recipe all along. I guess it kind of, uh, slipped Darla's mind when

Jane brought it up."

Darla's snide expression told me it had not, in fact, slipped her mind.

Ty was on his feet. "This is incredible news! Did you bring it with you?"

"I didn't know it belonged to your family." Gil sounded defensive. "Or that one of our ancestors, you know, stole it. Darla didn't mention it until after his, uh, skeleton turned up. By then, everyone knew about it. It was all over the news."

"That's all right." Ty's eyes shone with excitement. "It's all in the past. Where's the recipe now?"

Amy tugged on his arm, urging him to sit. He did so, with obvious reluctance.

"I never even knew the darn thing existed," Gil said. "I never heard of an old punch recipe. No one in my family ever—"

"Gil!" Ty was making a conspicuous effort to rein in his impatience. He leaned forward and spoke slowly and clearly. "Where is it?"

"I don't have it."

Ty's jaw tightened. "Stu knew how much that recipe meant to me, but I can't believe he'd have destroyed it, just to spite me."

"No, no, nothing like that," he said. "I mean I, uh… I know where it is."

Darla rolled her eyes. "For the love of God, can't you just say it? The recipe was buried with Stu."

At that instant, the front door swung open and two couples in their seventies entered, chatting and laughing and having a merry old time—until they spied our little group, sitting there in thunderstruck silence.

One of the newcomers, a portly gentleman who appeared to

have enjoyed a couple of cocktails with dinner, quipped, "Whatsamatter, folks? You related to that stiff they found in the basement?"

He guffawed at his own wit until Darla skewered him with a hard stare and said, "Yes. Also the stiff they found in the hot tub. Any more questions?"

They say you can't sober up instantly. I'm here to tell you they lied.

The jokester bleated something unintelligible as his friends yanked him through the entrance to the drawing room. Seconds later I heard them scurry into the enclosed porch and slam the door.

Ty took a deep breath and let it out slowly. His voice was dangerously calm as he said, "How is that possible, Gil? That the recipe was buried with him?"

"It's not my fault. I was just following Stu's instructions."

"What instructions?"

Darla said, "The instructions in his will. My brother-in-law had very specific requirements regarding his burial."

Not specific enough, I thought, remembering that sad excuse for a funeral.

Amy said, "I'm guessing one of those requirements involved the recipe for Sybbie's Punch."

"Well, uh, he called it Peg Leg Punch," Gil said, "but yeah, he said it had to be buried with him."

"Let me guess," I said. "It was the only copy in existence."

Gil nodded. "His will told us where to find the recipe. It was in a sealed envelope in his home safe. I was, uh, forbidden to open the envelope or make a copy of the contents. I had to place the envelope in the inside breast pocket of his suit jacket. You know, the suit he was buried in. So, uh, that's what I did."

Amy was casting furtive glances at her father. It was clear she was worried about him, hoping he wouldn't get too worked up.

Darla said something last week that I didn't give much thought to at the time. Maybe I should have. *We did the right thing, even following his kooky burial instructions to the letter.*

Okay, I've seen kookier, but this one definitely earned its place on the kooky spectrum.

"I felt obligated," Gil told Ty, "to follow the instructions in Stu's will. I, uh, saw it as my final duty to my brother, never mind that we didn't get along so well. But I want you to know, I never would've done it if I knew how important that old recipe was to you, or, uh, that one of my people stole it from one of your people."

Darla couldn't let that alone. "I'd say Sybille got back at Percival, and then some. I never heard of anything so wicked in my life as what that woman did to him."

"Ty already told us how bad he feels about that," Gil said, in the first display of backbone I'd witnessed from him. "It wasn't his fault, what his ancestor did way back when, but he's trying to make it right, and I appreciate that."

Ty acknowledged this with a small nod, pointedly avoiding Darla's malignant glare.

"And our Percival," Gil continued, "he was no saint either. He deliberately got Sybille's husband killed. And can I just point out? All this happened hundreds of years ago. I'd say it's time for everyone to move on and start getting along."

If Darla compressed her lips any tighter, they'd fuse together. Hey, it's just science.

Amy looked relieved. "That's what we want, too. Right, Dad?"

Ty appeared preoccupied. "Of course."

"Anyway..." Gil stood, prompting the rest of us to do the same. "I, uh, figured you and your family had a right know, Ty. About what became of that old recipe."

"Gil," Ty said, "how certain are you that the envelope you buried with your brother contained the recipe? Isn't it possible you put the wrong envelope in his pocket?"

Gil shook his head. "There was writing on the outside of it. 'Percival Ruskin's recipe for Peg Leg Punch, 1668.'" After a moment he added, "Nothing any of us can do at this point."

"That might not be strictly true," Ty said.

Amy placed her hand on his arm. "Dad? I know you don't mean..." She glanced nervously at the Ruskins.

"Why not?" Ty said. "It could be done very discreetly, when the cemetery's closed to the public. You wouldn't even have to be there, Gil, you'd just need to give permission. I'll cover all expenses, naturally."

"Now, wait a minute, Ty." Gil frowned. "I'm not about to disturb my brother's final rest for a piece of paper."

"The very idea—" Darla snapped her mouth shut when her husband shot her a stern look I suspected she hadn't seen very often. The message was clear. *I'll handle this.*

"Please just consider it," Ty said. "The burial's still fresh. It's been, what, just over a week. The exhumation would be done with the utmost respect, I give you my word."

"You're asking too much, Ty. If you, uh, feel the need to take back your offer to bury Percival, I'll understand—"

"No, of course not. One has nothing to do with the other." Ty appeared crestfallen as he opened the front door. "Thank you for coming by, Gil. Mrs. Ruskin."

16
We're Going to Teach That Rat a Lesson

MY CEREBRUM REFUSED to shut the heck up as I flopped from side to side in my bed that night, struggling to fall asleep. I just knew I was *this close* to answering the big question that had preoccupied me for the past two weeks, having concluded early on that Stu Ruskin almost certainly did not take his own life.

The man had made enemies. Well, that's what happens when you live your life as an unrepentant cheat, schemer, and user of women. For sure, Ty Collingwood saw him for what he was, and was filled with impotent fury over his daughter's refusal to break off her relationship with him. Little wonder Amy kept the news of their engagement from her dad; he didn't find out about it until after Stu was dead.

Ty might have had a reason to eliminate Stu, but he also had the most robust alibi. He was enjoying live jazz at a club in Southampton, seventy miles away, when Stu was killed. The thing is, it was a solo excursion, so there was no one to corroborate his story. If the police were so inclined, they could interview the club's staff and customers, look for a credit-card charge, and check cell-phone records to see if he was where he said he was when Shelley called him that night. But since the chief of police had pretty much convinced herself it was suicide, that was unlikely to happen.

So getting back to that user-of-women thing, it was the ladies who interested me most. If it's alibis you're looking for, theirs were, let's face it, tissue-thin.

Case in point: Having been forced to admit she was with Stu behind The Gabbling Goose that night, Amy now asked us to believe she threw on her clothes and jogged the mile to her apartment building, leaving Stu stewing over her abrupt departure.

Let's say her ex-fiancé was indeed alive when she left him in the hot tub. By that point, she would have been really steamed. Okay, that pun was unintended, but it was pretty good, don't you think? Anyway, I could see her slipping around the corner, out of earshot, and calling her new friend Georgia Chen, who had also been ill used by the infuriating man.

Georgia, home alone binge-watching rom-coms, gets all *Oh my Gawd!* and *How dare he!* and *Why didn't you steal his clothes?* and finally, *Wait there for me, Amy. We're going to teach that rat a lesson.*

And maybe they didn't intend to kill him at first, but things got out of hand and his gun was right there, and between the two of them, it wasn't all that hard to do.

Taking this murder-buddy thing further, who's to say Henry really was at his mom's doing handyman chores? (Well, his mom would probably back him up, but, I mean, she's his mom.) Georgia said he got in just before midnight. What if he was, in fact, home when his ex-wife got the call? Georgia says, *Oh my Gawd, Henry, you'll never guess where that rat Stu is at this very minute.*

And the two of them race over to The Gabbling Goose, with or without murder in their hearts because maybe they just wanted to tell him off, and things got out of hand.

I'd considered Henry a suspect from the start, based on how thoroughly Stu had torpedoed his life. But how could he have known that his nemesis was lounging in the hot tub behind the B&B unless someone clued him in? That someone would almost certainly have to be Georgia.

So now the three of them converge on the hot tub, browbeating Stu as he sits naked and vulnerable in the warm, swirling water.

But wait, there's more. We know that Woody has informed his wife that their darling Amy's detested ex-fiancé has taken up residence in The Gabbling Goose's spa. Shelley goes charging out there to chase the scoundrel off the property, and now it's a real party, four against one.

Someone discovers the gun and starts waving it around, threatening Stu, who, based on what I now know about him, probably laughs off the danger until it's too late.

Of course, this scenario depends on four people keeping a Very Big Secret once the deed is done.

As my overwrought mind finally drifted into sweet oblivion, the hot-tub party got into full swing, complete with a jazz ensemble, a platter of MegaMunchGigantiKookies, and Hot Tub Homicide cocktails for everyone. Somehow we all managed to squeeze into the tub, and boy, were we having a swell time—even Stu, who, despite looking a little pale, was laughing uproariously.

Yeah, that's right, I was there, too, and so was Sexy Beast, who kept tugging on my collar, trying to pull me out. The musicians were playing the lively, Latin-flavored tune "Tequila," which struck me as an odd choice for a jazz ensemble. And dang if it didn't sound just like the original 1950s version, performed by The Champs.

My sleep-numbed brain was happily bopping along to the familiar tune for a good long while before my eyes finally creaked open in the darkness of my bedroom and I registered the fact that the "Tequila" I was listening to was my cell phone's custom ringtone.

I fumbled around on the nightstand, nearly knocking over my water glass, before I managed to locate the phone, which informed me it was 2:47 in the a.m. I didn't recognize the caller's number, but no matter. I instantly concluded one of my parents was in the emergency room. Middle-of-the-night logic. My heart slamming painfully, I croaked a guttural hello.

"Jane! You have to help me!" It was a frantic female voice. I knew that voice. It wasn't my mom's.

"Um... Amy?"

"My mother just called. She can't find my dad."

I sat up and turned on the bedside lamp. I scrubbed a hand over my face, struggling to make my brain work. "Okay, but, well... I'm not sure how I can help you with that. Do you think something happened to him?"

"No. Yes. I mean..." Amy took a deep breath and let it out slowly. "Earlier this evening, after you left The Gabbling Goose, Dad was... well, he was beyond upset. He went on and on about that old recipe, and how he needed to get to it. You probably don't know this, Jane, but he's been obsessed with that recipe his whole life. It's his white whale."

"Yeah," I said, "I kinda knew that. So tell me what happened."

"Mom tends to go to bed before dad," she said, "but he

always turns in by midnight. She woke up a little while ago, and his side hasn't been slept in. She looked all over the house for him, then checked the garage. His car is missing. She has no idea when he left."

"Okay, so he drove somewhere," I said. "Has he ever done this before? I mean, you know, in the middle of the night?"

"Never. And he didn't leave a note."

"I assume he took his phone and wallet," I said, "and that she tried to call him."

"Yes to all of that," Amy said. "No answer. I tried, too. It went straight to voicemail."

Sexy Beast stared at me from his plush doggie bed, probably wondering what could possibly be important enough to disturb our slumber. Well, I was wondering the same thing. Why on earth was Amy calling *me* with this?

"You said your dad was very upset," I said. "Maybe he went for a drive to cool down."

"There's more," she said. "When Mom was still in the garage, she noticed that something's missing."

"What?"

"A shovel."

I squeezed my eyes shut for a moment. "He wouldn't," I said.

"I know it sounds crazy," she said, "but if you could've seen him ranting after you left… Jane, I think he would. I think he went to the cemetery. I'm so worried about him. His heart…"

"The cemetery gate is locked at night," I said. "How would he even get in?"

"He'd scale the fence or something, I don't know," she said. "You always hear about kids doing it, especially on Halloween."

"I'm still not sure why you called me," I said. "If I were you,

I'd drive over there and—"

"He hasn't listened to me yet on the subject. He's not going to start now. Trust, me, my presence would only make things worse." Amy took a shuddering breath. "I want to hire you to dig up Stu Ruskin and get that recipe for my father."

I was vigorously shaking my head, despite the fact that she couldn't see me.

"Not that you'd do the actual digging," she quickly added. "Obviously you'd have to bring in some muscle for that."

"You know that's illegal, Amy. I don't break the law for clients."

Okay, there are gray areas, but I wasn't going to get into that. Grave robbing was not on the Death Diva's menu of services.

My attempt to harden my heart against the sound of muted weeping was not altogether successful. "Then just reason with him, Jane," she sniffled. "He'll listen to you. He respects you. Whatever your fee is, I'll pay it. I'll pay you double."

"I won't let you pay me, Amy. Not for something like this." Holy cow, it almost sounded like I was agreeing to her nutty request.

"You mean you'll do it? Oh, thank you, Jane. Thank you so much. You're an angel." Now she was blubbering in earnest. "I'll be waiting for your call."

After I hung up, I turned to Sexy Beast and said, "Janey's certifiable. Just in case you ever doubted it." Then I called Martin. Not only was he my newly minted significant other (well, almost), but the man was, as I'd recently discovered, an honest-to-goodness bodyguard. Always a handy thing to have when sneaking into a boneyard in the middle of the night.

Not that I imagined I was in any real danger. Amy had asked

me to reason with her father, and I was pretty confident in my ability to do so. In more than two decades as the Death Diva, I'd had plenty of practice conversing with a variety of people on the most sensitive of subjects. I'd gotten pretty good at it, if I do say so myself.

As for Ty, he was obsessed, but he wasn't insane. I wouldn't be surprised if the fresh air cleared his head and he turned around before he even reached the cemetery.

Martin didn't answer his phone. I left a voicemail telling him where I'd be, as well as how to sneak into the cemetery without having to climb any fences. Yeah, that's right, yet another handy-dandy bit of insider knowledge I'd picked up during my strange career.

I hoped he'd get my message soon, but I couldn't afford to wait for him. Amy didn't know when her dad left his house. It could have been just a few minutes ago. If I hurried, I might be able to nip his foolish escapade in the bud.

I threw on jeans and a sweatshirt, assured Sexy Beast I'd be back soon (he'd already gone back to sleep, but it made me feel better), and took off for Whispering Willows Cemetery.

The roads were practically empty and I got there in record time, circling around the cemetery to park on a side street behind it. The graveyard was surrounded by a very old, tall, wrought-iron picket fence, each picket capped by an ornate, lethal-looking spear point. This rear section of the fence was concealed behind a yew hedge. Starting at the corner and counting posts, I knew just where to breach the hedge to avail myself of a gap between two pickets, just wide enough to squeeze through.

I might have been the only living person who knew about this gap, created in 1936 when a milk delivery truck was run off the road by a drunk frat boy driving a maroon Buick Roadmaster. The delivery truck was making its early-morning rounds, while the frat boy was headed home after a night of nonstop partying.

No, I did not make that story up. Why would you even think that? Okay, I know why you would think it, but let me assure you it really happened. The milk-truck driver, a delightful World War II veteran named Harold Barden, was one of my first clients back when I was still in high school, and he thought this budding Death Diva might appreciate knowing how to sneak into the boneyard in the off hours. And dang if the knowledge hasn't come in handy on a few occasions.

Harold, who at that point was quite old and infirm, had been looking for someone to deliver flags and floral arrangements each year on Memorial Day to the graves of his friends and relatives who'd made the ultimate sacrifice for their country. Most of them had no one left to remember them except Harold. After he died, I continued to decorate those graves, as I would do five days hence when the holiday rolled around again.

As for Harold, I acknowledge his birthday each year by sprinkling a box of Good & Plenty candies on his grave. That man sure did love his licorice.

As I jammed my hindquarters through the gap in the fence, wondering why this had been so much easier when I was eighteen—don't you even think of commenting!—I recalled how I'd mentally tsked when Martin shared his adventures in criminal trespass.

Suddenly I didn't feel so smug.

But it was all for a good cause, right? If I could keep Ty from making a monumental mistake, one that would scandalize his family and no doubt culminate in his arrest, then I would have done a good deed. Which, in turn, would help me relive that lovely smug feeling.

The newer section of the cemetery, where Stu was buried, wasn't too far away. The half-moon provided sufficient illumination to allow me to make my way there.

And since you ask, no, I was not terrified to be wandering around a cemetery in the middle of the night. Yes, I know it's more or less the definition of a scary setting, at least in grade-B horror movies. What can I tell you? I spent so much time at Whispering Willows, it was kind of a second home. I had no hesitation navigating the paths and assorted landmarks in the moonlit gloom.

An unwelcome thought did, however, bubble to the surface as I walked across the lawn toward Stu's grave. Let's say Amy was, indeed, the murderer. If our roles were reversed, I might be regretting how open I'd been during our earlier conversations, how much information I'd shared with that nosy Death Diva—who perhaps now knew too much and needed to be eliminated.

Amy could have been calling me from the cemetery earlier, just pretending to be distraught. She could be waiting behind a tree or monument at that very moment, waiting to shoot me or stab me or who knew what.

That thought stopped me in my tracks. I pulled my phone out of my back jeans pocket, intending to call Amy. If she was anywhere nearby, I might hear her phone ring.

Just then, the cool breeze shifted and a repetitive sound registered. Unless I was very much mistaken, it was the sound a shovel makes when slicing into dirt and then tossing that dirt onto more dirt.

Dang. So much for nipping Ty's demented project in the bud.

I was still some distance from Stu's grave. As I got closer, I stared into the shadows, looking for some sign of Ty. I hoped he was just getting started. When I finally spied him in profile, however, I saw with dismay that he was already standing inside the open grave. Obviously he'd been digging for some time. He'd probably left the house as soon as his wife, Jeanette, fell asleep.

Whispering Willows Cemetery did not require grave vaults or liners, and—spoiler alert—cheapskate Gilbert had declined to spring for one. Which meant there was nothing between Ty's shovel and Stu's casket except a couple of feet of earth. I saw him set aside the shovel and crouch inside the grave, and I assumed he was working the latches on the casket.

As I crept closer, it occurred to me that anything I said or did at that point would probably just make things worse. When I was about ten yards from the grave, I planted my feet, mentally debating whether to proceed or to turn around and slink away before he noticed me.

I heard the casket lid creak open and, about a half minute later, slam shut. Ty straightened, and I saw he was holding something, something that gleamed white in the moonlight.

An envelope.

"Yes!" he crowed. "So much for getting the last word, you worthless piece of crap." He laughed exultantly as he tore open the envelope.

The laughter abruptly ceased as he studied the paper it contained, squinting to read it by moonlight. Then he threw back his head and screamed like a wounded animal, raising the hairs on my nape.

Obscenities filled the night air. "You can't do this to me! You do not get to do this to me, you son of a bitch. If I'd known you planned a stunt like this," he told the dead man under his feet, "I'd have made it a lot worse for you than a bullet in the brain." He wadded up the paper and randomly hurled it in my direction. Then he went very still, peering into the shadows.

"Who's there?" he shouted.

Slinking away was no longer an option. I ran. Unfortunately, Ty ran faster. I'd gone just a few yards when pain detonated inside my skull.

IT WASN'T MY idea to wake up. It hurt too darn much. My head throbbed in time with my heartbeat. I didn't remember what happened, I only knew that I needed to go back to sleep. It was the only way to make the pain go away.

I was lying facedown, and gradually it dawned on me that I wasn't in my own bed—unless my bed had become a lot harder and grittier than I remembered. More gritty stuff rained down on me, and then again, and again, in a rapid rhythm. I felt the weight of it accumulate on my back, my legs, my head. I tried to move, but my entire body felt leaden.

The smell of earth filled my nostrils. Eventually, the danger of my situation began to register. Whatever was happening, instinctively I knew I had to do something about it. I turned my face downward in an unsuccessful attempt to shield it from the dirt quickly piling up. I forced my eyes open. Utter darkness surrounded me, but I was starting to orient myself.

Think.

I remembered getting a call from Amy. Sneaking into the

cemetery. Watching Ty read a piece of paper and scream in frustration.

I remembered what he said. *If I'd known you planned a stunt like this, I'd have made it a lot worse for you than a bullet in the brain.*

Shovelfuls of earth continued to fall, one after the other. Belatedly my groggy brain identified the rigid surface beneath me as Stu's casket.

Ty was burying me in Stu Ruskin's grave. Stu's corpse lay a few inches under me, the two of us separated by a layer of flimsy fiberboard covered in blue cloth.

My heart was a jackhammer. Automatically I tried to scream and only succeeded in sucking in a mouthful of soil. I needed to overcome the weight of the earth piling up on me, to try and grab the shovel from Ty. To fight back. It was my only chance. But my muscles refused to cooperate. Every attempt to move was met with waves of dizziness and nausea, and more skull-skewering pain. I had a bad concussion, at the very least. He must have clobbered me with the shovel.

With some effort, I managed to tug the neckline of my sweatshirt up over my nose and mouth. It was a temporary solution. Before long, my air would run out.

The sound of falling dirt was now muffled under the deep layer already covering me. It pinned me down, compressed my lungs. Panic was a living thing, sucking my air and stealing my wits.

Think, Jane. Dammit, this is not how it's going to end for you.

My phone! It was in the right back pocket of my jeans. If I could manage to call 911, I might get out of this horror show alive.

I forced my right hand through the soil to reach my pocket.

It was empty. Ty had relieved me of my phone before throwing me into the hole.

In desperation, I pulled in a lungful of the little air I had left, and screamed, *"Ty! Don't do this."*

I was sobbing now, trying with all my might to dig myself out, but it was useless. The distant sound of falling clods of earth and the immobilizing pressure weighing me down told me how deeply I was buried.

Already it was difficult to breathe. I inhaled another precious lungful, and yelled, *"Please, Ty, I'm begging you! Don't leave me to die like this."* I reasoned that since I could still hear the dirt landing, he might hear my desperate pleas.

Several moments later, the sound stopped, and that's when I knew it was hopeless. Ty had finished the job. He would have made sure Stu's grave was slightly mounded with earth, precisely the way the cemetery staff had left it after the funeral, to allow for settling of the ground and eventual seeding with grass.

In my mind's eye I saw Ty sprinting through the cemetery with his shovel, scrambling over the fence and heading for his car.

My initial weakness was beginning to abate, aided by the adrenaline coursing through me. I continued to struggle against the earth pressing down on me, which succeeded only in squandering my paltry air supply. But what choice did I have? It wasn't in me to simply give up.

After what seemed an eternity but was probably about two minutes, I heard the sound of digging directly above me.

Was it possible? Had Martin gotten my message and somehow figured out what Ty had done? The rapid shovel strikes came closer and closer. Finally, when most of the soil had been removed, I felt someone jump in next to me and frantically clean off my face. I blinked against the grit, eager to lay eyes on the padre.

"God forgive me." It was Ty. He was panting, his moonlit face sheened with sweat and tears, as he pushed dirt off me. "Don't die, Jane. Please don't—"

His features twisted in pain. He started to stand, but his legs buckled and he landed heavily on top of me, unmoving. After a stunned moment, I remembered Ty's heart condition. With a herculean effort, I gradually dragged myself out from under him and pushed him onto his back. The excruciating pain in my head brought me perilously close to passing out myself. Through sheer force of will I managed to both remain conscious and keep from vomiting my taco dinner all over Ty.

He wasn't breathing, and I couldn't detect a heartbeat. I knew CPR, but I also knew that job one was to call for help. Ty had a cell phone in each of his back pockets. One of those phones, of course, belonged to me. I called 911 and briefly explained the situation and our location ("Please speak more clearly, ma'am—it sounded like you said you're in a grave") before starting chest compressions and rescue breathing.

The seconds ticked by like hours as I battled pain and exhaustion trying to save the life of the man who'd just buried me alive. Ultimately his conscience had won out, which was fortunate for both of us. His heart probably would have failed him even if he hadn't dug me back out of that grave, and then there would have been no one around to help him.

After a few minutes, my strength began to fail me. Just when I thought I was going to keel over right on top of Ty, I heard the sound of running feet and Martin calling, "Jane! Jane, where are you?"

"Here," I croaked, then took a deep breath and hollered,

"I'm here, Martin," while waving an arm high enough for him to spot me.

The padre stopped short at the edge of the open grave. If the situation hadn't been so dire, I would have laughed at his gobsmacked expression.

"I'm waiting for the ambulance," I said. "Do you know CPR?"

Without a word, he jumped down onto the casket and started chest compressions on Ty while I shakily crawled out of the hole and collapsed onto the cool grass. He knew better than to demand an explanation, except to ask, "Where are you hurt, Jane?"

Gingerly I touched the back of my head, through the layers of dirt and matted hair. Martin cursed when he saw my fingers. Yep, blood still looked black by moonlight. He started to move away from Ty, to attend to me.

"Don't you dare," I said. "He's in worse shape than I am."

We both heard it then: a distant siren that grew louder and louder until it reached the cemetery. "It's about time," the padre said.

"How's the ambulance going to get in here?" I asked. "That gate is padlocked."

Still doing chest compressions, he said, "They've got a bolt cutter."

A small white object winked in the moonlight several yards away. Half crawling, half stumbling, I made my way over to it. Kneeling, I smoothed out the crumpled piece of paper Ty had furiously tossed away, and read Stu's final message to his blood enemy.

17
Making a Killing with Booze

AMY MET ME on the porch of The Gabbling Goose and ushered me inside. "Thanks for coming, Jane."

"No problem." It was a lie, of course, the problem being that two and a half weeks after that hellish scene in the cemetery, I was nowhere near ready for a nice, civilized sit-down with her dad. He'd asked very politely, through her, for the meeting, promising it would be brief. Part of me wanted to refuse—well, can you blame me?—but another part, the elusive, mature part that's better at adulting, knew that if I did that, I'd regret it. So there I was.

And face it, if ever any two people had unfinished business, it was Ty Collingwood and me.

Physically, I'd recovered from my concussion, but getting to the point where I no longer slammed awake in the middle of the night, convinced I was suffocating under tons of earth, inhaling dirt and listening to the rhythmic *chunk, chunk* of a shovel… well, that would take a little longer.

I'd spent one night in the hospital. The next morning, Martin brought me back to my house and essentially moved in for two weeks, waiting on me hand and foot instead of going to work. Maxine Baumgartner, the owner of Murray's Pub, covered his late-night shifts, and he persuaded her to give Georgia Chen, self-described fab mixologist, a try during the afternoon and early-evening hours, after her bakery job. Georgia happily accepted the part-time gig and proved herself a skilled and popular bartender.

During my convalescence, the padre cooked my meals, monitored my pain meds, kept my house neat and tidy, and ran interference, ensuring my privacy while I convalesced. The only other people who had regular access to me were Sophie and my folks. Dom wanted to come see me, but I gently declined.

Martin even took over my Death Diva duties on Memorial Day, delivering flowers and flags to graves on behalf of my clients who'd requested that service. He included the graves I still decorated out of love and respect for my deceased client Harold Barden, the milk-truck driver responsible for that convenient gap in the cemetery's fence.

And if you're wondering why Martin didn't answer his phone when I tried calling him in the middle of the night, it's because he had it set to vibrate only, and it failed to wake him. He didn't get the message until about an hour later when he just happened to wake up and check his phone.

The padre's personal service did not, alas, include anything *too* personal. He slept in a guest room and never once tried any funny business. Once the waves of dizziness were a thing of the past and my skull no longer throbbed twenty-four seven, I commanded him very firmly to move out of my house and go back to work. And yes, that firm commandment was accompanied by a very thorough kiss of gratitude for all he'd done for me. That was four days ago, and we hadn't seen each other since, though we spoke and texted several times each day.

I had not told Martin about this visit to The Gabbling

Goose. He would have had some strong opinions on the matter.

Amy leaned closer and murmured, "I'm so sorry, Jane." Her eyes glistened. "If I'd had any idea…"

She didn't finish. Well, what could she say? *If I'd had any idea my father was a deranged killer, I never would have asked you to go to the cemetery at three a.m. to stop him from digging up his victim.*

She nodded toward the adjoining drawing room. "He's waiting for you. Do you want me to, um, stay with you?"

"No, it's fine." I gave her a tight smile and entered the drawing room, a cozy sitting area I'd passed through on several occasions but hadn't spent much time in.

Ty Collingwood sat in an upholstered wing chair by the cold hearth, which now housed a cluster of live plants. It was a warm afternoon in early June. A breeze wafted through the open windows, carrying the mingled scents of roses and the nearby bay.

Ty came to his feet when I entered, folding the newspaper he'd been reading and setting it on a coffee table, next to a glass of orange juice and a prescription bottle. He removed his reading glasses and tucked them into his shirt pocket.

He appeared to have lost weight, and now looked older than fifty-six—his age according to the various news stories. He'd been released on bail, which had been set at a million dollars.

"Please." He indicated a matching wing chair. "What can I get you, Jane? I think Shelley put a pot of coffee on. And Georgia baked some blackberry tarts."

"Nothing, thanks." This stilted politeness was agony.

Once we were both seated, he said, "I must admit, I was relieved when you agreed to meet with me. God knows you don't owe me such a kindness."

As I attempted to formulate a response, Toby strolled in from the enclosed porch and leapt onto his lap. The big cat gave a few chirps and let her eyes drift shut as he stroked her long fur.

"No words can ever..." He stopped and shook his head. "I was out of my mind that night. This lifelong obsession of mine, to claim that old family recipe—it took over my whole being. That's not an excuse," he hastily added. "It's not much of explanation either, but it's all I can offer."

Well, it wasn't *all* he could offer. "That's why you dug up Stu's body," I said, "but not why you killed him. And almost killed me."

He didn't answer immediately, and I briefly considered assuring him I wouldn't share anything he told me in a court of law. It was not a promise I could keep, so I remained silent. Of course, it was just the two of us there, so he could always deny having made any self-incriminating remarks. Not that that would count for much. The case against him was too compelling.

His lawyer, Carlos Levine, was reputed to be the best, but unless he could produce bona fide miracles, Ty would be found guilty of murder once his case went to trial. Considering the state of his health, it was reasonable to assume he'd die in prison.

Finally he said, "You heard what I said that night, after I read the note Stu left me. You knew I killed him, so I had to... well, I *thought* I had to silence you. Of course, thought had nothing to do with it. I didn't think, I acted."

Quietly I said, "Then you changed your mind."

He dragged in a deep breath and let it out slowly, staring out the window at the rosebushes. Finally he looked at me and said, "I came to my senses when I realized I was doing to you what my ancestor Sybille did to Percival Ruskin."

Well, not precisely. In my case it was more like the story "The Premature Burial" than "The Cask of Amontillado," but suffice it to say, Edgar Allan Poe would have approved—of the familiar plot line if not the act itself.

Ty closed his eyes for a long moment. "I'm so very sorry, Jane. Sorry for all of it, but mostly for what I did to you."

I nodded, a wordless acknowledgment. It was all I could manage.

His brow creased in concern. "Are you fully recovered? Your head?"

"Yes. It was a bad concussion, but I'm all better."

"I'm glad to hear it." After a moment he added, "You saved my life. After what you endured, no one would have blamed you for letting me die. I wouldn't be here if you hadn't performed CPR." Ty's eyes glistened, and he struggled to compose himself. Finally he cleared his throat and quietly said, "Thank you, Jane."

"I'm glad I could do it. My friend Martin also pitched in." The bizarre circumstances notwithstanding, I couldn't have lived with myself if I'd sat by and not at least attempted to save a fellow human being. I wondered if Ty would be as thankful when he found himself spending the rest of his life behind bars.

I said, "Tell me what happened the night Stu died."

Ty hesitated, but only for a moment. I sensed him deciding he owed me this. "We all know what kind of man Stu Ruskin was," he said. "And no, that doesn't excuse what I did. But at that moment, it seemed like there was no other way to stop him."

"To stop him from what? From trapping Amy in a blighted marriage and getting that much closer to owning…?" I spread my arms to indicate our surroundings, the Collingwood ancestral property. "You didn't even know about the engagement."

"I did, as a matter of fact," he said, "though I was the last to learn of it. I called here that evening, just checking up on things, and spoke with Woody. He told me Stu was sitting back there in the hot tub as if he already owned the place. He referred to him as 'Amy's fiancé.'"

I'd asked Woody whether he'd told anyone besides Shelley that he'd seen Stu in the hot tub. He thought he might have, but wasn't sure.

"Where were you when you made this call?" I asked. "Not Southampton, I presume."

"No, I was at home. Jeanette was at her sister's house in Sea Cliff. They get together every Wednesday evening with friends to play cards. Later I told her I went to the jazz club while she was out. I don't make a habit of lying to my wife, but it was either that or ask *her* to lie for *me*. To the police."

I said, "Knowing they'd probably ask her where you were when Stu died."

"That's right." He continued to stroke Toby, who expressed her appreciation with her musical, trilling purr.

"So you came over here to deal with him?" I asked.

"After I got off the phone with Woody, I was so angry I couldn't see straight," he said. "I jumped in my car and gunned it all the way here. It's a wonder I didn't get into an accident. I parked around the block and unlocked the gate at the back of the property. No one could have seen me from the house."

"Why sneak around? Were you already planning to, you know, do something to him?"

"No," he said, "I just wanted to get the drop on him. Confront him. Let him know he might've fooled Amy, but he wasn't fooling me. I knew what he was really after. My daughter, she's, well, she can be somewhat naïve."

"Amy has a good heart," I said, "and something tells me her naïveté is a thing of the past. Did you know she'd been out there earlier? In the hot tub?"

"No. Woody didn't mention seeing her—just Stu. I did notice the martini glass on the rim. I just assumed it was his. If I hadn't been so worked up, I might've wondered where Stu Ruskin, of all people, had gotten ahold of a cocktail at The Gabbling Goose. I didn't find out the drink was Amy's until a week later when the cops found her fingerprints on the glass." Ty glanced toward the entrance to the kitchen and lowered his voice. "Shelley thought Amy did it."

"What, you mean…" My eyes widened. "She thought Amy murdered Stu?"

He nodded grimly. "Shelley knew Amy had been back there using the hot tub."

"But she also knew Stu was alive after Amy left," I said. "Woody told me she went out there to try and chase him off."

"For all the good it did her," Ty said. "After you discovered his body, Shelley decided Amy must've come back later and shot him. Amy had just broken up with him that morning and was pretty upset."

"And Shelley never said anything to Amy about it? Never asked her if she did it?"

He shook his head. "Meanwhile, Amy kept her own suspicions to herself. She thought Shelley killed him."

"Good grief. They were protecting each other." While all of them pretended to believe the suicide theory. "So Woody told you about the engagement but not the breakup?"

"He didn't know about that," he said. "Either he wasn't told or he was told and forgot."

"Which is why you thought they were still engaged when

you confronted him," I said. "What were you hoping? That he'd willingly give up your daughter? Abandon his rotten scheme?"

"It was a long shot," I said, "but I had to try. Of course, I had no way of knowing she'd already dumped him."

"Did he clue you in?" I asked.

"Just the opposite. Once he realized I didn't know about the breakup, he taunted me about their upcoming marriage and how all this would be his once I was dead. And how that would be sooner rather than later because of what he referred to as my 'bum ticker.'"

"Lovely." I shook my head in disgust.

"But he didn't stop there," he said. "He knew how much the Sybbie's Punch recipe meant to me, how I'd spent my whole life searching for it."

"I think I see where this is going," I said. "He told you he had it in his possession, didn't he? That it had been handed down in his family."

"That's right," Ty said. "He offered to sell it to me for a hundred thousand dollars."

"You told me you didn't believe the Ruskins held on to that recipe over the years."

"I *didn't* believe it," he said, "not until Gilbert showed up here a week after the funeral to tell me he buried it with his brother."

"But until then, you figured Stu was lying about having the recipe," I said, "that he was just trying to rip you off."

Ty nodded. "Which he was, of course. I told him to go to hell, only I didn't put it that politely. I was boiling mad by that point, as you can imagine. That's when I noticed this small leather backpack lying there next to his clothes. Out of his reach. I said something like, gee, a valuable recipe like that, I'll bet you keep it with you at all times. I opened the backpack and dumped its contents onto the grass."

"Were you surprised when a gun fell out?" I asked.

"At first, yes," he said. "Then it kind of made sense that a self-important thug like Stu Ruskin would feel the need to strut around with a weapon like that."

"What did he do then?"

"What *could* he do?" Ty said. "He was sitting there in his birthday suit, about as vulnerable as a guy can be. He tried to laugh it off, even while I calmly pawed through his gun paraphernalia and screwed the suppressor onto the Glock. At that point I was just trying to rattle his cage."

I took a slow, calming breath, knowing where this story was heading. "That's all he did? Laugh?"

"For some reason," he said, "Stu thought that would be a good time to double down on the taunts. He ridiculed me and my obsession over the recipe. He insulted my daughter in the most degrading way. He said he was going to end up with Amy and The Gabbling Goose and my precious recipe, and there wasn't a damn thing I could do about it."

Ty fell silent, his blue-gray gaze unfocused as he mentally relived Stu Ruskin's final moments. He'd stopped stroking Toby, who tried to remind him what his hand was for with impatient head butts. Finally the exasperated cat sprang off his lap, prompting Ty to blink and clear his throat.

"It happened so quickly," he said. "And it was so… easy. Too easy, really. Stu wasn't expecting it."

I swallowed hard. "Did you mean to do it, Ty?"

"I must've asked myself that question a thousand times since that night." He looked even older now, practically gaunt. "I don't recall making the decision, but part of me must have wanted to do it. To eliminate him."

Most people have wondered whether they're capable of murder, under the right circumstances. Ty Collingwood had learned the answer, and it would haunt him for the rest of his life.

"So the note he left you," I said. "I'm no stranger to death-related practical jokes. I've seen a few of them in the course of my odd career. Well, I've actually seen a whole bunch of them. I had an assignment not too long ago that involved a reading of the will, only it turned out the deceased woman was very much alive."

Ty frowned in perplexity. "So then, what was her point?"

"Her point was to eavesdrop on how her relatives really felt about her," I said. "Not that she didn't already know, but she wanted to rub their noses in it while disinheriting them, face-to-face. This is one mean lady."

"I suppose you're implying," Ty said, "that's Stu's request to have the punch recipe buried with him was his version of a 'death-related practical joke.' Did you notice I wasn't laughing when I tore open that envelope?"

"You have to admire the planning that went into it, though," I said. "To dummy up the sealed envelope containing the 'secret recipe,' to stash it in his safe and leave those specific instructions in his will."

"This so-called joke would only work if I was still around when he died—not a given by any means, considering the state of my health and the difference in our ages."

"But he must have assumed," I said, "that if he did predecease you, you'd eventually discover the recipe had been buried with him. I mean, supposedly buried with him. You know."

"He was right," Ty said. "I would have. Stu knew I was convinced none of the Ruskins had the recipe, but he also had to know that at some point I'd have gotten desperate enough to question Gilbert, just on the off chance they'd found it stashed in Great-Great-Grandma Ruskin's recipe box or something."

Okay, here's the thing. Stu had been dead for fourteen days, and in the ground for nine, when Ty dug him up to get that recipe. Now, a two-week-old corpse is… well, it isn't something I'd choose to snuggle up with, but trust me, I've seen worse. However, Ty seemed to be implying that even if he'd found out, say, ten years from now that the secret recipe for Sybbie's Punch resided in Stu Ruskin's moldering jacket pocket, he still would have snuck out to the boneyard in the middle of the night with his shovel.

I didn't know whether to applaud his dedication or quietly upchuck into my purse.

I said, "I read what was in the envelope."

"Ah yes," he said, "the envelope enticingly labeled, 'Percival Ruskin's recipe for Peg Leg Punch, 1668.'"

"You have to admit," I said, "it was a pretty clever limerick. 'Goodwife Collingwood I do accuse'… um…" I tried to recall how the rest of it went.

Ty recited Stu's note from memory. "'Goodwife Collingwood I do accuse / Of making a killing with booze / A dude named Percy / Was shown no mercy / And now Ty is singing the blues.'"

"That last line is obviously a reference to the trick he played on you," I said. "Making you believe the recipe was buried with him. He seemed to be confident you'd dig him up to get at it."

"He knew how far gone I was," he said, clearly chagrined to admit it. "That old recipe took on an almost mystical significance for me. I'd have done anything to get my hands on it—up to and including grave-robbing, as it turned out."

"It would seem," I said, "that Stu was more or less okay with having his final resting place not be so, well, restful."

"All that mattered was him getting the last word," Ty said. "He probably laughed himself sick composing that limerick and devising a plan to get me to exhume him."

"So I have to ask," I said. "Your offer to foot the bill for Percival's funeral and burial—was that prompted by guilt over killing Gilbert's brother?"

"That was part of it." Ty gave a weary sigh. "Okay, it was a big part of it, along with horror over what Sybille did. I thought for sure Gilbert would change his mind and refuse my offer, now that he knows how Stu died. I'm glad he didn't. And I'm grateful you didn't back out either. Percival Ruskin is owed a decent burial, no matter what he did in life."

"And he certainly wouldn't get one from his descendants," I said, "so I'm glad that worked out."

I'd thought long and hard about whether to cancel my involvement in Percy's long-overdue funeral. If I backed out, then Gilbert and Darla would take over the planning, and I couldn't see that turning out well. Even worse, having decided to go ahead and let Ty pay for it, they'd be forced to deal directly with the man who'd murdered Gilbert's brother. So, in addition to sharing my vast experience at arranging funerals, I'd also be a welcome buffer between the Ruskin family and the person who was signing the checks. In the end I'd decided to see it through.

Ty's cell phone emitted a musical tone, which he silenced with a touch.

"Do you have to answer that?" I asked.

"It's just my medication reminder." He lifted the pill bottle from the coffee table, shook one out, and swallowed it with a sip of orange juice.

I'd noticed this coffee table before, in passing. It was rectangular, with a glass top that protected an embroidered cloth placed under it. I leaned closer and lifted the newspaper to get a better look. "Sybille must have made this."

"She sure did." He moved his glass and pill bottle to a side table so I could take a closer look at this example of Sybille Collingwood's artistry. "This piece has been displayed in this room since well before I was born."

I said, "It's exquisite."

The length of linen was about two feet by three feet. Like the inn's antique kitchen towels, it revealed its age in yellowed patches and a frayed hem. But those flaws in no way detracted from the beauty of the embroidery, which depicted the exterior of The Gabbling Goose in its original seventeenth-century incarnation, before the expansions and renovations that had helped it survive into the twenty-first.

The inn had been rendered in minute detail, from the myriad bricks to the colonnaded porch to the original red clay-tile roof. The Gabbling Goose's roof was now slate, the shutters on the leaded-glass windows now painted Colonial blue rather than muted green. And apparently there was once a large birch tree in the front yard, along with a profusion of colorful flowers, attesting to Sybille Collingwood's skill as a gardener as well as a needlewoman. The image included a blue sky, drifting clouds, and a pair of goats nibbling grass.

"It's in incredible condition," I said.

"This is considered Sybille's masterpiece," Ty said, "plus it's the only record of how The Gabbling Goose originally looked, so her descendants always took care to preserve it. It's been kept out of direct sunlight, and once UV-filtering glass became available, they started using that."

"How is it possible," I asked, "that the person who created this magnificent embroidery, with such loving attention to detail, was capable of such cruelty?"

"Her legacy will forever be tainted." He grimaced. "As will mine. Future generations of Collingwoods will remember us both as cold-blooded murderers."

I knelt next to the coffee table to peer more closely at the needlework. "The border is as interesting as the picture of the house."

All along the edges of the linen were scenes of vegetable gardening, apple picking, bread baking, carpentry, beer brewing and cider pressing, weaving and sewing, milking and cheese making, chickens and goats—the various types of industry required to maintain an active Colonial inn.

Ty said, "I used to stare at that thing for hours when I was a kid. I was fascinated by the pictures of old-fashioned people doing old-fashioned work, right here at The Gabbling Goose. It's been years since I really looked at it."

The corners bore four different circular images, depicting foodstuffs. One was a teacup surrounded by a wreath of green tea leaves. The next was half of a brown, oval nut sitting on a curved metallic device with holes in it, and ringed by a swirl of brown specks.

Not being an experienced cook, it took me a moment. "Is that nutmeg?"

"Very good. We still have that old grater."

"Of course you do." I looked at the next corner, a tiny still life executed in colored thread: a pair of dark glass jugs, labeled *Rum* and *AJ*, placed next to a red apple. This tableau was encircled by several jointed plant stalks topped by long, thin leaves.

"Those stalks look like sugarcane," I said, "which makes sense since rum is made from it. But what does AJ stand for?"

He smiled. "Applejack, or apple brandy. The Collingwoods owned a lot of property back then, including a huge orchard."

Moving on to the last corner, I saw eight lemon halves arranged in a circle around yet another piece of sugarcane and a bowl heaped with a beige substance I assumed was sugar—the minimally processed kind, tinged with molasses.

"More sugarcane?" I said. "Doesn't that seem redundant, to have the same item in two of the four food pictures?"

"I never thought about it." He unfolded his reading glasses and put them back on, leaning over the table to examine the image. "Maybe she liked embroidering sugarcane."

I studied the lemon halves, gorgeously rendered in several shades of yellow, dripping juice. And next to the sugar bowl, a couple of yellow curls similar to the ones I'd seen not that long ago at Murray's Pub, adorning the rims of Amy's and Georgia's cocktails.

Strips of lemon peel.

You know how sometimes you'll be working a jigsaw puzzle and you'll find yourself getting more and more frustrated and nothing seems to fit and then all of a sudden a piece just snaps into place? And then all the rest of the pieces slide home, and just like that, the picture comes into focus.

I sat back on my heels and stared at each of the four corners in turn. I only realized my mouth was agape when Ty said, "Jane? Are you all right?"

I blinked up at him. "I found your recipe."

"SO WE'RE TALKING *dark* rum, right?" Martin asked. "Seems to me that's what they would've used in the colonies back then."

"I think you're right," I said.

We were in Murray's Pub. It was late. The locked door sported a CLOSED sign, and the padre had already balanced the cash drawer and cleaned up. The two of us were perched side-by-side on barstools, perusing the list of punch ingredients I'd scrawled on Gabbling Goose stationery.

We weren't alone in the pub. Georgia and her ex, Henry, were snuggled together on one side of a booth, quietly talking. They'd been like that for two hours, gradually scooting closer to each other, their conversation now punctuated by secret smiles and light touches.

Martin didn't have the heart to kick them out, and since Georgia had agreed to fill in behind the bar on occasion, thus cementing her status as a kinda sorta employee, he figured if she wanted to hang out after closing to rekindle her fragile relationship with her ex-husband, who was he to play the heavy?

The two of them finally abandoned their booth to join us at the bar. Henry had his arm around Georgia's waist.

"I didn't realize how late it was getting," she said. "You shoulda booted our butts out the door."

Martin shrugged. "I'm in no hurry."

Henry peered over our shoulders. "What are you working on?"

I handed him the list. "It's ingredients for a Colonial-era punch The Gabbling Goose used to serve. We're wondering how to turn it into an actual recipe."

"Oh my Gawd!" Georgia snatched it from him. "Where'd they find it?"

"You know about this?" I asked.

"Amy says her family's been looking for that recipe *forever*."

I told her about my discovery at the B&B that afternoon. "I took pictures," I said, tapping my phone to bring up photos of the embroidery, including close-ups of the four corners.

Henry said, "But how can you be sure these are the ingredients for the punch?"

"Well, Ty's been researching Colonial drinks for decades," I said, "and he's come across these ingredients plenty of times, though not in this particular combination. He has no doubt this is the basis for Sybbie's Punch."

"But why embroider them into a picture of The Gabbling Goose?" he asked.

The padre said, "It actually makes sense if you think about it. The inn was known for this punch. It ended up costing two men their lives and starting the whole Collingwood-Ruskin feud."

"As far as Ty's concerned," I said, "Sybbie's Punch is a crucial piece of the Collingwood legacy, which is why he was so determined to hunt it down. He once told me he hoped to set eyes on the recipe before he died."

"Turns out it was staring him in the face his whole life," Martin said, "though I wouldn't call it an actual recipe. I mean, we have the ingredients, but not the amounts or instructions."

Henry grinned at his ex-wife. "I happen to know a skilled mixologist who just loves inventing cocktails. Think you're up to the challenge, beautiful?"

Georgia was already sprinting around the end of the bar.

"Martin, make some tea. Strong."

"Yes, ma'am." He joined her behind the bar and grabbed a few teabags, while she perused the bottles of booze.

"I'm thinking this is closest to what they would've used." She held up a bottle of fifteen-year-old dark rum for his inspection.

"Good choice." He plucked another bottle off the shelf. "This company claims they've been making applejack since the eighteenth century."

"Close enough." She slapped several lemons on the bar, along with a glass canister filled with coarse, light brown crystals.

"What kind of sugar is that?" I asked.

"Demerara," she said. "It's a kind of raw sugar, and most likely what Sybille used in the punch. Nowadays it's still used in some cocktails, which is why we keep it here. Martin, we're going to need some strips of lemon peel."

"I'm on it." He produced a vegetable peeler and went to work.

"Jane, show me those pictures again," she said.

I handed over my phone and she scrolled through the images, her brow knitting in concentration. She made a writing motion, and Martin placed a pen and writing pad in front of her.

As Georgia scribbled notes, muttering to herself, Henry said, "I love watching this lady get creative."

After a few minutes of work, she put down her pen. "Okay, Sybille would've mixed up a whole bowl of punch at a time, but I'm going to try making just four servings. Let's start with equal parts rum, applejack, and tea. Maybe half as much lemon juice, and just enough sugar to sweeten it without being cloying."

Martin set a glass pitcher in front of her.

"So, what did Sybille use that for?" I nodded toward the lemon peel. "Just garnish?"

Georgia shook her head. "In the picture, the peel is shown next to the sugar, which tells me step one is to muddle those two together. So let's get to it."

From behind the bar she produced a wooden muddler, which looked like a miniature baseball bat. We watched as she tossed four strips of peel into the pitcher, added a few spoonfuls of the crunchy demerara sugar, and used the muddler to vigorously mash them together. Meanwhile Martin squeezed the lemons into a bowl.

"What does the muddling do?" I asked.

"The sugar acts as an abrasive," she said. "When you crush them together like this, you're extracting the flavorful oils from the lemon peel."

Once she was satisfied with the result, she poured in the rum, applejack, tea, and lemon juice, added some ice, and stirred the golden-brown mixture.

Martin set four copper mugs on the bar, the kind normally reserved for Moscow mules. "We don't have pewter cups, so these will have to do."

Georgia lifted the frosty pitcher. "Who's ready to sample the first batch of Sybbie's Punch made since, well, since who knows when?"

The rest of us hollered for her to get on with it, whereupon she divided the contents of the pitcher between our four cups.

"Not yet!" Georgia admonished as we reached for our drinks. "Were you raised in a barn?"

Martin ceremoniously handed her a small Lucite-and-chrome contraption, which housed a nutmeg. She held it over one of the mugs and turned the crank on top. Ground nutmeg drifted onto the drink. She repeated the process three more times.

Henry said, "*Now* can we taste it?"

She gave him a look that was equal parts stern and suggestive. "Impatient as always. Haven't you learned by now, Henry? Some things are worth waiting for."

He reddened slightly, while chewing back a grin. The padre and I pretended not to notice.

Georgia raised her mug. *"Genbei!"* She laughed at my perplexed expression. "That's Mandarin for 'bottoms up!'"

Henry lifted his drink. *"A votre santé!"*

The padre gave it a Gaelic spin. *"Sláinte!"*

"I was going to do that one!" I complained. "That's okay, I'll just pretend to be Italian. *Cin cin!"*

We all took a sip.

"Oh my Gawd, it's *good*!"

My eyebrows jerked up. "Well, dang if this isn't a mighty tasty cocktail."

Martin took a second sip. "The flavors are nicely balanced. Well done, Georgia."

"Well done, *Sybille*," she corrected. "I was thinking I'd probably have to tweak this first try, but I don't know, I'm kinda happy with how it came out."

"Even if it isn't an exact duplicate of the original Sybbie's Punch," I said, "I doubt it's far off. Shelley will be thrilled. She can't wait to start serving it at The Gabbling Goose."

"So will they keep the recipe secret?" Henry asked.

"How would they even manage that?" Georgia said. "I mean, all of us here know how to make it, and unless they shove that beautiful piece of embroidery in a closet, anyone who visits the B&B can work it out on their own."

"Ty and Amy are in agreement," I said. "Sybbie's Punch belongs to the world. As far as they're concerned, secret recipes have caused nothing but heartache and tragedy."

"Amen to that," Henry said.

"I have a feeling customers are going to start coming in here asking for this drink," Martin said. "Georgia, can you tell me how to make a single serving?"

"Sure thing." She recited the recipe while the padre jotted it down:

SYBBIE'S PUNCH

Ingredients:
1 strip of lemon peel
2 teaspoons demerara or turbinado sugar
1 ounce dark rum
1 ounce applejack or apple brandy
1 ounce strong black tea
1 tablespoon lemon juice
Ground nutmeg

Instructions:
1. *Using a muddler or wooden spoon, muddle the lemon zest with the sugar.*
2. *Add rum, applejack, tea, and lemon juice.*
3. *Stir and serve over ice, sprinkled with ground nutmeg.*

Henry drained his mug. "Well, we definitely have a winner here."

"Speaking of winners, Henry," Martin said, "I caught a couple of episodes of your new web series."

"What's this?" I said. "I had no idea. What kind of series?"

"It's a baking show." He shrugged. "I teach the basics. You know, cakes, pies, breads, pastries. Nothing special. Each episode is about fifteen minutes."

"Oh my Gawd, listen to this idiot. 'Nothing special'?" Georgia reached across the bar to smack his shoulder. "It's named after Henry's bakery, The Cranky Crumb, and he uses all these crazy video techniques and you never see his face, he's like this disembodied narrator, a *cranky* disembodied narrator, and it's *so funny*. But also really educational for the home baker."

"You're biased," he said.

"Yeah, I'm biased," she scoffed. "That's why two different cable networks have put out feelers. He already has a sponsor, one of those home-delivery meal-kit companies."

"Wow," I said. "That sounds promising."

"We'll see." Henry tried to sound casual, but I could tell he was excited. A brand-new career path, and it had nothing to do with any secret recipes. On the contrary, it was about sharing his baking expertise with the public.

"All those times his friend Steve came over," Georgia said, "I thought he was helping Henry make videos for job applications. I had no idea till I stumbled over his series on YouTube!"

After we finished our drinks, we all pitched in to clean up. Then Henry and Georgia said good night and left together, holding hands.

"I'm happy for them." I lifted my straw basket tote.

"So am I." Martin did one last check and turned off lights. "It was a messy situation, but if any two people belong together, it's Henry and Georgia. Why are you lugging that big thing around?"

I ignored the question. We exited the pub into the cool late-spring night. A streetlamp cast a circle of light on the deserted road.

"Where are you parked?" he said, as he locked up. "I'll walk you to your car."

"I took a Lyft," I said. "Good thing I didn't drive. That Sybbie's Punch really went to my head. I'm going to need to sleep it off."

"Seriously?" he said. "That's the only booze you had all night. Before that, you were knocking back iced tea."

"I really think I need to sleep it off."

"If you say so." He walked the few steps to the next door, behind which was a staircase that led to his over-the-bar apartment. "Maybe you're getting sick. I'll drive you home."

I turned him to face me and stared into his gorgeous, clueless eyes. "I'm telling you, I know what I need, and right now I need to sleep it off."

He started to respond, and stopped. He glanced into my tote bag, which happened to hold a variety of overnight essentials. Finally he offered a slow, sexy smile. "Are you sure?"

"Ever the gentleman." I smiled. "I'm sure. Sexy Beast is bunking with Sophie. We have all night. All morning, too, if we want it."

Martin slid his fingers around the back of my neck. His chest expanded on a slow, deep breath as he stared into my eyes, making no effort to conceal his emotions. His voice was husky as he said, "I need to tell you something first. Before we go upstairs. I love you, Jane."

My eyes stung. "And it's a darn good thing, Padre, because I love you, too."

The kiss that followed was so good, I lost my grip on the tote bag, which crashed to the sidewalk, disgorging its contents. I shoved my hairbrush and bra back inside while the padre held up a particularly filmy article of clothing I'd procured that very morning at UnderStatements, the high-end lingerie store on Main Street.

I sat back on my heels as he examined my new purchase. "I'll wait," I said. "Got nothing better to do."

At last he folded it carefully and returned it to the tote, which he lifted, while helping me rise. "We have all morning, you said?"

"All afternoon, too, if we want it. Sophie enjoys SB's company, and there's nowhere else I need to be."

"What a coincidence." He unlocked the door and held it open. "Me, either."

About the Author

Pamela Burford comes from a funny family. You may take that any way you want. She was raised in a household that valued laughter above all, so of course the first thing she looked for in a husband was a sense of humor. Is it any wonder their grown kids are into stand-up comedy and improv? Oh, and here's another fun fact: Pamela's identical twin sister, Patricia Ryan, aka P.B. Ryan, is also a published novelist. Patricia is the Good Twin, and yeah, Pamela knows what that makes her. But hey, Evil Twins have more fun!

It should come as no surprise that everything Pamela writes is infused with her own quirky brand of humor, from her feel-good contemporary romance and romantic suspense novels to her popular Jane Delaney mystery series, featuring snarky "Death Diva" Jane, her canine sidekick Sexy Beast, and a fun love-triangle subplot. Pamela's own beloved poodle, Murray, wants you to know that any similarities between himself and neurotic, high-strung Sexy Beast are purely coincidental.

Pamela is the proud founder and past president of Long Island Romance Writers. Her books have won awards and sold millions of copies, but what excites her most is hearing from readers. Swing by and say hi at pamelaburford.com.

Made in the USA
Monee, IL
21 May 2022